KT-234-969

TEARS WILL NOT SAVE THEM

TEARS WILL NOT SAVE THEM

Linda Sole

severn
House

This first world edition published 2010
in Great Britain and in 2011 in the USA by
SEVERN HOUSE PUBLISHERS LTD of
9–15 High Street, Sutton, Surrey, England, SM1 1DF.
Trade paperback edition first published
in Great Britain and the USA 2011 by
SEVERN HOUSE PUBLISHERS LTD.

British Library Cataloguing in Publication Data

Sole, Linda.
  Tears will not save them.
  1. Great Britain–Armed Forces–Nurses–Fiction.
  2. World War, 1914-1918–Medical care–Great Britain–
  Fiction. 3. World War, 1914-1918–Casualties–Fiction.
  I. Title
  823.9'14-dc22

ISBN-13: 978-0-7278-6979-1   (cased)
ISBN-13: 978-1-84751-312-0   (trade paper)

Except where actual historical events and characters are being
described for the storyline of this novel, all situations in this
publication are fictitious and any resemblance to living persons
is purely coincidental.

All Severn House titles are printed on acid-free paper.

Severn House Publishers support The Forest Stewardship Council [FSC],
the leading international forest certification organisation. All our titles that
are printed on Greenpeace-approved FSC-certified paper carry the FSC logo.

Typeset by Palimpsest Book Production Ltd.,
Falkirk, Stirlingshire, Scotland.
Printed and bound in Great Britain by
MPG Books Ltd., Bodmin, Cornwall.

One

'I'm glad to see you're well wrapped up today. It's bitter cold and I shall be glad to get home to a fire!'

Jane Shaw turned her head as she heard her neighbour's voice. She was standing outside Woolworth's in the main street of March, the small railway town where she had lived for the whole of her eighteen years, wondering whether she could afford to buy a penny bar of chocolate for her young brother.

'Have you been to work this morning, Aggie? I thought you were working nights at the pub?'

'My boss asked me if I would go in this morning.' Aggie Bristow bent over the shabby pram Jane had parked on the pavement. 'How's young Charlie then?'

'He isn't at all well.' Jane looked anxiously at her brother. 'He hasn't got over the chill he had at Christmas. He isn't as strong as other children of his age.'

'If it hadn't been for the care you lavish on him, lass, I think the poor lad would have been gone before now. You're better to him than most mothers, though it ain't fair you have to stay home and look after the boy.'

'I don't mind taking care of him.' Jane smiled as her brother waved his gloved fist at her. People thought he was retarded. The doctor had told Jane that it might be something to do with him having been born to a mother in her middle years whose health was poor, but Jane thought he was just slow at learning. Charlie *was* sometimes difficult to control but he had a lovely nature. 'I was just wondering if I should buy him a bar of chocolate. I promised Amelia she could have some new pencils for school but Charlie deserves a treat, because he is so poorly.'

Aggie put her hand into her coat pocket and pulled out a threepenny piece. 'Here, take this, Jane. The lad deserves— Good gracious me! Look at that horse . . .'

Jane glanced in the direction Aggie had pointed out and gasped. A horse was careering down the High Street, its reins hanging loose. Even as she was wondering what had happened to the rider, she saw that a young boy playing with a wooden hoop was standing right in its path.

'Look after Charlie!' Jane yelled at her neighbour and rushed out into the road in front of a cyclist, who had stopped in confusion to avoid the horse, and a parked van, whose driver was in one of the shops. She caught the boy by the arm and dragged him clear, pushing him towards the path just as the horse brushed past them both, knocking her forward so that she landed on her knees in the road.

Winded and shocked, Jane remained on her knees for a few moments after the horse had raced on down the road. She was vaguely aware of shouting and screaming, the sound of a car braking hastily, a hooter blasting, and then a man wearing riding breeches running after the maddened horse and yelling at the top of his voice. The boy she had saved was crying noisily and being comforted by a large woman in a smart coat with an astrakhan collar.

'Are you all right, miss?' A man in a grey overcoat and trilby hat came up to Jane as she struggled to her feet. 'You might have been killed.'

'I was afraid the boy would be knocked over.' Jane winced as she looked down at her coat and saw the muddy stains. Her knees felt sore where she had fallen, though she didn't think she had any other injuries. 'I'm not badly hurt. I was lucky.'

'It's a miracle no one was killed,' the van driver had been examining the side of his vehicle and now came to join the little crowd around Jane. 'Horses are damned dangerous beasts if they aren't kept under control.'

The sound of shouting and cheering made them all turn round and look. A man in working clothes had launched himself at the horse and grabbed the reins as the beast crashed into a stall selling vegetables at the side of the road. Potatoes, cabbages and other goods had spilled out into the road and several vehicles had halted suddenly, causing confusion and noise, but the horse was now restored to its rider.

'Thank goodness someone stopped it before it did more damage,' Aggie said as Jane joined her in front of Woolworth's. 'That was a foolish thing to do, love. What would have happened to young Charlie if you'd been killed?'

Jane was shaking. 'I was afraid the boy would be trampled. It didn't occur to me that I might be hurt . . .'

'You want to get straight home, love,' the woman in the brown coat came up to Jane and touched her hand. 'You saved my Tom's life. I reckon you deserve a medal.'

'It was just instinct.' Jane blushed, as she became aware of people looking at her curiously. She caught sight of her reflection in a shop window. Her dark hair was tucked under a red felt cloche hat and her skin had a greyish tinge, her eyes slightly dazed. 'Yes, I should get home, Aggie. I'll walk with you if you don't mind?'

'Course I don't mind.' Aggie took hold of the pram handle. 'I'll look after Charlie. You can pop into the corner shop and get him a bar of chocolate on the way home. What you need now is a cup of hot sweet tea, my girl.'

'Where have you been?' Jane's mother was in the kitchen when she wheeled the pram into the big room and lifted Charlie out, sitting him on the shabby but comfortable sofa. 'I wanted a drink and you weren't here. I had to come down and make it myself.'

'I'm sorry I was out when you needed me. I had a cup of tea with Aggie . . .'

'I thought I told you I didn't want you going round there?' Helen Shaw's sharp eyes went over her. 'What happened to your coat? It looks as if you've been rolling in the mud.'

'I fell over. Aggie was there and she saw I was a bit shaken so she insisted on making me a cup of tea.' Jane wouldn't dream of telling her mother that she had pulled a young lad clear of a charging horse. No sympathy would be given; she would simply be lectured for reckless behaviour. 'I'm sorry I was so long. I popped back to the corner shop and got Charlie some chocolate.'

'Why you want to waste money on him I don't know. He doesn't appreciate it.'

Jane held back the retort that sprang to her lips. Arguing with her mother was a waste of time and might bring on one of Helen Shaw's bad heads.

'He loves chocolate, Mum, you know he does.'

'What he loves is neither here nor there. I don't think it is good for him to be indulged.'

Jane sighed as she put some water in a saucepan and set it on the range. Charlie might eat a soft-boiled egg if he felt well enough. She had baked earlier that morning and he enjoyed bread and butter cut into soldiers.

'I'm going to fetch the coke in now,' Jane said and picked up the bucket. As she moved it, a stack of fairly recent newspapers used for lighting the fire fell over. She picked one up, glancing at the headline about Joseph Chamberlain deciding to retire from parliament.

'Well, get on with it,' Mrs Shaw said. 'I'm not very hungry but you can make me some cheese on toast. You can bring it to me in bed.'

'Will you watch Charlie while I fetch the coke?'

'For goodness sake! Am I expected to do everything? Be quick then. I have a headache coming on . . .'

Jane heard the church clock striking twelve. It was midnight and she had been up most of the night with Charlie, because he had been crying and miserable all day. He hadn't seemed too bad the day they went shopping in the High Street, and he had eaten the chocolate bar she'd bought with Aggie's threepence. However, his cold seemed to get worse that night and he seemed really ill when she got him up in the morning. Jane had asked her mother twice during the day if they should have the doctor but Mrs Shaw thought it a waste of money.

Outside the cottage the rain was lashing down, beating against the small windowpanes; the wind made an eerie sound as it howled about the eaves, drowning the sound of a train pulling into the marshalling yards across the embankment. Yet the noise of the wind was nothing compared to the sound of Charlie screaming.

'Hush, Charlie sweetheart,' she begged as she bent over his cot and stroked his head. His skin felt hot and dry. He had been crying for hours and nothing she did would stop his pitiful wailing. 'Please don't cry, my love. You'll wake Ma and she needs her sleep.'

Charlie stared at her without comprehension. He was three years old and could still not walk properly, though he managed to speak a few words when desperate for attention.

'What's wrong with him, love?'

Jane's father entered the small bedroom. She turned her head to look at him. He was dressed in a pair of old cord trousers held up by black braces and a grey shirt.

'He hasn't been well all day, Pa.'

John Shaw walked to the cot and bent over to look at the child. He lifted Charlie under his arms and held him up to look at his red face, then pressed the thin body to his shoulder, patting the child's back as he began to walk up and down the small room. The child's wails waned to a mewling cry, tears trickling down his cheeks.

'You get off to bed, Jane. You've been up half the night with him.'

'You look tired to death yourself.' Jane watched him, noticing how gentle and loving he was to the little boy. 'You work too hard – all those long hours at the office.'

Her father was a clerk to a solicitor in the small but thriving town of March. They were situated a few miles from the cathedral city in the Isle of Ely, which could be reached by bus or train. A longer train journey would take them into the city of Cambridge with its ancient colleges and green parks, but Jane had visited the city no more than a few times in her life. Her father worked hard for them but his wages were sufficient only to keep them respectable.

She was eighteen and ought by rights to have been at work for the past three years, but Jane's mother insisted she stay at home to look after her and her brother. Helen Shaw clung to her bed most of the time, and though she was able to come down and even go out if she felt inclined, she seldom did.

'It isn't fair on you, Pa. I should be able to work to help with the bills . . .'

'Now then, Janey, love,' he said and smiled at her with faint reproof. 'You know your mother can't cope with Charlie. If it were just Melia and us, she might let you go to work but this little feller needs too much attention.'

Charlie let out a wail of misery. His father put a hand to his forehead and frowned.

'He is burning up. His skin was dry but now it feels clammy. I think I had best fetch the doctor in case he is really ill.'

'Thank you. I should have fetched him earlier.'

'Don't blame yourself.'

They both knew whose fault it was but neither of them would

say a word to the culprit. Helen Shaw suffered terrible headaches and her family lived in fear of distressing her.

'The weather is atrocious tonight. Wrap up well, Pa. We don't want you catching cold.'

'Don't worry, Jane. I'll be as quick as I can. Just do your best to keep Charlie from waking your Ma.'

Jane hushed her brother, putting him back in the cot, but he started to scream immediately and she had to pick him up once more.

'Hush my darling.' She rocked him gently in her arms. 'Yes, I know you feel bad. Your poor little tummy aches, doesn't it?'

There was the sound of hurried steps down the stairs and then the door closing sharply.

'Rock a bye baby in the tree tops . . .' Jane was singing softly to her brother and did not hear the shuffle of slippers on linoleum.

'Can't you keep that brat quiet? How am I supposed to sleep with that racket going on all night? I can feel one of my headaches coming on. Leave him alone to cry and fetch me a hot drink.'

'If I put Charlie down he will scream again. I'll take him with me while I make your drink, Ma. Perhaps a little hot milk would help Charlie too.'

'That's right, put that little monster first.'

Jane swallowed her protest. Mrs Shaw felt herself hard done by no matter how hard they all tried to make her life easier. Jane was tied to the house most of the time, though she went shopping when she had the chance. Her only free time came when her sister Melia was home from school to run errands for their mother.

She carried Charlie pressed close to her shoulder and went down to the kitchen. His tears soaked into her nightgown, his whimpering cries a relief from the terrible screaming. The kitchen range was still warm but the fire needed making up to heat the milk. Jane settled her brother on the sofa, placing soft cushions all round him to keep him from rolling off. Charlie continued to sniffle when she left him, but his screams had stopped for the moment.

It was warmer in the kitchen than in his own room, which might be why he seemed easier now. Jane wondered if the damp cold atmosphere of the bedrooms was part of his troubles, the reason he was so often ill.

The cottage was old and undoubtedly needed repairs but the landlord said there was nothing he could do. Jane's father had done what he could to improve things himself. It was he who had run a pipe into the house from the standpipe in the yard so that they at least had a deep stone sink with running water. That saved Jane the trouble of going out to the yard every time she needed to fill the kettle. The kitchen was decently furnished with a large stripped pine dresser, a big table and enough chairs to seat all the family together, but the old sofa had seen better days.

Jane wished they had an inside toilet instead of having to walk down the yard to the outhouse where a primitive wooden-seated lavatory had been installed just before the railway sold the cottages. It actually had a cistern and chain, which was better than some people had and something Jane was truly grateful for. As long as she kept it clean with disinfectant it didn't smell too awful. Carrying the bedroom slops out in the morning was something she hated but it had to be done.

She hovered near the black range, appreciating its heat. As soon as the milk was warm enough, Jane divided it between two mugs, giving Charlie a third of what she was taking for her mother. She topped her brother's milk up with a little cold water so that it would not be too hot for him.

'Stay there, darling,' she told him, pushing the mug into both his hands. He could feed himself though he often refused to eat unless she put each spoonful into his mouth. 'Hold the mug tight, darling. Drink your milk. I will be back in a minute . . .'

'No! Jane stay . . .' Charlie wailed and tipped the milk over his chest. He screamed as it touched his skin, though Jane knew it wasn't hot enough to hurt him. She put the tray for her mother on the large scrubbed pine table and fetched a towel, moping up the liquid Charlie had spilled. 'Jane not go . . .'

'I have to take this for Ma,' Jane said. 'Sit there and don't move until I get back . . .'

Charlie set up a wail of protest as she picked up the tray and went out, but she decided to leave him to cry for a while. She couldn't possibly carry him and the hot milk. Perhaps her mother was right. Perhaps she did spoil him, but it broke her heart to see him in distress. He wasn't like other children; he couldn't do much for himself and sometimes, when he tried to walk, his body seemed to just flop over. The doctor had told her he would never improve.

'You have to face it, Jane. Charlie is retarded. I know he seems to understand and you think he is just backward, but the chances are that he will get worse not better.'

Jane resented the doctor's plain speaking. She prayed every night that her brother's condition would improve.

'You took your time,' Helen Shaw grumbled as Jane carried her drink into the bedroom. She sipped the milk and pulled a face. 'It is almost cold.'

'I'm sorry. Charlie spilled some of his and . . . I can heat it again if you want?'

'I'll drink it as it is . . .' A loud scream came from downstairs. 'See what is wrong with that brat now!'

Jane needed no urging from her mother. She rushed down to the kitchen, discovering that her brother had fallen from the sofa and crawled to the range. He must have tried to get into the bucket of coke and tipped the contents over himself.

'Charlie . . .' Jane carried him back to the sofa. Pulling the nightgown over his head to change him, she planted a kiss on his hot little body. Usually, he giggled when she did something like that, but he was too distressed. 'All better now . . .'

Carrying Charlie, she went to the window and looked out. The rain was still sheeting down. Her father would be soaked to the skin. 'Your daddy will be back soon,' she promised as Charlie started to sob again. 'Poor little boy . . .' She paced up and down the kitchen, occasionally glancing out of the window. The wavering light of a carriage lamp made her sigh with relief. 'Thank goodness . . .'

Her father was with the doctor in the gig and he jumped down, leading the way into the kitchen.

'I saw the light,' John Shaw said. 'Is he worse?'

'He woke Ma. I came down to fetch her a hot drink.'

'I see . . .' He reached for a towel from the airing line above the range and began to rub vigorously at his dark hair. 'Let the doctor look at him, Jane.'

Jane placed her brother amongst the cushions on the old sofa, standing back to watch anxiously as the doctor began his examination.

'How long has he been like this, Jane?' Doctor Martin gave her a concerned look.

'The fever started yesterday. He was miserable when I got him up first thing, but he only started to scream an hour or so after I put him to bed this evening.'

'Why didn't you send for me earlier in the day?'

'I thought it was just a tummy ache. Is he really ill?'

'I think he should be in hospital.' Doctor Martin glanced at her father. 'Are you prepared for the expense? Charlie has a putrid fever. If he stays in this damp cottage I think this chill could turn to pneumonia. Of course in the circumstances you might feel the expense is too much . . .'

'What do you mean in the circumstances? Of course Charlie is worth it – isn't he, Pa?' Her eyes appealed to her father. 'I'll go to work . . . anything to help Charlie . . .'

'I'll manage somehow, Jane. My son has to have his chance, Doctor. I'll find the money to pay but I will need time.'

'I can arrange for you to have time to pay at the cottage hospital; they owe me a few favours.' Doctor Martin looked at Jane. 'Can you wrap him up warm, please? You had better get dressed your-self. I shall need you to come with me.'

The next few hours were long and anxious ones for Jane. Her brother was taken into the doctors' care after what seemed a desperate dash to the local cottage hospital, and she was asked to wait in a cold little room that had only a small window high up. The walls were painted in glossy dark green to halfway up and then a dull cream.

She paced up and down as the minutes ticked by at a snail's pace, feeling helpless. What were they going to do to her brother and why had no one come to tell her what was going on?

Jane had no means of telling the time but she could hear a clock striking sometimes, and when it struck eight times she decided to go in search of someone. Seeing a nurse in a long, dark grey skirt and white apron, she called to her.

'Yes, miss? What are you doing here? Visiting times are not until this afternoon between three and five.'

'We brought my brother in as an emergency last night. I was told to wait but no one came to let me know how he was getting on.'

The nurse frowned. 'It isn't usual for family to wait. You should have been told to go home and come back this afternoon. I suggest you do that now, Miss . . .?'

'Jane Shaw. My brother's name is Charlie. Please, could you find out where he is and how he is? Charlie isn't like other children and he will be upset without me to look after him.'

The nurse looked impatient and then her expression softened. 'He will be in the children's ward. Stay here and I will enquire for you.'

Jane thanked her, watching anxiously as she went off. She was gone for a while but at least there was a window here that Jane could look out of, and she contented herself with gazing at some damp rose bushes and water dripping from the trees.

'Did you think I had forgotten you?' the nurse asked her on her return.

'Did you find out anything? Is Charlie . . .?' she stopped, suddenly fearing the worst.

'He was sleeping peacefully. Sister said he had a bad hour or so but the doctors gave him something for his chest infection and she thinks the crisis may have passed. You can visit him this afternoon.'

'Couldn't I see him now?'

'Sister is getting ready for Matron's rounds. I've told you, he is being well cared for. Please go home now and come again this afternoon.'

'It was all a fuss about nothing.' When Jane entered her mother's bedroom, she was sitting up in bed, reading a copy of Ethel M. Dell's book, *The Way of the Eagle*. Jane had paid tuppence at the library to get it for her mother because there was a long waiting list. 'I told you he didn't need the doctor and he certainly didn't need to go to hospital. What is that going to cost? Besides, it would be a relief for us all if that imbecile . . .' Seeing the angry look in her daughter's eyes, she scowled. 'I know you care about Charlie, but he takes up too much of your attention.'

'Don't call Charlie an imbecile, Ma!'

'You should face the truth, Jane. He is mentally and physically retarded. One of these days we are going to have to put him away in an institution. It would be better to let him die when he is ill.'

'I'm going to do some washing while Charlie is away,' Jane turned away. 'Call me if you need something.'

If she had stayed another moment she would have accused her mother of being lazy. Jane suspected that her mother was perfectly capable of doing work in the house, at least of making a cup of tea for herself and cooking dinner. She didn't doubt that her mother's headaches were terrible at times, but she had used them as an excuse to become an invalid.

Melia was sitting at the kitchen table, eating a slice of toast and strawberry jam.

'Ma is in a terrible mood. She told me I had to stay home today in case you didn't get back to look after her.'

'I'm here now so you can get off to school.'

'It's too late . . .'

'You can tell your teacher that your brother was ill and you had to get Ma's breakfast. He will understand . . .'

'Mr Hastings is wonderful.' Melia's face lit up as she began to gather her school things. 'He says that I am bright enough to go to college and be a teacher.'

'That would be wonderful for you, Melia. I would have liked to do something like that but . . . All the more reason for you to get off now. You don't want to get behind with your lessons.'

'It's rotten luck for you,' Melia said, suddenly moved to hug her sister. 'I feel mean sometimes knowing that you had to give up your plans to stay home and look after Charlie . . .'

'I love Charlie. I care about you too, Melia. I want you to make something of your life.'

'But what about you? Won't you want to have a life of your own – get married one day? You're really pretty, Jane. At least you would be if you ever had time to do your hair and wear a decent dress . . .'

'Thanks for the compliment.' Jane glanced in the spotted mirror above the sofa and grimaced as she saw what Melia meant. 'Don't worry, love. I know you meant well. Get off now and tell Mr Hastings that I would like to talk to him about your future.'

'Why? You know Ma thinks I should leave school this summer so that I can look after her and you can go to work.'

'If it doesn't cost too much to go to college perhaps Pa would persuade her that you should stay on at school.'

Melia's face lit up. 'Do you mean it, Janey? Would you do that for me? I thought you would jump at the chance of going to work?'

'I don't have the chance to be a teacher. The best I shall do is work in a shop.' Jane sighed inwardly. 'Besides, Charlie isn't happy with anyone but me. It makes sense that you should have your chance, Melia.'

'I'll ask Mr Hastings to come and see you one evening. You will like him, Jane.' Melia hesitated, then, 'I heard something about you from Tom Brown's mother. She says you pushed him out of the way of a bolting horse the other day. You didn't tell me, Jane?'

'Because it was nothing. I just pushed him out of the way.'

'Mr Hastings says it was an act of heroism.'

'And he will be cross if you're late for class. So hurry and get ready. I've got a lot of work to do . . .'

'I've been worried about Charlie all day,' John said when he came into the kitchen that evening. 'How is he, Jane?'

Jane looked at him in silence, then, 'The nurses told me that he was recovering well when I visited this afternoon, but he was asleep all the time I was there. I think . . . they have given him something to keep him quiet.'

'For his own good I expect. I suppose they think it is better to sedate him for a while. Just until he is over his illness.'

'Yes, perhaps . . .' Jane had got the impression that the nurses on duty seemed to think that her brother was less important than other patients, because he was backward and unable to walk or talk as he ought at his age. 'Charlie is worth saving, Pa. You know how loving he is when he is well.'

'You worry about him too much.' He put his arm about her shoulders. 'When he was born I was warned that he might not have a long life.'

'I know – but he should be allowed to enjoy what he has . . . shouldn't he?'

'Yes, of course he should.' John turned away, lifting the lid on a saucepan. 'The stew smells good, Janey . . .' He broke off and sneezed, his shoulders shaking.

'I hope you haven't taken a chill? You were soaked through last night.'

'I'll be all right.' He arched his brows as Jane hovered. 'What is it? Something is on your mind.'

'It's about Melia. Ma says she should leave school in the summer when she is fourteen and take my place so that I can go to work . . .'

'It is only fair she should take her turn. I thought you wanted a job?'

'If Ma could look after Charlie I would jump at it, but . . . Melia may have a chance to go to college and learn to be a teacher . . .'

'Wouldn't that cost a lot of money?'

'There might be some sort of scholarship. I think it is free if you pass the exams and win an assisted place.'

'That would mean we would have to go on managing on my wage. I was counting on you to bring in something when Melia left school.'

'It would be a good life for her, Pa.'

'Yes . . .' He drove his fingers through his dark hair. 'Let me think about it, Janey. I might find a way of earning extra.'

'You already work too hard. Perhaps we should forget it – but Melia isn't very good with Charlie.'

'I'll see what I can do. Don't say anything to her for the moment.'

'Miss Shaw?' Jane stared at the young man standing at her front door a couple of days later. She had been in the middle of making a fruit cake when the bell rang. 'Your sister Amelia asked me to call. You wanted to talk about her chances of becoming a teacher.'

'You are Mr Hastings?' He was young and very good looking with his dark blond hair and inquiring blue eyes. She put a hand up to her own dark locks, feeling conscious that she had dragged her hair back into a knot to keep it out of her eyes. 'Please come in. I wasn't expecting anyone. I've been cleaning and now I'm baking.'

'If it isn't convenient I could come back?'

'Please, come in now you are here. Melia is out and my mother is asleep.' She led the way into the kitchen, pleased that it wasn't full of wet washing for once. 'Do you mind talking here? The front parlour fire hasn't been lit and it's cold there.'

'The kitchen is fine for me.' Robert Hastings glanced round
the big, comfortable kitchen. 'I understand that you care for your
mother and small brother?'

'Yes, I do. Charlie is in hospital at the moment. The doctor
thought he might have pneumonia . . .' She paused, then, 'I know
you think Melia is bright enough to train as a teacher, but I am
not sure it will be possible.'

'That is a pity. Melia seemed to think there was a chance.'

'I hoped there might be. I'm afraid I gave her the impression
that it might be possible, but my father seems to think we couldn't
afford to let her go to college.'

'She has the chance to win a scholarship. If she gets it – and
I think she has every chance – her tuition would be free.'

'Yes, I thought it might be.' Jane looked wistful as he arched
his brows. 'I once hoped to go to college myself but it wasn't
possible.'

'You had to leave school to look after your mother and
brother?'

'Yes, but that isn't important. I would like to give Melia the
chance, Mr Hastings but . . . my father is expecting me to bring
in some money once Melia leaves school and takes my place.'

'It would be the waste of a bright girl's life, don't you agree?'

'Yes, I do but . . . My father works hard for us but he doesn't
earn much and my mother needs expensive medicine. Charlie's
hospital fees will be difficult enough to find.'

'Yes, I see.' Robert's tone expressed sympathy. 'I do understand
how hard it is, Miss Shaw. I had to work to put myself through
college. Melia is lucky to have this chance. If she doesn't take it
I shall have to offer it to another girl.'

'Can you give me a few days? My father said he would see
what he could do . . .'

'One week is as long as I can delay it. I have been asked to
put forward the names of girls wishing to stay on and take further
education. If I call next Saturday morning – would that give you
enough time?'

'I'll ask my father when he comes home. If he says we can
manage I'll let you know next week.'

'Very well. I shall delay making my report for one week.' He
smiled at her. 'I think Melia is lucky to have a sister like you,

Miss Shaw. We all think you were very brave to pull that young lad out of the way of that horse the other day.'

'The man who stopped the horse was the brave one. I could never have done that!'

'You wouldn't have had the strength but your action was equally courageous.' He smiled at her in approval. 'Well, I can see you are busy so I shan't delay you any longer.'

'Oh . . .' It wasn't often that Jane had a chance to speak to a young man, especially one as attractive as Robert Hastings and she felt a pang of regret. 'I should have offered you a cup of tea.'

'Perhaps next week. I hope your brother is better soon. Good morning, Miss Shaw.'

'Thank you. Goodbye, Mr Hastings.'

Jane did not get a chance to speak to her father that afternoon. He returned home feeling ill, sneezing and coughing. He had brought a miniature bottle of whisky, to which he asked Jane to add hot water and sugar in a cup. He took it with him to his tiny room, where he slept alone these days because of his wife's bad headaches.

Jane peeped in on him later to ask if he needed anything but he merely moaned and asked to be left alone. Jane's mother came out of her bedroom as she walked away.

'What is wrong with him? I suppose he took a chill the other night.'

'I am sure he will be better by Monday. I'm off to the hospital in a few minutes, Ma. Can I get anything for you before I go?'

'Your sister can bring me a hot drink at three o'clock.'

'Melia went to the church bazaar. I made some buns for her to take for the cake stall this morning.'

'You are always wasting money! Wait until you're earning a wage before you start giving what little we have away.'

'Everyone takes something – even Aggie Bristow sends a cake for the church bazaar.'

'What that common tart does is her business,' Helen drew her top lip back. 'We all know where she earns her money. How many times do I have to tell you to have nothing to do with her, Jane?'

'Aggie isn't a tart and it isn't fair to call her names.'

Jane's mother lashed out at her. 'Don't forget I am your mother and I won't put up with being spoken to in that manner.'

Jane stared at her, putting a hand to her cheek. Her mother nagged her every day of her life but it was the first time she had hit her. She turned and ran downstairs. If she didn't get out of the house, she would scream!

'The doctors would like to do some ability tests on Charlie,' Sister Norris told Jane that afternoon when she visited the hospital. 'We know he is retarded but with the proper treatment he might learn to do more for himself.'

'I have tried to teach him to feed himself, and sometimes he can toddle about the kitchen on his own . . . but then he seems to lose control and just flops over.'

'What happens then?'

'He just lies there and screams until I pick him up.'

Sister Norris nodded. 'He has learned that screaming gets him his own way. You may think you are doing the right thing by giving him attention, but in the end it is causing him harm.'

'I can't bear to see him distressed . . .' Jane felt uneasy. 'How much would it cost to do the tests? I'm not sure we could afford for Charlie to stay in hospital for several weeks.'

'This would involve him going to a special home where they have time to look after the boy. He would live there, though you might be able to take him home now and then for a few days.'

'You're talking about a mental institution! No! Charlie isn't going anywhere like that!'

'It really would be the best for him. If your family isn't able to pay there are state funded places, though they are not as good as the private home we were thinking of.'

'You've been drugging him, haven't you? He looked at me when I spoke to him earlier and he didn't know me.'

'It was necessary. The child is uncontrollable . . .'

'You shouldn't have done that!' Jane was so angry that she barely knew how to control her rage. 'My brother may be slow but he has a lovely nature when he is well. He was frightened in this place without me.'

'I've told you, it isn't good for him to be picked up all the time. What are you doing?' Sister Norris glared at her as she picked Charlie up and wrapped him in the shawl she had brought with her. 'You cannot take the boy without the doctor signing him off.'

'My brother is better off at home with me. I should never have let Doctor Martin send him here.' Charlie's body was flopping all over the place; he obviously had no control over his limbs. 'I can't believe what you've done to him. He has never been as bad as this . . .'

The nurse looked offended, angry. 'Your brother has been properly cared for. He was ill when he came in and would probably have died without treatment.'

'He would be better off dying at home than living the way you seem to think right!' Jane's dark eyes narrowed in contempt. 'My father will pay the bill but I'm taking Charlie home.'

'The hospital will not be responsible if you take him now.'

'Charlie will be better with me.'

How dare they treat Charlie as if he were an imbecile? Didn't they understand that he had feelings? She would fight tooth and nail to keep her brother from going to a mental institution.

'I told you it was a waste of money to send that child to the hospital.' Helen Shaw watched Jane nursing her brother on the old sofa in the kitchen. 'You won't agree, but the nurse was right.'

'How can you stand there and say that about your own son? What kind of a mother are you? They were giving Charlie drugs to keep him quiet. Look at him – look at his eyes. He has never been like this, Ma. You know he hasn't.'

'At least he isn't screaming. Your father is ill, Jane. Really ill! I heard him coughing and went in to look at him. He may need the doctor but I don't see how we can afford it.'

'I'll put Charlie in his cot. Then I'll go up and see if Pa wants the doctor.'

She went upstairs and settled Charlie in his cot, tucking the blankets round him. He wasn't an imbecile! He knew when he was with people who loved him. He closed his eyes and she left him, hurrying to her father's room along the landing. John Shaw was tossing restlessly in the narrow bed with iron rails at the head; he had pushed the candlewick cover back, his face and neck red and flushed.

'Are you very ill, Pa?' Jane asked and stroked his forehead. 'Do you want me to fetch the doctor?'

'I ache all over,' her father said. 'I don't want the doctor. Just go to the shop and ask for something for a cold – aspirin will help.'

'Are you sure you don't want the doctor?'

'I just need something to help with the aching. Did I hear you talking to Charlie?'

'I brought him home from the hospital. They were drugging him to keep him quiet – and the nurse said the doctors thought he should be in a special home.'

'I couldn't afford to pay, Jane.'

'Sister said there was a state home but you know what that means. Those places are awful, Pa.'

'We shan't let him go there. He's better off with you, Janey.' Her father coughed and moaned, moving restlessly.

'Try and rest, Pa. I'll fetch you something from the shop.'

'That's a good girl. If you could make me a hot drink when you get back please?'

'Jane!' Hearing her sister call, Jane turned and waited as she left the corner shop after purchasing a strip of tablets for her father. Melia came running up to her. Her expression was petulant, resentful. 'Why did you tell me I could stay on at school and go to college if you knew I couldn't?'

'I thought it might be all right. I'm sorry Melia. I suppose Mr Hastings told you what I said?'

'You promised me! I told my friends I was going and now I can't!'

'It isn't certain yet. Pa is going to think about it, but he can't for the moment, because he is ill.'

'I don't want to leave school and take your place. I don't mind looking after Ma sometimes – but I won't look after Charlie. He messes himself and he smells . . .'

'Stop it! Stop that this minute! I'm sick of people finding fault with Charlie. He can't help it if he can't control himself some-times. He *is* retarded, Melia. I can't deny that and I won't apologize for it. His condition isn't his fault and he can be lovely when he is well . . . you know. he can.'

'I know . . .' Melia wiped a tear from her cheek, a look of shame in her eyes. 'I just don't want to spend my life looking after him and Ma.'

'It's Ma's place to look after him, but she says she can't. One of us has to do it, Melia. I don't mind staying home but Pa may not be able to manage. He needs someone else to work and bring in money.'

'Mr Hastings says I could go as a pupil teacher in another year or so. I would get a small wage. I wouldn't be qualified and I would have to go to college later, but it would be something.'

'I'll talk to Pa when he is better. Please don't cry, Melia – and don't blame Charlie. It isn't his fault.'

'Sorry . . .' Melia looked ashamed of herself. 'I didn't mean to say that about Charlie.'

'Even if you can't go to college you don't have to take my place. In a few months you could find a job and I'll carry on as usual.' Jane smiled at her sister as they went into the house together. 'Go up and see if Ma wants anything and then take a look at Charlie. I'm going to make a hot drink for Pa.'

'All right. Even if I have to leave school and go to work I'll still be luckier than you . . .'

Jane took her coat off and went into the kitchen. Filling the kettle at the sink, she put it on the range. She was about to take the tray upstairs when she heard a cry from above her. Then Melia's feet sounded on the stairs as she came running down.

'It's Charlie,' she gasped. 'I went into Ma, as you said, then took a look at Charlie. He had turned over on his stomach the way he does sometimes and . . . his face is blue.'

'Charlie!' Jane left the tray, rushing up the stairs to her brother's room. She turned him over, looking at him anxiously. He had a strange bluish colour about his lips and his eyes had rolled upwards. She stroked his face, tears trickling down her cheeks. 'Oh, Charlie! Charlie . . .'

Melia had come into the room behind her. Jane turned to her, her face streaked with tears. She could scarcely speak let alone think calmly. She should never have left him even to go to the corner shop, but he had smiled at her and she had thought he would be fine once the drugs wore off, but now he was dead.

'I should never have left him . . .' she whispered. 'I should have been with him.'

'It isn't your fault, Jane. Charlie was ill. It could have happened at any time.'

'No, it is my fault. I brought him home and I knew something was wrong. I should have been with him.'

'You couldn't be with him all the time. You've got Ma and Pa to think of too.'

Two

'You must not blame yourself, Jane,' Doctor Martin told her after he had made his examination. 'Charlie was weakened by his illness. Somehow he turned over and suffocated himself.' He paused, choosing his words carefully. 'You won't think so now, my dear, but perhaps it was for the best.'

'Please don't say that! I loved Charlie. He was never too much trouble for me.'

'He might have become impossible to control. You would not have wanted to see him restrained in a mental institution?' Jane shook her head. 'While he was a small child you were stronger but as he grew his strength would have outstripped yours.'

'I shouldn't have left him alone.'

'Charlie's death was an accident. You must comfort yourself as best you can. In time you will know I was right. While I am here, I'll take a look at your father.'

'Thank you. I wanted to call you earlier but he said an aspirin would do . . .'

'Very likely it will, but I should like to make certain.'

After he left the room, Jane bent over her brother's body, stroking his face. Tears trickled down her cheeks. Poor, poor little boy!

'He isn't suffering any more,' Melia said from the doorway. 'Don't cry, Jane. Charlie was lucky to have you. Ma would have had him put away years ago if you hadn't looked after him. You loved him even if no one else cared much.'

'Ma hasn't even been to look at him! She said her head aches too much.' Jane blew her nose, fighting her bitterness. 'At least you can stay on at school now, Melia. I'm going to find myself a job.'

'I had to pop round and ask if there was anything I could do,' Aggie said when she came to the house that afternoon. 'I'm real sorry for your loss, Jane. I know you loved that boy.' She deposited a brown earthenware casserole on the kitchen table. 'It's a bit of chicken and some vegetables. If there is anything I can do for you, lass, you have only to say.'

Jane held her tears back. Aggie wasn't the only one of their close neighbours to pop round and offer food or sympathy and she was grateful for their kindness.

'My father is going to make the arrangements for the funeral so I think we shall manage, but the casserole will save me going shopping and I didn't feel like it today.'

'I should think not either. You have a bit of a rest, lass.'

'I've got some ironing to do later. My father needs a clean shirt for tomorrow. His best suit will need steaming and pressing too.'

'Well, if you feel better doing something.' Aggie looked at her with sympathy. 'I'm next door if you need me, Jane.'

'Will you stop for a cup of tea?'

Aggie glanced up at the ceiling. 'Is your mother in bed?'

'She knows people are visiting and won't come down.'

'Well, just a quick one then.' Aggie picked up the newspaper from the kitchen table. 'I see they've completed the memorial to the old Queen in front of Buckingham Palace. She was a lovely lady, our Vicky, though dreadfully sad after her husband died. King Eddie is a bit of a ladies' man, so they say.'

'Yes, he is. I'm not sure what Queen Victoria would have thought if she had seen some of the stories in the papers.'

'Whom were you talking to just now?' Jane's mother demanded as she took her in a cup of tea later. 'I wish people would keep their noses out of our business.'

'People are kind; they want to help,' Jane replied. 'I've been glad of some company.'

'Well, just remember I am trying to sleep.' Helen Shaw glared at her. 'I've used the pot so you had better empty it.'

Jane was tempted to tell her mother to get up and empty it herself, but she held her temper. 'I'll fetch the slop bucket.'

'Well, don't be long. I may go to sleep and I don't want to be disturbed.'

Jane sighed as she went downstairs. Why was it that everyone else could be generous and sympathetic and all her mother did was grumble.

She lifted her head, refusing to feel sorry for herself as she went into the scullery to fetch the slop bucket. There was a large wicker basket of ironing on the table, waiting for her; she might as well make a start now as later.

She saw that one of Charlie's nightgowns was on top. Bending down, she took it out and cradled it to her cheek, imagining she could smell him and thinking of the last time she had pulled it over his head. The tears started to trickle down her cheeks but she brushed them away.

As soon as she had emptied the slops, she would get on with her work and perhaps then some of the pain would ease.

The rain had fallen steadily all night, but it stopped soon after dawn. Jane saw the light strengthen. She had been standing by the window for ages. It was the day of the funeral and in a few hours Charlie would leave his home for the last time. It was breaking her heart to think of his tiny body in the cheap coffin.

Ever since she'd brought Charlie back from hospital the anger had been growing inside her. Maybe things would have been different if her father hadn't had to work so many hours. Perhaps her mother would have been more loving to Charlie if she hadn't suffered terrible headaches.

She pulled on a shabby dressing gown and went down to the kitchen. At least it was warm here, because her father had banked up the range to keep it going overnight.

She was filling the kettle when she heard something behind her and turned to see her father. He was already wearing trousers and a shirt, his braces black because of the occasion.

'You couldn't sleep either?'

'I've been awake hours. I thought I would make a hot drink but you beat me to it, Janey.'

'I keep thinking . . .' Jane sighed. Her father was through the worst of his chill but the phlegm had settled on his chest. 'I'm going to look for a job, Pa. It will make things easier for you.'

'What about your mother?'

'Melia can help in the house. She'll get tea when she comes home after school, and Ma can manage the rest. She always could but she didn't see why she should when I was here to do it.'

'That's harsh, Janey.'

'Harsh but true. I didn't mind being here all day while I had

Charlie but now I'm going to work – and Melia is staying at school so that she can train as a teacher.'

Her father's weary grey eyes settled on her. 'You sound like your Ma . . .'

'God forbid!' Jane said and watched his face darken. 'I'm sorry. I know you don't like to hear a word said against Ma but she is selfish – and you know it.'

'I loved her once. She was a good wife and mother before these headaches started.'

'Perhaps she was, but I can't forgive her for ignoring Charlie. She could have kept an eye on him while I was out.'

'Stop blaming your Ma – and yourself. Charlie has gone. You can't bring him back.'

'I'm sorry, Pa. I don't want to hurt you, but I've made up my mind – and nothing you or Ma can say will change it . . .'

John Shaw took the mug of steaming strong tea and held it in both hands. 'I can see that, my love. I shan't try to change you, and your Ma can manage if she has to – but please don't let what happened to Charlie make you bitter.'

The grass in the churchyard was soggy underfoot, water squelching through the thin soles of the black button boots Jane was wearing. Most people hadn't bothered to follow the family out to see the burial, because it had started to rain again during the service. Helen Shaw hadn't even come to church. Her excuse was that she had a headache, but she had been acting strangely since Charlie died. Once or twice she hadn't been able to look her daughter in the eye. Jane thought she was feeling guilty for having neglected her son and knew an unworthy satisfaction.

Jane's father had refused to let Melia attend the funeral.

'You can stay home and get some sandwiches ready in case our neighbours call after the funeral.'

Melia hadn't resisted. 'All right,' she said, throwing a look of apology at her sister. 'Jane has made a big cake and some buns. I'll make paste sandwiches, and egg ones too.'

'There's a good girl.' John Shaw smiled at her.

Jane wouldn't have stayed home even if her father had told her she should, so he hadn't wasted his breath. He looked at her as she threw the small bunch of violets into the open grave and nodded, seeming to approve.

Outside the church one or two people had lingered: Aggie Bristow amongst them. She was wearing black in respect of the occasion, her cheeks bearing no trace of the rouge she wore in the evenings. Jane was hardly aware of her or anyone else, until a man came up to her, offering his hand. She gave him hers and he closed both hands over hers, the pressure of his fingers somehow warm and comforting.

'I am most terribly sorry, Miss Shaw. I know this has been an unhappy time for you. You will miss your brother very much I think.'

'Yes, I shall. Thank you, Mr Hastings.'

Jane saw the genuine sympathy in his eyes and some of her hurt eased. He was the one person who hadn't tried to tell her that Charlie's death was for the best.

'Will you come back for a cup of tea? You might like to talk to my father about my sister. He knows that Melia wants to go to college and train to be a teacher, but if you explained how clever she is I am sure it would help him to understand why she deserves a chance.'

He adjusted his tie and then smiled. 'Yes, I should like to meet your father. Melia talks about you a great deal, Miss Shaw, but she doesn't say much about her family.'

'I suppose that is because I've been closer to her for the past few years. Our mother is an invalid and Pa has to work long hours. However, I shall be able to help him in future. I have decided to find a job.'

'Indeed? What kind of work are you looking for – will you work in a shop or go into service?'

'I'm not sure what I can do. I need a reference but I've never worked outside my home . . .'

'I am sure Doctor Martin would give you a character reference and Mr Johnson told me that you were an excellent pupil.'

'I hadn't thought of asking Mr Johnson.' Jane remembered her former headmaster with a little frown. 'I might ask Doctor Martin – though I'm not sure if that would do . . .'

'It might if you had thought of service. I happen to know of someone looking for help in the nursery. My aunt knows the family cook. Mrs Stratton has a seven-year-old son as well as two older daughters. The nanny can't cope with him on her own so the family needs a nursemaid.'

'Looking after a young boy . . .' For a moment Jane's soft brown eyes clouded. 'I'm not sure if I am quite ready for that yet.'

'Forgive me. I thought the idea might appeal, but it is too soon.'

'Please, do not apologize. I know you meant it kindly and it does sound as if I might be able to help – but I need a little time to think.'

'Yes, of course. I'll write down the address in case you want to apply. It is in King's Lynn in Norfolk . . .'

'I should need to go away, leave Cambridgeshire.' Jane was thoughtful as she considered the idea. It might be exactly what she needed – a complete break from everything she had known and a chance to put the heartbreak of Charlie's death behind her.

Jane didn't say anything about going out to work to her family for a few days after the funeral. She got up early the next morning and started to spring clean the house from top to bottom, doing all the jobs she had been meaning to do for ages.

Her mother looked in on her when she was cleaning Charlie's room. Helen Shaw's expression was strange, somehow guilty, but the moment passed and Helen glared at her.

'We could sell the cot, pushchair and some of these things. Charlie doesn't need them now and the money would help to pay your father's bills.'

Jane left the room without answering, and went out to sweep the backyard, secure in the belief that her mother wouldn't follow her.

After two days of scrubbing and polishing her hands were sore and she felt exhausted when she tumbled into bed that night. However, her mind was made up. The address Robert Hastings had given her was in Norfolk, some distance from her home. She would need to catch a train and then perhaps a bus, because she thought the house might be out in the country.

She had decided to ask both Doctor Martin and her old headmaster for references and to write applying for the job of nurse-maid at the Stratton household. The house was called Stratton Hall and Jane thought Mrs Stratton might be well to do, which made her a little nervous. However, the Shaw family was respectable and Jane's father had paid for both his daughters to be educated. Surely she had a chance?

Jane posted her letter after she had been to the doctor's house. She had caught him just before he began his surgery and he'd promised to give her a glowing testimony.

'You were excellent with Charlie. I think you would do very well as a nursemaid, Jane.'

Encouraged by his kindness, Jane decided to visit the school and speak to Mr Johnson. The children were in the playground, laughing and screaming as they played games of hopscotch and skipping. The girls were in grey dresses that skirted their ankles, aprons and black shoes, the boys in short trousers with grey socks and scuffed boots.

As Jane walked towards the building that housed the headmaster's study, Robert Hastings came up to her.

'Good morning, Miss Shaw. Are you here to see the headmaster?'

'I hoped he might have a moment during the children's playtime.'

'I'll take you to him,' Robert said. 'Are you going to follow my advice?'

'I have written to Mrs Stratton. She may prefer someone with more experience but I have been quite honest about my situation.'

'I am sure you have. Mrs Stratton is a widow. Her husband died last winter of a putrid chill that turned to pneumonia.'

'I am very sorry to hear that. It isn't surprising that she needs more help with her children.'

'She isn't an invalid. I believe she entertains often but the boy has been disruptive since his father died.'

'Grief can make you feel angry.'

'Is that how you feel?'

Jane met his steady gaze. He was an attractive man with a quiet manner that she liked.

'Yes. Angry because life is so unfair. Why should Charlie have to suffer as he did?'

'I can't give you an answer, Jane. Life is often cruel.' They had reached the headmaster's room. He knocked at the door. 'It is Hastings, sir. I have someone who would like to speak with you.'

The door was opened promptly by a gentleman with white hair and a stooping figure. Jane was surprised by how much he had aged since she left school and her fear of him melted away.

'Forgive me for disturbing you, Mr Johnson. I dare say you don't remember me.'

'Of course I remember you, Miss Shaw. Please come in.' His faded blue eyes glanced at Robert. 'Was that all, Hastings?'

'Yes, sir. Good luck, Miss Shaw.'

Jane followed the headmaster into his study. He indicated a chair and she sat down. He took his own chair at the opposite side of the cluttered desk and folded his hands in the steeple position.

'I have heard good things of you, Miss Shaw. According to one of our mothers you are quite a hero. Now, what may I do for you?'

The letter inviting Jane to an interview came at the end of the week. She showed it to her father on Sunday morning when they returned from church.

'It doesn't mean I shall get the job, but at least they were interested enough to offer me an interview.'

'I know Stratton Hall. I was sent there some months ago, to deliver some documents for Mrs Stratton to sign after her husband's death, because they were too important to trust to the post. You'll need to walk after you leave the train . . .' He looked at Jane thoughtfully. 'There was something about her I didn't like. It's an isolated place, probably twenty minutes walk from King's Lynn.'

'I don't mind that, Pa. I can get myself a cheap bicycle and cycle to the village, and I can catch the train when I want to visit you or Melia.'

'And your mother!'

'Yes, Ma too. Ma wanted some lavender water. I didn't have any money to spare so she told me to sell Charlie's cot and things. I put a card in the newsagent.'

'You didn't have to do that, Janey.' He put his hand in his pocket and brought out a handful of coins. 'I can give you ten shillings. Buy your Ma what she wants and ask me when you need more.'

'But you have a lot of bills to pay. Can you manage?'

'I earned a few bob extra. Not much but enough to pay for your ma's lavender water.' Her father turned away to cough.

'Are you all right, Pa? Are you sure you should have gone back to work so soon?'

'I can't afford to be away from my job.' He gave her a look she couldn't interpret. 'Don't worry, Janey. And don't forget to buy the lavender water for your Ma.'

Jane put the money in the pot on the mantelpiece. Her father would always find money for his wife's needs somehow.

'I'll get the lavender water on Monday morning. My interview isn't until the afternoon.'

'Are you sure you want this job, love? You might find something in a shop in town. You wouldn't have to leave us then.'

'I think I want to go away, Pa. Norfolk isn't the other side of the world, is it?'

'No . . .' He looked regretful. 'Seeing your face makes the day brighter, Janey. No, I shouldn't make you feel you have to stay for me. You want to get away and it's right you should – but I'm not sure Stratton Hall is the right place for you.'

'I'll go to the interview. If she is a monster I shan't take the job – if she offers it to me, of course.' Jane laughed. 'Let's face it, Pa. I don't have many qualifications.'

'It is lovely to hear you laugh again. Take no notice of me, Janey – and I think they will be lucky to get you.'

'You would.' Jane moved impulsively towards her father and hugged him. 'I do love you, Pa.'

His arms closed about her. 'I hope you will always think well of me. I love you, Janey. I loved Charlie. You know that, don't you?'

'Yes, I do,' she said. 'If I get this job I can help you pay what you owe, Pa – and then you won't have to work so hard.'

'I doubt if they will pay you much, and you may have to wait months for your first pay day,' he smiled. 'But it will be good for you to see how the other half lives . . .'

Jane's knees went weak when she saw the size of Stratton Hall. It was the largest house she'd ever been close to, with its main building of depressing grey stone and two wings of a slightly different shade, and small paned windows. Situated within walking distance of King's Lynn, it stood at the end of a long gravel drive, looking slightly forbidding. She thought there must be at least ten or more bedrooms, several reception rooms plus the servants' quarters. She stood outside the house for a few minutes, trying to take it all in and wondering where she ought to go. Should she knock at the front door or find another at the back of the house?

'You look lost. Can I help you?'

Jane spun round as she heard the deep voice and found herself staring at the most attractive man she'd ever met in her life. He had pale silver-blond hair, deep blue eyes, a straight nose and lips that looked soft and inviting.

'I am Jane Shaw. I've come to an interview with Mrs Stratton about the position of nursemaid and I'm not sure where to go.'

'Away from here as fast as your feet will take you,' he said. 'Maria's son is a monster. I wouldn't wish such a fate on a nice girl like you.'

'Oh . . .' Momentarily lost for words, she recovered, 'I am sure he can't be that bad. He is only seven years old!'

'You don't know the brat.' He offered his hand. 'I'm Maria's little brother David Heron. I didn't mean to offend you. Ned can be a little monster but I am sure he will respond to the right person. Maria neglects him and Nanny is an old fusspot.'

'I see . . . you were just teasing. I thought you were being unkind but you didn't mean it.'

'You are forgiven. I think a girl like you would always be forgiven anything. Has anyone ever told you that you have eyes as soft and brown as melting chocolate?'

'No! Of course not.' Instinctively, she felt that he was a dangerous flirt. 'Could you please tell me where I should go?'

'I'll take you in myself. Don't look at me like that, Jane. I'm not in the habit of seducing decent girls like you – at least not at the first meeting.'

'No, I'm sure . . .' She stopped abruptly, feeling all kinds of an idiot, because he was teasing her. 'Thank you.'

'It is really my sister you have to watch out for,' David said as he ushered her towards the front door. 'She isn't always kind to—'

His words were lost as the front door opened and a woman came out. She was wearing a long flowing garment with wide sleeves that came to a point, making it look a bit like a Chinese mandarin's gown. Her hair was a deep honey blonde, much darker than David Heron's, her lips too red to be natural.

'David, darling. I saw you from upstairs. It is ages since you visited. I thought . . .' her words trailed away, her greenish-blue eyes going over Jane with a look of suspicion. 'I hope you haven't brought your latest tart to visit me?'

Jane's cheeks felt hot but before she could speak, David Heron laughed. 'You have a bad mouth, Maria. I sometimes wonder what goes on in that beautiful head of yours. Does this perfectly respectable young woman look like a tart?' He arched his brows in ridicule as her eyes narrowed. 'This is Jane Shaw – the latest innocent to offer herself up as fodder for your son's evil pranks.'

'Don't call my poor boy names!' Maria Stratton cried, a red flush sweeping into her cheeks. 'I beg your pardon, Miss Shaw. It is your own fault for arriving with my brother. He has a penchant for picking up unsuitable women.'

'We met a moment ago. I was wondering where I ought to go?'

'I don't interview servants myself. Mrs Buller will do that . . . but you might as well come in now you are here. You can wait in the hall. I'll tell her you are here.'

'Forgive my sister,' David Heron gave Jane a rueful look. 'She is often unspeakably rude.'

'David!' Maria hung on his arm, drawing him into a room at the right of the hall. 'You are horrible to me. I have no idea why I love you so much . . .'

'Because I am irresistible to all women . . .'

Jane heard their laughter as the door closed behind them. It was even colder here in the hall than outside. Her eyes travelled over the heavy Victorian furnishings, which gave the hall a depressing feel. The hallstand was of dark carved oak; chairs of a similar style stood against the wall and there was a large over-powering mirror. The saving grace that attracted Jane's attention was the painting of mountains further down the hall. She was still studying it some minutes later when she heard something behind her. She turned and saw a tall thin woman dressed in black, her iron-grey hair pulled into a severe knot.

'Miss Shaw?'

'Yes, I'm Jane Shaw.'

'I am Mrs Buller. Mrs Stratton asked me to interview you. If you will come into my sitting room, Miss Shaw.'

'Please call me Jane . . .' Jane was aware of her sharp glance. 'If that isn't presuming too much? I'm sorry but I haven't been into service before.'

'That's honest enough, Jane. I'm Margaret Buller but you call me Mrs Buller. My husband is Buller. He is in overall charge of the servants – of which there are currently seven, including Nanny and the outdoor man.'

'That sounds a lot but for a house this size it probably isn't?'

'Lord love you, Jane.' Mrs Buller gave a snort of derision. 'In the place I had before this there were nearer twenty. Make no mistake, you'll be expected to pull your weight and more. Nanny knows her business but she is too old to have charge of a lad like Master Edward. He leads her a merry dance I can tell you.'

'Is he really as naughty as he sounds?'

'He is an unhappy child,' Mrs Buller said when the door was shut behind them. 'Please sit down, Jane. Tell me why you haven't worked before – and why you applied for this position . . .'

'I must have misjudged Mrs Stratton. She seemed a sharp-tongued woman to me,' Jane's father said when she offered him twelve and sixpence that evening on his return from work. 'I wouldn't have expected her to pay in advance.'

'Mrs Buller gave me twenty-five shillings in advance against my wages, but I don't get the rest until I've been there six months.'

'Seems odd if you ask me. Still, never look a gift horse in the mouth.' He shook his head as Jane pushed the money into his hand. 'Nay lass. I'll not take your first wages from you. You might have to pay for your uniform.'

'Mrs Buller told me they are free. Take this, Pa. You must have several bills to pay.'

'I had a bit of luck,' her father said, his gaze sliding away from hers. 'Give your sister half a crown if you can spare it and keep the rest for yourself.'

'But it's the reason I'm going to work,' Jane argued. 'I'll give two and sixpence to Melia, as you said – and I'll put the five shillings I owe you in the housekeeping.'

She took the pot down and discovered there was already five half crowns and several shillings.

'I thought we were down to the last shilling for the gas, Pa . . .' Jane was puzzled. 'You gave me money for my bus fare and to pay for Ma's lavender water . . .'

'If you must know we had a little sweepstake at the office. There was a horse running at Newmarket . . . and I drew the winner. There's no big mystery.'

'That's wonderful, Pa!' Jane cried and hugged him. 'It will pay the rent we owe and it might pay the hospital bill too.'

'Don't strangle me, love,' he unhooked himself from her arms, giving her a peculiar, almost guilty look as he pushed her away. 'So – when are you starting your new job?'

'I shall be leaving in the morning. I shall catch the twelve o'clock train and then catch a bus.'

'Where is Jane going? And where have you been all day, miss?' Jane turned to face her mother's sullen stare. 'I'll get your supper, Ma – but after today Melia will do it. I shan't be here.'

'Why not? I can't be here all day on my own!'

'I'm sorry, Ma, but you will have to manage. I shan't be living at home. I've got a job looking after a young boy. He is difficult to manage and his nanny is getting too old.'

'When you said you wanted a job I thought you meant in a shop – so you could pop home in the middle of the day and get me a drink.' Mrs Shaw glared at Jane. 'You can just tell them you've changed your mind.'

'Mrs Buller paid me my first wage and I signed for it. I couldn't walk away from the job now if I wanted.'

'You wretched ungrateful girl! After all I've done for you!'

'I'm sorry, Ma, but Melia can leave you a jug of water by the bed. You'll have to manage somehow.'

'You could give the money back.'

'It says on the paper I signed that I am obliged to work for six months if I take the money.'

'It's a way of making sure you don't walk out on them too soon. I'm not sure it is legal but you could be in trouble if you try to break the agreement.' John looked at her thoughtfully. 'You've been paid for a month, Jane. If you hate it there they can't make you stay longer whatever they say.'

'I'll remember that but I think it will be all right. Mrs Buller isn't too bad. She asked me if I would help out when Mrs Stratton gives dinner parties – after the child is in bed.'

'Slave labour! I hope you said no,' Mrs Shaw said, her expression scornful. 'Well, I think you have behaved in a disgraceful, deceitful manner, Jane. You don't care about my feelings at all.'

'Of course I care – but I wanted to help Pa pay the bills and save for Melia so that she can go to college. Besides, the job is a decent one.'

'I'm glad you think being a servant is a decent way of earning your living. My parents were shopkeepers and your father works for a solicitor. I should have thought you would value yourself more highly – but it is obvious that my opinion counts for nothing.'

Mrs Shaw walked from the room. Silence descended for a moment.

'I did mean it for the best, Pa.'

'Your money will help – but I wish you'd chosen to work somewhere else. I told you I didn't much like Mrs Stratton when I met her.'

'I know she isn't very nice, Pa – but my place is in the nursery with the child. I have to help Nanny with his care and his clothes, play with him, see he does the lessons he is set – and help out in the kitchen when they have guests. I don't see anything threatening in that – do you?'

'Not when you put it that way. But remember what I said – they can't hold you to the six months if you hate it there, Janey.'

'I can give Melia a few shillings now and then. She can save them for when she goes to college.'

'I dare say we'll find the money between us.' Jane's father turned away to fill his pipe with tobacco – a rare treat for him. 'You'd best get on with the supper . . .'

Three

'I was afraid you would change your mind.' Nanny Mowbray looked approving as Jane entered the nursery on her first morning, wearing a striped blue and white dress and white starched apron, her hair twisted neatly into a pleat at the back and covered by a cap. 'I've been thinking I would have to leave but didn't want to let the family down. I was *her* husband's nanny, you know. My poor boy! It was so tragic, and him in his prime. I'll never understand how a strong man could die so suddenly of what seemed just a chill.' Nanny wiped a tear from her wrinkled cheek. 'He asked me to come when Miss Sara was born and I stayed to nurse Miss Angela and then Master Edward – but the girls were no trouble. Master Edward is a handful, too much for me on my own.'

'I am sure it must make a lot of work for you. What would you like me to do first?'

'We'll have a chat for a start.'

Jane hadn't met her charge yet, because her train had been late and she'd had to wait for a bus when she got to King's Lynn the previous afternoon. Master Edward had been in bed by the time she arrived and she hadn't wanted to disturb him.

'Where are the girls? How old are they?' Jane saw a pile of dried washing in a basket and began to sort it out ready for ironing.

'Miss Sara is seventeen and at finishing school in Switzerland. Miss Angela is twelve and she goes to a private school near Norwich. She boards during the week but comes home for the weekends – at least she can if she wants . . .'

'Oh, that is nice for Mrs Stratton.'

'You wouldn't think so by the way they carry on. Miss Angela likes her own way and so does Madam.'

'Are there any other relatives – anyone who takes an interest in Master Edward?'

'Only Mr Heron – that's Mrs Stratton's younger brother,' Nanny pursued her mouth. 'I can't deny he is good with the boy. Edward responds to his uncle more than anyone else, but . . . he is not to be trusted.'

'I met him yesterday.' Jane looked about her. 'Where is Master Edward now? Should I help him get dressed?'

'Lord love you, no. He can manage that well enough himself. He was up early this morning so that he could go riding with his uncle. Mr Heron is staying for a few days . . .' Nanny was disapproving. 'He is probably in some kind of money trouble. He knows where to come when he wants something.'

'Ah . . .' Jane remembered the way Mrs Stratton had greeted her brother. 'Shall I take these things to the kitchen and iron them?'

'We've got a special place for our ironing. I'll show you where everything is and then you can make a start.'

Jane finished the ironing and looked round for something to do. She had been told that the maids did the sweeping and dusting twice a week, but it was obvious that no one had tidied up the schoolroom for a long time.

'Good morning, Miss Shaw,' a cheerful voice addressed her from the doorway, making her turn with a start. 'Say good morning to Miss Shaw, Ned.'

In his riding clothes, David Heron was even more striking than when she'd seen him the previous day. Her dark gaze sought out the young boy she had come here to care for, noting the fresh colour in his cheeks and the sparkle in his eyes – greenish blue like his mother's.

'Why has she come?' the boy asked and looked sulky. 'I don't need another nanny.'

'That's just as well then, because I'm not your nanny. I'm here to help Nanny with her work – and to oversee your lessons. I've been looking at your books, Edward. You haven't done any of the exercises set for you by the Rector this week.'

'You can't tell me what to do! If you try I'll kick you and if you smack me my mother will dismiss you.'

'Ned!' David Heron looked at him with disapproval. 'That was extremely rude, young man.'

'Edward is establishing the boundaries,' Jane said calmly. 'I have no intention of smacking you, Edward – but I can deprive you of privileges. If you do not attend your lessons you may not be able to go riding with your uncle or play the games you enjoy.'

'You can't do that – can she, Uncle David?'

'I rather think she can, old chap . . .'

'I shall come with you whatever she says. I don't have to do what she tells me!'

'I on the other hand shall take my instruction from Miss Shaw. If you wish for the game of cricket I promised for this afternoon I rather think you must do some work first.' David Heron turned his beguiling smile on Jane. 'Would you come and field for us? I believe your duties include taking Ned out for walks and playing games with him – after he has done his school work, of course.'

'I should be happy to play cricket with you and Edward, Mr Heron – if Edward does some of this work first.'

'I shan't do anything if you call me Edward. I hate that name! Uncle David calls me Ned.'

'Would you prefer me to use Ned?'

The boy stared at her mutinously and then nodded. 'I haven't done the arithmetic, because I don't know how to . . .'

'I think I can show you how. You look intelligent, Ned. Why don't we see if you are as clever, as I think?' She raised her brows at him. 'What is it you don't understand about these sums? They are what we call algebra, but it is really just a case of multiplying, adding and then dividing. You have to work out what number each letter stands for and then it is easy if you know how to multiply and divide . . .'

'Of course I do. I'm not a baby.'

'I didn't think you were. Shall we do this one together? Then you can do the others yourself.'

A soft chuckle made her look at David Heron.

'You are quite the teacher, Miss Shaw. I shall see you both later.'

Jane saw the ball fly through the air towards her. She caught it neatly, smiling inwardly as she saw the surprise and swiftly hidden annoyance in David Heron's eyes.

'I believe that is out. Wouldn't you say so Sam?' Her eyes turned on the gardener's boy, who looked at her apprehensively, not daring to venture his opinion. 'It is Ned's turn now.'

'That's the first time anyone has caught Uncle David,' Ned's eyes gleamed with triumph. He admired his uncle a lot, even so he couldn't hide the triumph he felt in taking the bat from him. 'You were lucky, Miss Shaw.'

'Was I?' Jane hid her amusement. 'I played cricket at school. There weren't always enough boys who wanted to be in the team so girls had to stand in, and I was quite good at it.'

'Can you bowl as well?'

Jane looked at David Heron, trying to read his mind. 'Underarm, I am afraid. I'm better with the bat.'

'You'd better stay where you are then. You had a lucky catch, as Ned said. If you catch Ned as well we might let you have a turn with the bat.'

Jane had realized instantly that the game was between Ned and his uncle. The gardener's boy was a permanent fielder and evidently that was also meant to be her role.

She watched as David Heron bowled to his nephew, approving the way he gave no quarter. Ned took a wild swing and missed the first ball completely but it bounced high and his wicket survived. He gripped the handle with both hands in determined fashion and struck the next ball dead centre. It flew through the air towards the gardener's boy. Sam managed to miss it, deliberately Jane thought. She frowned as he darted after it and hunted in the shrubbery while Ned took five runs. His uncle had notched up ten before being caught and the boy was grinning ear to ear when Sam finally threw the ball to David.

Ned hit the third ball in the same direction and the same thing happened again. Jane frowned, because she was quite certain that Sam could have caught both balls if he had tried. She wasn't sure if David knew what was going on or not but she certainly did not approve. When the fourth ball came in her direction she dived to catch it, landing on the ground with the ball safe in her hand.

'That's out! You are hitting the ball too high, Ned. You should try to keep it low and sweep it to the side . . .'

'It wasn't out. You dropped it!' Ned claimed, his cheeks red with temper.

'I assure you I did not. It is Sam's turn to bat now.'

'No! He doesn't bat. He is a fielder. I'm not out because you cheated.'

'I did not cheat, young man – and you know it.' Jane stared him in the eyes. 'I think perhaps someone else has been cheating but we won't say any more about it if you give the bat up to Sam.'

'I don't want to play any more.' Ned threw the bat to the ground in disgust and walked towards a fallen tree, sitting down with his knees hunched.

'All right. We shall play without you. Sam – come and take the bat, please.'

Sam hesitated, looked nervously at his employer's son, coming slowly to take the bat she offered. David paused for a moment and then took up his stance, bowling a slightly harder ball at Sam than he had for his nephew. Sam hit out catching it squarely and sending it flying into the shrubbery. He started to run between the wickets. Jane went into the bushes and hunted. She found it and rushed back as Sam completed his fourth run.

David bowled again. Sam hit it straight at Jane and she caught it. She suspected that he had done it deliberately, and when she saw him glance anxiously at Ned she was certain.

'Right, you've caught us all out,' David said. 'Now it's your turn, Miss Shaw. We'll see what you can do with the bat.'

Jane accepted it from Sam. She was surprised when David went over to his nephew and said something to him in a low voice. Ned rose to his feet, took the ball and came back to face her. She saw the gleam of malice in his eyes, and was not surprised when he threw the ball straight at her. It was aimed at her head and all she could do was put up her arm to protect herself. The ball struck her with force and she gave an involuntary yelp of pain.

'That was a foul throw,' David said. 'Jane gets two runs for that, Ned. I told you to bowl hard but not at her face.'

'Sorry. It slipped from my hand.'

Jane was quite certain Ned had meant to hurt her but she rubbed at her arm and said nothing. Ned's second ball flew through the air, bounced and Jane swept it to her right. She hadn't noticed that David had moved in closer and could not help admiring the way he dived to catch the ball and hold it up in triumph.

'That is out!' he shouted, clearly pleased to have proved his point. 'It is my turn again now.'

'All right – but this time everyone tries harder.' Her eyes were on Sam. 'This is a game of skill and the object is to get the person in bat out before he achieves too many runs. There is no point in playing unless everyone follows the rules. Winning undeservedly isn't worth doing – and gentlemen do not cheat. ' The young gardener's boy flushed red, his eyes darting at Ned. 'It's your turn again, Mr Heron.'

'Thank you, Miss Shaw. I do believe you missed your vocation in life.'

Jane ignored the challenge. She handed him the bat and then gave the ball to Sam.

'Let's see if you can bowl as well as I believe you can bat.'

Sam's gaze flew to her face and then he grinned. Jane knew that she had touched a chord in him and suddenly the game looked exciting.

'I had no idea that the youth could play like that,' David said to Jane as they walked back to the house later. 'He made every one of us look like an amateur. How did you know he could play?'

'I guessed,' Jane said and laughed. 'Before he went back to work, Sam told me he plays for the village team. He has been offered a chance of playing for the county cricket team but unfortunately he cannot afford to take it up.'

'That is a shame. I shall have to speak to his father – see if anything could be arranged.'

'It would be kind of you to take an interest but I expect the family need his wage.'

'I dare say there may be a way round it. If it was worth my while . . .'

Jane met his intense gaze, feeling a little shock run through her. 'What do you mean?'

'Now what should I mean, Jane? What has Nanny been telling you about me? I know she thinks I am the devil incarnate. She was devoted to Maria's husband. I seldom visited when Vernon Stratton was alive. He thought I was a bad influence on his wife but it was always she who influenced me, of course.'

'Are you suggesting . . .' Jane broke off, her cheeks faintly pink. 'Do you enjoy mocking me, Mr Heron?'

'Oh yes, Jane, very much. You amuse me more than you can possibly know.' He grinned and ran after his nephew, who had gone on ahead, placing an arm around his shoulders for a moment before turning away.

Ned looked at Jane as they went into the house. 'You knew that Sam deliberately let me score runs, didn't you?'

'Yes. Are you cross because I told Sam to play properly?'

'He plays much better than I do.'

'He is a lot older. Your uncle is older and so am I – but you scored more runs than I did. If people let you win you will never know if you're any good at something.'

'Uncle David caught you out both times. You shouldn't have caught him the first time. No one else ever has.'

'Maybe I was lucky, as you said.'

'I'm sorry I hit you. I shouldn't have done that – it wasn't the way a gentleman behaves.'

'No, it wasn't. I forgive you, but think before you do it again.'

'The last governess told Mother I was impossible. Am I impossible, Jane?'

'I don't know you yet. So far I think there may be hope for you.'

Ned stared at her for a moment then ran on ahead up the stairs.

Jane followed, feeling pleased with her afternoon. Ned seemed a bright, somewhat spoiled lad but decent enough deep down.

Staring at the frog sitting on her pillow that night, Jane realized that she had congratulated herself too soon. She pulled the top covers down and found two pinecones and, more seriously, a stinging nettle. If she had got into bed without looking she might have had a nasty surprise. The nettles would have been painful on her bare legs, and, had the frog not crawled out on to the pillow she might have lain on the poor creature.

Jane had never been frightened of frogs. She picked it up carefully, wondering what to do for the best. Complaining to Mrs Stratton or Ned's uncle was something she would be loathe to do – but if she just let him get away with it he would imagine he could carry on with his silly tricks.

Carrying the frog gently, she went along the passage to the nursery where Ned slept. A small lamp was burning on the dressing table. Nanny had told her that he hated to sleep in the dark. Ned's eyes were closed but as she approached him, he opened them and looked at her. An apprehensive look came to his face as he saw that she had the frog in her hand.

'Did I wake you? I'm sorry. I found this darling little frog in my room and I thought he might be your pet. He was on my pillow. It was a good thing I didn't lay on him, because I might have squashed him.'

'Squashed frog.' Ned had an expectant look in his eyes now. 'Aren't you afraid of frogs?'

'No. Should I be?'

'Most girls are. Angela hates them. She screams if I put them in her bed.'

'Poor Angela. I like frogs. I don't like stinging nettles though. I am allergic to their sting. Once, I had a terrible rash all over me from touching a nettle. My face swelled up and the doctor said I could have died.'

Ned's face went white.

'I didn't know people could die from stinging nettles.'

'I'm not sure they can. I made it up.'

Ned stared at her uncertainly. 'To punish me?'

'Do you think you deserve to be punished?'

He scowled at her but with an underlying apprehension. 'Will you leave? Will you tell my mother I'm impossible?'

'Would she be cross with you?'

'She might hit me. She did last time.'

'I shan't tell her. Do you want me to leave here? Would you rather have someone else?'

'No . . .' Ned paused, then. 'I think I like you.'

'Shall I leave the frog here in this box of yours?'

'He likes to crawl about the room. Just put him anywhere. I'll take him outside in the morning.'

'Right. Shall I put the light out?'

'No! You wouldn't?' Ned's eyes widened in fear.

'No, I wouldn't do that,' Jane said. 'Did someone do it to you to punish you?' Ned nodded. 'That was unkind. I shan't be unkind to you, Ned. Go to sleep now and don't worry. I think the Rector will be pleased when he sees all the sums you've done.'

'Do you really like frogs?'

'Yes.' Jane smiled. 'I really do. Goodnight, Ned. Sweet dreams. There aren't any bogey men you know – and I'm just down the hall if you need me.'

★   ★   ★

Over the next few days Jane gradually settled into her new life. She rose early to help Nanny tidy the nursery, and then fetched Ned's breakfast from the kitchen. The first morning Cook was surprised to see her.

'You had only to ring for it.'

'It is no trouble for me to get it myself – if I shan't be in your way? Ned told me he likes his bread cut into soldiers and his egg not too runny – and he wants honey with his toast not marmalade. He doesn't like the thick bits in the marmalade.'

'Now there's a thing.' Cook stared at her in surprise. 'No one has ever told me that before. I could send the clear marmalade if he would prefer it?'

'We'll have the honey today, please – if there is some?'

'Yes, of course there is, Miss Shaw. Madam likes it herself.'

Cook was a plump lady with dark brown hair peeping from the front of her cap.

'My name is Jane. I would rather you didn't call me Miss Shaw – and I'm sorry. Nanny didn't tell me your name.'

'I'm just Cook to everyone, but my name is Sally Brent.' Cook smiled and nodded. 'That egg should be just right. I was thinking of chicken soup and a ham sandwich for the lad's lunch. What do you think?'

'That sounds lovely to me. What else is there?'

'Well, he could have a mutton chop or some pork pie with potatoes and greens, but he doesn't eat his greens as a rule.'

'He should have them sometimes. I'll ask him what he likes later and we'll discuss his menus tomorrow. The soup and sandwich will do very well for today.'

Ned ate most of his breakfast that morning, but when lunchtime came he refused both the soup and the sandwich, pushing his spoon around the dish and pulling a face.

'Don't you like soup?' Jane asked.

She had taken her meal with him and found the soup tasty. The ham sandwich was delicious.

'Not this sort. I like the tomato one and the asparagus – and there's a clear one with bits in it.'

'I'll ask Cook to make one of those for you another day. This ham is lovely. We never have ham that tastes this good at my home. We couldn't often afford it at all. Sometimes all we had was bread and dripping.'

'Ugh! That sounds horrid. Why couldn't you afford it?'

'Because my father didn't earn enough money and by the end of the week we had to make do with what we had.'

'Were you very poor?'

'There were other people I knew who had less. We always had chickens in the yard so if they laid enough eggs there was something to eat.'

Ned was silent. 'Am I lucky? Someone told me I didn't deserve to be lucky.'

'Who was that?'

'One of the maids before she left us.'

'She shouldn't have said that to you. You are fortunate to have a nice home and plenty to eat but it isn't your fault that other people don't have the same.'

Ned picked up his sandwich and ate a mouthful. 'I like tomato sandwiches and I like them on toast. Mother has them for tea sometimes – and she has salmon too. I like that better than ham.'

'Well, I expect you can have it. Do you like any vegetables?'

'Peas are all right – but I like them raw. I like to go scrumping with Sam from his father's allotment. I love gooseberries and raspberries.'

'Oh yes, I loved doing that too! Especially when there were gooseberries and strawberries.'

Jane smiled. Ned wasn't really that much different from Melia when she was his age.

'Well, that's quite an achievement,' Cook said when Jane handed her a list of Ned's likes and dislikes. 'He has quite sophisticated tastes for a lad of his age, don't you think?'

'Ned certainly knows what he likes and what he doesn't.'

'Nobody else ever told me.' Cook looked at her thoughtfully. 'I reckon that boy has had a stroke of luck for once with you coming here. Some folk wouldn't think he deserves better than he gets – but he misses his father. He wasn't half the trouble before Mr Stratton took that chill and died so mysterious.'

'Why do you say mysterious?'

Cook turned red and turned away to stir a pot of sauce on

the stove. 'A fine strong man like that shouldn't ought to die of a chill . . . I'm sayin' no more.'

Nanny had said something similar but Jane wasn't sure what their hints were meant to convey and it wasn't her place to speculate.

His uncle took him riding after lunch and he came back with a healthy colour in his cheeks. He told her that Uncle David was getting a new car and would be taking him out for a spin soon, chattering on about the model and how fast it would go until Jane tucked him into bed that evening.

There were no nasty surprises in her bed when she pulled the sheets back that night. She didn't imagine the war was won for a moment, but Ned seemed to have called a truce.

David Heron came up to the nursery with his nephew after the drive in his new car. He was still wearing a leather helmet and goggles, which he had pushed up out of the way.

'Look at the pair of you!' Nanny clucked her tongue as she saw them. 'It's a bath for you, Master Edward – and you should do the same Mr Heron.'

'Thank you, Nanny. I dare say I shall before dinner,' David said, grinning at Jane as the elderly lady took her charge away. 'Nanny's opinion is that automobiles are nasty dirty things and she may be right. We had the top down and we're both covered in dust.'

'Nothing that a little soap and water won't cure.' Jane was amused but tried not to show it. 'Was it fun? Ned looks as if he enjoyed himself.'

'He loved it. I shall teach him to drive when I come down again. It will be safe in our own grounds.'

'Are you leaving so soon?' Jane blurted the words out and then blushed. 'Ned will be disappointed. It will be dull for him with just Nanny and me.'

'You can rope Sam in for a game of cricket if the weather is fine and he loves to visit the horses. We went down to the river today. Did you know that it is tidal? If you want to paddle when it is hot you are better off with the stream on the estate.' David's eyes gleamed. 'Shall you miss me, Jane?'

'No not at all. Why should I?'

'Now that's just plain mean. I thought you liked me, Jane?'

'You are Ned's uncle and kind to him. It doesn't matter what I think. I'm just a servant.'

'Have I ever made you feel like a servant?' David reached out; his fingers curled about her arm, pressed into her flesh so hard that she almost winced. 'Answer me!'

'No, you haven't – but I am your nephew's nurse come governess. Your sister employs me.'

'That doesn't make you a menial.' His eyes narrowed. 'You certainly don't behave like any servant I've ever known.'

'That is because I have no experience of how to behave in service.'

'It is your natural pride. I told Maria you would be good for Ned and you are. You care about him, don't you?'

'Yes. Yes, I do . . .' Jane looked at him proudly. 'But it still doesn't matter what I think of you.'

'It matters to me. I've done something to make you pleased with me.'

'Oh . . .' she was wary as she waited. 'What?'

'I've arranged for Sam to have a trial for the county – and if he is accepted he can take time off to practise and play in matches. He will keep his job and the same wage as he has now, but has to put in extra hours to make up for it.'

'You did that for Sam?'

'I did it for you, Jane – so that you would think I'm not such a bad chap after all . . .'

'You shouldn't have done it for me . . .'

Jane was suddenly nervous. She half suspected what was coming but wasn't quick enough to move before he grabbed her, pulling her into his arms. His kiss was hard, punishing and demanding. She did not respond to him and when he let her go his expression was angry.

'Why didn't you kiss me back?'

'Because I didn't want to kiss you.'

'You won't admit it you liked it yet, because you're a stubborn prude, but you felt it from the start – just as I did.'

'I felt nothing,' Jane said but knew that she lied. 'You had no right to do that . . . someone might have come in.'

'Next time I'll make sure we're alone – and I shan't take no for an answer. I want you, Jane, and I always get what I want . . .'

★   ★   ★

Ned was a bit subdued for the first couple of days after his uncle left. Jane took him on long rambles through the countryside, refusing to let him sink into himself – or to acknowledge that she missed seeing his uncle. They picked wild flowers so that they could study them; at other times they cycled into King's Lynn and walked by the river, watching as the boats struggled against the tide. Sometimes, they took the ferry to the other side and went exploring further afield. She discovered that he had a talent for drawing and praised the studies he did of flowers, fir cones and his frog. He had formed a habit of carrying the frog in his jacket pocket, and Jane suggested that he draw his pet.

'He won't stay still long enough,' Ned objected. 'I've tried but it didn't look right.'

'Supposing I hold Frog on my lap so that you can see him?'

'I could try.' Ned's face was alight with interest. 'I want to be an artist like my father. Did you know he had his paintings shown at an academy in London?'

'No, I didn't – but I noticed a painting in the hall downstairs. Did your father paint that?'

'Is it the one of mountains? Mother put it at the back of the hall, because she doesn't like Father's work – but I think it is wonderful.'

'Yes, it is. No wonder you can draw so well. Was your father a professional?'

'Someone told him he should have an exhibition and he was thinking about it – then he was taken ill . . .' A shadow fell over his face. 'Mother put most of the paintings in store. She says it upsets her to look at them but I think she is just being spiteful because I love them.'

'Ned! You shouldn't say that about your mother.'

'She doesn't care about me. She didn't care about my father either. I heard her shouting at him just before he got ill.'

'Ned, you really shouldn't talk about your mother that way.'

'I hate her! She killed him. I know she did.'

'You don't truly believe that your mother killed your father? He was very ill. A lot of people die with pneumonia. It is very sad but the doctors don't know how to make them better.'

Ned looked at her hard. 'You're not just making it up – like the stinging nettles?'

'I wouldn't lie to you about something important. Believe me, Ned. It was just a little joke the other night, but you did put the nettles in my bed and I had to try and make you see it was wrong.'

'I won't do it again.' Ned suddenly threw himself at her, the sobs shaking his body. 'I loved my father. It hurts so much when someone you love leaves you. He loved me. Mother doesn't love me.'

Jane's arms closed about him. Tears trickled down her cheeks as she kissed the top of his head, rubbing his back gently in an effort to comfort him.

'I know it hurts, Ned. I lost someone I loved just before I came here . . .' He looked up at her curiously. 'My little brother was three years old. I don't know what was wrong with Charlie. I thought it was just a nasty chill but he died suddenly.'

'But you loved him, didn't you?'

'Yes, I did. Very much.'

'Then he was lucky,' Ned said. 'No one loves me – except perhaps Uncle David, a bit.'

'I am sure your uncle loves you, Ned.' Jane hugged him. 'I am becoming fond of you, too.'

'Are you?' Ned's eyes gleamed speculatively. 'Can we go walking again tomorrow?'

'You know the Rector comes tomorrow to mark your books and set more lessons. Don't you want to hear what he says about your work?'

'Suppose so . . .' Ned shrugged. 'My father used to read me a story sometimes. Will you read to me tonight, Jane?'

'Yes, of course I will. Pick the book you want and we'll start it this evening – and if the weather is fine we'll have a picnic the day after tomorrow . . .'

Angela came home that weekend. She was a pretty girl with soft fair hair and intelligent eyes, but her mouth had a sulky look. Jane met her when she went into the schoolroom and found the brother and sister arguing. They were fighting over a book and as they struggled a page was torn out.

'That is a bit silly, isn't it? Why are you arguing over Ned's book?'

'It isn't Ned's it is mine. He is always taking things that don't belong to him.'

'You don't want it any more. You know I like it.'

'Surely, it is more of a boy's book than a girl's,' Jane said as she rescued the copy of *Treasure Island* that had now fallen on the floor between them. 'Ned, you should ask your sister's permission before you take her things.'

'It doesn't matter. It is ruined now,' Angela said and looked at Jane coldly. 'He might as well keep it . . .'

She turned and rushed from the room.

'She is going to cry. She always cries if she doesn't get her own way.'

'You shouldn't have taken the book if you knew it was important to your sister. It is her book . . .'

'It was Father's book,' Ned said. 'Angela took it after he died. She knew I wanted it but she wanted it too.'

'Ah, I see. Perhaps you could agree to share it.'

'It is spoiled now . . .' Ned looked miserable. 'I didn't mean to tear it, Jane.'

'I know you didn't. Don't be upset. I can mend it for you – but I think you should go and say sorry to your sister, don't you?'

Jane knocked at Angela's door. For a moment there was silence and then she was invited to enter. The girl looked up as she entered but didn't smile, nor did she get up from the bed where she was sitting.

'Did you tell Ned to apologize to me?'

'He didn't mean to tear the book, Angela. I've stuck the page back in and it won't show if you don't look too carefully.'

'I don't care. I've told Ned he can keep it.' She got up from the bed and went to the window, gazing out. 'I hate coming home. As soon as I can leave school I'm going away . . .'

'I am sure your mother likes to see you.'

'You know nothing about my mother or me.' Angela turned accusing eyes on her. 'I hate her and she hates me. Sara is lucky. She went away and she won't come back ever.'

'Why do you hate your mother?'

'Wouldn't you like to know?' Angela turned back to the window. 'You wouldn't believe me if I told you. No one would, except

Nanny. She knows. Please go away. Ned thinks you're all right but I don't want anything to do with you.'

'If that's what you want . . .' Jane hesitated, then, 'You know where I am if you want to talk.'

'I shan't – to you anyway. Why should I? You're just a servant.'

'Yes, I am, but I'm here if you want me.'

Four

'You sent for me, Madam?' Jane stood in the small sitting room Mrs Stratton used in the mornings. 'I hope I haven't done anything wrong?'

Maria's eyes went over her with unconcealed dislike. 'You have survived longer than I expected. My son normally makes the life of his nursemaid as uncomfortable as he possibly can. What have you done to change that, Miss Shaw? If you are caning him you can stop.'

'I have not lifted a finger to hurt Ned,' Jane said and realized she had made a mistake as she saw her employer's frown. 'I meant Master Edward.'

'I should just think so! Remember your place, Miss Shaw. I took you on the flimsiest of recommendations. Do not imagine I will stand for impudence.'

'No, Madam. I am sorry. It won't happen again.'

'It had better not.' Maria's eyes narrowed. 'Your six months comes to an end in four weeks' time. Will you sign another contract?'

'Yes, if you wish, Madam — but my father says the contract was not binding. You don't need to try and force me to stay. I should like to stay while Ned needs me. I beg your pardon, I meant Master Edward.'

Maria Stratton's eyes darkened with anger, but she turned away to glance out of the window.

'You will be needed until after Christmas. He goes to boarding school in the New Year. I would have sent him sooner but he was distraught over his father's—' She broke off and turned to face Jane, a look of anguish in her eyes, 'My brother is coming to visit us. He has recently joined the army. I suppose you did realize that there is going to be a war soon?'

'Yes, Madam. I read the papers and my father thinks it is almost inevitable. His last letter to me says the assassination of the Archduke Franz Ferdinand and his wife will definitely lead to war. According to the papers, the assassins may have been Serbian.'

'I was not sure whether you took an interest in such things. Mrs Buller told me that you've spent most of your free time in the house. Are you hiding from something or someone?'

'I enjoy my work, Madam. I read when I have an hour or two to myself and I take Master Edward for long walks.' A few days earlier she had taken Ned to a restaurant in King's Lynn for cream cakes and tea, spending some time wandering around the fleet, a narrow, muddy inlet where the fishing vessels were harboured. 'Master Edward is very clever at drawing. I wondered if he could have some paints for his birthday?'

'His father played at being an artist.' Maria's mouth thinned. 'My son will go to a good school and learn how to be a professional man. He will inherit a fortune left in trust for him when he is twenty-three. Painting is a waste of time.'

Jane didn't agree but it wasn't for her to tell his mother she was wrong.

'Very well, you may go,' Maria said. She exclaimed with annoyance as the brooch she was wearing suddenly fell to the ground. As she bent to pick it up, Jane saw that it was a large diamond star. 'The catch has broken again. I shall have to send it to a jeweller in London.' She opened the drawer of a desk that stood in the bay window and tossed the brooch carelessly into it. 'What are you waiting for?'

'Nothing, Madam. Thank you.'

Maria sent her a look that made her spine tingle. Jane sensed that her employer did not like her. She was being given a further term of employment only because Ned had improved so much.

'Nanny said there is going to be a war.' Ned looked at Jane as they sat on the grassy bank and ate their picnic. 'What does that mean? Why do we want to fight the Germans? Is it just because that archduke got killed?'

'No, I don't think it's just that, Ned. The papers have been warning of trouble in the Balkans for months. My father wrote me that it is to do with treaties and things of that sort – all rather complicated. Yesterday's paper said that even if war happens it will be over in a few months.'

Ned picked a long stem of grass and chewed the end. The day

was warm; a still, lazy day when the only sounds to be heard were bees buzzing amongst the shining petals of yellow buttercups and a thrush singing in a copse of beech trees nearby.

'Did you know that my uncle has joined the army?'

'Your mother told me yesterday.'

'Will he have to fight the enemy?'

'Don't worry too much. It may not happen.'

'Nanny says it will. She remembers the Crimea War. A lot of men died in that war. We read about it in the history book you borrowed from the library.'

'That war was ages ago.' Jane reached forward to touch his hand. 'Your uncle is a clever man. Even if he goes to war, he will come back safe and sound.'

Ned drew his hand away. 'Don't pretend, Jane. You don't know if he'll come back. You told me men should face the truth and behave like gentlemen. Uncle David will fight because he isn't a coward. He would never become a *cons-scientious* objector.'

'That is a big word for a hot day,' Jane said, smiling. 'Your uncle is going to visit us soon. You can talk to him about what is happening.'

'Do you think it was because he joined the army that he hasn't been to stay with us for months?'

'I imagine so. He must have been training to be a soldier.' She lifted her face to the sun, basking in its warmth. 'Do you want to paddle in the stream?'

'Yes.' Ned started taking off his shoes and socks.

Jane wasn't wearing stockings because it was such a warm day. She slipped her shoes off and went down to the shallow stream that wound through the grounds of Maria Stratton's home.

Lifting her skirt and tucking it up so that it only just covered her knees, she waded into the water. It felt deliciously cool and the sandy bed was firm beneath her toes. Ned splashed at her, kicking water over her. Jane retaliated. He bent down and scooped water in his hands, making a move towards her. She screamed and pretended to run from him but he caught her and threw the water over her.

'You little wretch! Just you wait . . .' She bent down to scoop up some water, throwing it at him.

'Is this a private game or can anyone join in?'

Jane hadn't seen the man approaching. She turned and looked

at him, the expression in his eyes sending a little flutter of apprehension through her.

'I didn't know anyone was watching . . .' Jane walked from the stream and let her skirts down.

'Uncle David . . .' Ned gave a scream of delight and charged past her, throwing himself at his uncle.

David grabbed him and swung him round. The two of them were obviously happy to see each other and by the time the rough and tumble of their greeting was over Jane had had a chance to recover her composure.

'When did you arrive?' she asked.

'An hour or so ago. Mrs Buller told me that you often have picnics. Ned is a lucky boy. I don't remember being taken on a picnic when I was his age. I went to boarding school and it wasn't much fun.'

'We learn a lot on our walks. The Rector is impressed with the improvement in his work. You should see some of the studies he did of the harbour in King's Lynn . . .' Jane glanced away as she saw the heat of passion in David Heron's eyes. 'Besides, Ned will be going to school next year.'

Ned stared at her, his face white. 'Who told you that? I don't want to go to boarding school.'

Jane was horrified as she saw his distress. 'I'm sorry, Ned. I had no idea your mother hadn't said anything to you.'

'It will be all right, old chap,' David said. 'Just because I didn't much like my school at first it doesn't mean you won't. You'll make friends with lads of your own age and—'

'I'm not going!'

Ned had finished putting on his socks and shoes, and before either Jane or his uncle were aware of what he meant to do he started running across the fields in the direction of his home.

'Ned! Please wait for me . . .' Jane slipped her feet into her shoes but David caught her arm. 'I have to go after him.'

'He isn't a baby. He will be eight in August. Most boys of his class have been at boarding school for a year now. Ned's father put his name down when he was born and Maria is determined he should go.'

'I thought you cared about him?'

'I do care for him, of course I do – but this is his destiny. It is what his father wanted and I think it is best for him.'

'You don't understand what he has been through. He feels things deeply. I'm not sure he could survive a boarding school . . . the initiations and all the other stuff that goes on.'

'It will make a man of him.'

'That is so harsh! He adores you. He was worrying about you having to fight if there is a war . . .'

'It is a matter of when, not if there is a war. I wish it didn't have to be this way, Jane – but I have no choice but to fight and Ned has to go to boarding school.'

Jane wouldn't answer him. She walked away, feeling angry with him for not understanding. He didn't know that Ned was afraid of the dark or about the way he clung to her because he was desperate to be loved.

Ned was in his room when Jane found him. His eyes were red and she knew he had been crying.

'Why didn't you tell me before?'

'I didn't know until yesterday – and I wasn't aware that you hadn't been told, Ned. Your father booked your place when you were born. I'm really sorry.'

'Why should you care? Looking after me is just a job to you . . . that's what Angela says.'

'Ned, you know that isn't true. I love teaching you and playing with you. I shall hate having to leave you.'

'Will you?'

'I will write to you at school – and I'll visit sometimes, if you want me to? We could go out to tea.'

'Why should you bother? No one else cares.'

'Your uncle cares. He just thinks school will be good for you – and perhaps it will. You will make friends. I'm just a servant . . .'

'You're not a servant! You are my friend!'

Jane laughed as she saw his stubborn face. 'I am glad you know that, Ned. I'm going to make you a promise now. I shall always be your friend. Whatever happens, wherever I am – wherever you are. I shall write to you and let you know where I am and what I'm doing. Will you be my friend?'

'I am your friend.' Ned smiled reluctantly. 'I don't care what Angela says. You won't break your promise?'

'We may be apart but I'll never forget you.'

'I suppose if my father wanted me to go to this school perhaps it will be best for me.'

'I think it was your father's own school. You will want to make him proud of you, won't you?'

'You promise you'll write and visit?'

'I give you my solemn word.' Jane laughed as he suddenly threw his arms about her. 'There's no need to strangle me. Why don't you go and find your uncle? He can tell you all about the army . . .'

Ned was spending a lot of time with his uncle. Because she kept everywhere spick and span there was little for her to do so she asked Mrs Buller if she could take her days off.

'How much time do you want?'

'Could I have three days – or is that too much?'

'You're entitled to them, Jane. I'll pay you your wages too. I trust you to come back and finish your time.'

'Give me four months. I'll have the last month when I've earned it.'

'You're as honest as they come,' Mrs Buller said and smiled at her. 'When do you want to go home?'

'I'll leave tomorrow. Mr Heron is here for another few days so—' she broke off as Buller came into the housekeeper's parlour.

He looked worried. 'I'm glad you're here, Miss Shaw. I want my wife to hear this, because I know she has a good opinion of you – and it's awkward.'

'Have I done something wrong, Mr Buller?' Jane asked of the small, rather ugly man.

'It is a serious matter, Miss Shaw. A valuable diamond brooch has gone missing from the drawer of the desk in Mrs Stratton's sitting room. She says she put it there when the clasp failed the day she interviewed you and . . . the implication is that you are the one most likely to have taken it.'

'I would never do such a thing!'

'I certainly don't believe it,' Mrs Buller declared stoutly. 'Nor should you, Buller. Jane is as honest a girl as you'll find.'

'The brooch has gone and Jane saw it put there . . .' Buller held up his hands as his wife's eyes took fire. 'I'm not accusing her – but the mistress wants to see her now in the sitting room.'

'I'll go right away.' Jane lifted her head. 'If you want to search my room, please do. I have nothing to hide.'

'Perhaps that might be as well.'

'If you search Jane's room you'll search mine and every other member of staff,' his wife told him.

'I would rather Mr Buller did make the search.' Jane did her best to contain her anger, because they were not to blame for the accusation. 'I am going to the sitting room immediately. Please search my things before I get back.'

She walked from the housekeeper's room proudly. Had she stayed a moment longer she might have said something unwise to Mr Buller and that would be unfair.

She knocked at the sitting room door and entered when invited. Maria Stratton's expression was one of anger and suspicion.

'You know why you are here, I presume? I placed my brooch in the drawer of this desk when you were here a few days ago and now it has gone. What have you to say for yourself?'

'I saw you place the brooch in a drawer. You said you were going to send it to a London jeweller. I have not entered this room since you told me I could go that day.'

'Why should I believe you?' Maria's eyes flashed with temper. 'I know nothing of you or your family . . .'

'My references were from people who knew me. You could have checked them had you wished.' Jane's anger got the better of her. 'You took me because you would have taken anybody at that time. Ned was too much trouble until I showed him a little love, which had been singularly lacking in his life since his father's death.'

'How dare you?' Maria took a step towards her and slapped her across the face. 'I will not stand for impudence. You may leave my employment this instant.'

'Yes, I shall, but I am giving in my notice. I am not a thief and you deserved what I just said to you for neglecting your son. It broke his heart when his father died and you couldn't even tell him he was going to boarding school in the New Year . . .'

'Get out!' Maria screamed. 'I don't want you in my house a

minute longer than necessary – and if that brooch isn't found I shall call the police.'

'I didn't take your brooch. Call the police if you wish but it doesn't change the fact that you are a bad mother.'

She walked from the room before Maria could think of a reply. Her anger sustained her until she was in her room, which she saw at once had been searched, but then she started shaking. Sitting down on the edge of her bed, she covered her face with her hands. Dismissed from her job for impudence and with the shadow of theft hanging over her, Jane knew that she might have difficulty in finding another job in the future.

What would Ned think when he knew she was leaving? A three-day absence while his uncle was here was one thing, but he still had more than four months before he went to boarding school. He would feel that she had deserted him, and Jane knew it was in part her fault

Nanny came in as she was packing. She looked upset and Jane could see she had been crying.

'You're not going, Jane?'

'We had words and she dismissed me.'

'She is a wicked, evil woman,' Nanny said. 'I'll stay until the boy goes to school and then I'm off to my sister. I wouldn't stay for a second longer if it weren't that I promised my boy . . .'

'I am sorry to leave you.' Jane embraced her and was surprised when Nanny held on to her with unexpectedly fierce emotion. 'Ned won't be so much trouble to you now. He has grown up.'

'This will upset him, put him back to where he was.'

'I'll write to him, Nanny.'

'He'll break his heart over it and that's a fact.'

'I know but there's nothing I can do.'

When Jane's bags were packed she went down to Mrs Buller's room. The housekeeper invited her in, her expression one of extreme distress.

'Jane! Why did you answer Madam back that way?'

'I know I shouldn't have done it. I was just so angry that I couldn't help myself.'

'She has a bad mouth but we all knew that when we came here.' Mrs Buller shook her head sorrowfully. 'I've been told not to pay you more than a month's money. She says that you've forfeited your wages and she still seems to think you took the brooch. I told her a search had been made and nothing found but she just screwed up her mouth.'

'When have I had time to sell it? I haven't left the house, except for the picnic with Ned that day.'

'Madam knows that in her heart but for some reason she has it in for you – and you saying that about Master Edward got to her. She says that he is to have his tea with her in the afternoons in future. She wants him to learn some social manners before he goes to school.'

'Poor Ned . . .' Jane said, her voice choked with emotion. 'I don't mind all the rest, Mrs Buller – but I hate leaving him. I've written him a letter. Will you see that he gets it?'

'Yes, of course.' Mrs Buller shook her head. 'I can only pay you what she told me, Jane – but she owes you another four months. I should speak to someone if I were you. Your father works for a lawyer, doesn't he?'

'Lawyers cost a lot of money. I think it might swallow up all I'm owed and more.'

'It is wicked that people like her can do this and get away with it!'

'The law should protect us but it doesn't. Perhaps one day when women have the vote things will change.'

'I'm not a suffragette,' Mrs Buller said. 'I think the way they go on is disrespectful and foolish, but it is time that working people were protected. I'll give your letter to Master Edward and I'll tell him you were upset at leaving him. I only wish I could do more.'

'Oh, Jane, that is awful.' Jane's father looked shocked. 'A diamond brooch is worth a lot of money. You will find it hard to get another job with something like that hanging over your head.'

'I didn't take it, Pa.'

'I know you didn't.' He thrust his fingers through his hair looking worried. 'It was too bad of her not to pay you what was owed. I was relying on that money . . .'

'I thought you only wanted some of it?'

John Shaw turned away to look out of the window. 'I did something foolish, Jane. Five pounds of your money might have put it right but now . . .' He turned to her, his face haggard with worry. 'I owe five pounds at work. I thought there was plenty of time but they've asked for an audit of the ledgers . . .'

'What do you mean you owe five pounds at work?'

John turned slowly to face her. 'You aren't a thief, Jane – but I am. I stole five pounds from the petty cash tin and I've taken a few shillings here and there since then.'

Jane's eyes widened in horror. 'I don't believe it! How could you? You've always taught us not to touch a penny that didn't belong to us. A thief . . . why?' Jane saw the shame and misery in his face. 'Was it when Charlie was ill? Oh, Pa, what made you do it?'

'I don't know, Jane. You don't have to tell me that I've let you down. I've let myself down. They are doing the audit next week. If they find the discrepancies I'll be sacked. I shall have no chance of getting another decent job.'

'How much have you taken?'

'Five pounds from the petty cash – perhaps three or four pounds at most from clients' money. I thought that once you got your wages, I could begin to put it back, bit by bit. It's years since Mr Sampson had an outside audit done . . .'

'If I'd been paid I would have given you all the money and welcome,' Jane said. 'I know why you took the first five pounds, Pa – but why take the rest?'

'I was saving for Melia's future. Some of it was spent on things your Ma needed, but I have four pounds in a box in the shed . . .' He raked his fingers through his thinning hair. 'I don't know what to do, Jane. I would put the four pounds back but it still wouldn't tally, though the petty cash money wasn't recorded. That's what made me take it – it shouldn't have been there.'

'Someone put it there and they must have wondered what happened to it, even if there was no record in the book. You must have realized you would get caught one day, Pa?'

'What has your father done now?' Helen Shaw's sharp voice made them both turn guiltily. 'What are you doing home? Did they give you the push?'

'Yes. A brooch went missing and I was more or less accused of taking it . . . Don't look like that, Ma. I swear I didn't touch it. My room was searched and Mrs Buller believed me but Mrs Stratton seemed to think I must have taken it. I lost my temper. I told her she was a bad mother . . .'

'No wonder she sacked you! Did you take leave of your senses? She won't give you a reference – and she might send the police after you.'

'They won't be able to prove anything. I didn't touch that brooch – but I was rude to her.'

'So you've come home to be a burden on us for the rest of your life. I hope she gave you your wages?'

'Mrs Buller paid me a month. I know I'm entitled to the rest – but Mrs Stratton won't pay me and it would cost too much to sue her for it, wouldn't it, Pa?'

'You would need more than you're owed!' Helen snapped and her husband looked at her sharply.

'It isn't Jane's fault. She has been unjustly accused. There might be some sort of appeal, Jane, but I'm not sure. I could ask if you like?' He turned away but not before Jane caught the expression of anguish in his eyes.

'I've got twenty-one shillings. You take that for the bills, Pa. I'll go out first thing in the morning and see if I can find a job . . .'

'Some hope of that,' Helen said. 'You were warned not to go to that place, but you had to have your way. Well, my girl, you will find something if you want to live here – even if it is scrubbing floors!'

Five

'Mrs Stratton must be horrible,' Melia said when she came in from school and heard the news. 'If I'd been you I would have left there ages ago.' She hugged her sister. 'I'm glad you're home. I've missed you.'

'I've missed you too but I liked looking after Ned. He is lonely and unhappy and he needs to be loved.'

'You needed him too, because of Charlie. Don't think I haven't missed him, Jane, because I have. I know I said things but I wish he were back with us. The house has seemed empty without you and Charlie.'

'It can't have been easy for you looking after Ma and doing your school work.' Jane smiled at her. 'I'll do what I can now but I have to find work of some kind.'

'Yes, I know. Why don't you ask Aggie? She might know if there is a job going somewhere.'

'I don't have a reference from my last employer.' Jane sighed. 'I was thinking of trying at Woolworth's but I know they are strict about references there.'

'You'll find something. You're clever and honest and someone will see what a good worker you would be.'

Jane didn't answer. Melia had no idea how hard it could be to find work, especially with the accusation of theft hanging over her. She was innocent but there was no way she could prove it.

'Miss Shaw . . . Jane . . .'

Jane stopped walking as she heard a man's voice call her. She had been trudging round the streets all morning and was on her way home. The nice man in Woolworth's had told her they might need a supervisor soon but she would need three references, including one from her last employer. She waited for Robert to catch up with her.

'I thought it was you – I understand you lost your job?'

'Yes. It wouldn't have been so bad but I didn't get paid all I was owed.'

'I am sorry I told you about the job, Jane. You might have found something here months ago.'

'You mustn't blame yourself. No one seems to be hiring at the moment. I think it may be because the idea of a war is bothering them.'

'I do know of something . . .' Robert looked away for a moment. 'I hardly like to suggest it, because it isn't good enough for a girl like you . . .'

'My father needs money. I'll do anything.'

'It is a cleaning job at the Royal Arms . . .' he broke off as a little gasp escaped Jane. 'It's not a nice place and certainly for a young woman like you. Forget I told you.'

Jane was silent, then, 'I was shocked when you told me the name of the public house but I shall go there this afternoon. I meant it when I said I would do anything.'

'I should like to help, Jane, but I have an invalid mother to support.'

'I couldn't accept financial help. You tried to help me last time, Mr Hastings – and now you've told me about another job. I am very grateful.'

'I almost wish I hadn't . . .' He gave her a rueful smile. 'I suppose you wouldn't call me Robert?'

'Why not? I know you've been good to Melia. She talks about you all the time.'

'Melia deserves her chance but so do you . . .'

'Please do not concern yourself over me. I am quite capable of managing myself.'

'Now I have offended you.'

'No . . .' Jane's expression softened. 'I appreciate your concern, Robert, truly I do – but I can manage.'

'Well, good luck then.' He hesitated as if he wanted to say more then sighed and turned away.

Jane's skin crawled as the man's eyes went over her, seeming to strip the clothes from her back. He was a tall, heavily built man with narrow-set eyes and an unshaven chin.

'So you need a job?' he leered at her from behind the bar and spat on the greasy wooden floor. 'You don't look the sort we usually get. Them pretty hands o'yourn won't take kindly to scrubbing toilets, I reckon.'

Jane smothered the desire to turn tail and run. The way he looked at her made her flesh crawl but the wages were four shillings a week and that money might make a difference.

'I can scrub floors and toilets. I don't think you will have cause to complain of my work.'

'Hoity toighty miss, ain't yer? I suppose I could give yer a try. I'll want yer here at six o'clock in the morning – and again in the afternoon to clean up before we open fer the night.'

'Yes, of course, Mr Jackson.'

'Yer can call me Ernie. If yer treat me right, Janey, you and me will get on just fine.'

'When do you want me to start?'

'Best go home and change into something else. Them toilets ain't been cleaned fer a week and the stink is somethin' horrible.'

'Jane!' John Shaw looked at his daughter in horror. 'You didn't take a job cleaning toilets in that place for four shillings a week! What were you thinking of? Surely there was something more respectable?'

'I've been everywhere. I know it isn't much but it is better than nothing, and once you get straight perhaps I can find something better.'

'If I do. The audit is set for next week.'

'If the worst happens tell them the truth, Pa. Explain about Charlie and the rest . . .'

'They wouldn't care, Jane. A thief is a thief and that's the end of it. I knew I was wrong and if they discover what I've done . . .'

'What have you done?' John swung round guiltily as he heard his wife's sharp voice. 'Didn't know I was there, did you? Well, are you going to tell me?'

'Pa borrowed some money from the petty cash tin,' Jane said, wanting to shield him from her mother's scorn. 'He is going to put it back tomorrow, aren't you, Pa?'

'Borrowed!' Helen Shaw's voice lashed at him. 'Stole more like! How could you bring shame to this house, John! I've put up with you all these years but if you lose your job I'm finished with you.'

'I would be worth more to you dead. There's a small policy amongst my things . . .' His expression was humiliated, desperate. 'I'll end it rather than cause more trouble.'

'Pa! Don't say things like that!' Jane whirled on her mother. 'And don't be so horrible to him. He took the money for you and Charlie. It isn't his fault that you're always ill.'

'That's all you know, miss. You can take his part but if he hadn't forced that imbecile on me in the first place none of this would have happened. Yes, that's what your precious father did – raped his own wife.'

'It wasn't like that,' John looked ashamed. 'I'd had a little drink and you were so cold . . .'

'That's it, blame me. I wish I'd never met you and the sooner you're gone the better.'

'Stop it, Ma! You have no right to say things like that—' Jane flinched as her mother struck her across the face. 'If you turn Pa out I'll take Melia and leave you to look after yourself.'

'Helen, that wasn't called for – and you shouldn't have spoken to your mother like that, Jane.' Her father gave her a look of disapproval. 'Your mother spoke in haste. Maybe they won't find out what I've done and if they do they might give me another chance.'

'Pigs might fly! You are a wastrel and a loser, John Shaw, but I never thought I was married to a thief.' Her eyes narrowed with spite. 'Is that the reason your family threw you out all those years ago?'

'It wasn't like that at all.'

'I know they wouldn't have anything to do with you. You told me you left home but I've seen the letters from Alice.'

'You had no right to read my letters! Besides, Alice doesn't know it all, no one does.' John Shaw's neck was red. He took a step towards his wife, his face working as he struggled to control his temper. 'You say you've put up with me – but I've had a shrew for a wife.'

'That's right, snivel like the cowardly worm you are. If I'd known that you wouldn't inherit anything from that tight fisted family of yours I would never have married you in the first place.'

'Damn you!' John caught his wife by the throat and shook her as if she were a rag doll. 'You cold bitch, I should have taught you a lesson long ago.'

'Pa . . . Stop it! Please stop this! You don't know what you're doing.'

'She deserves what she gets.' He thrust his wife backwards with such violence that she stumbled and fell, hitting her head against the black iron cooking range. 'Cold bitch . . .'

Jane knelt, her heart in her mouth as she bent over her mother's body. Helen's head was lying at a peculiar angle but her eyes were wide open and staring.

'Ma . . . Ma . . . please don't be dead . . .' Jane looked up at her father in shocked dismay. Everything had escalated so quickly that she hardly knew what had happened. 'She's dead. What are we going to do?' Jane could see that her father was stunned. He looked sick and bewildered, lost. 'It was an accident, Pa. She came over faint and struck her head as she fell, that's all.'

'I killed her, Jane. I wanted her dead and I killed her.'

'It was an accident. You didn't mean to do it.' Jane caught his arm. 'Melia is out with her friends. You fetch the doctor and I'll say Ma had a funny turn and fell against the range.'

'No! I killed my wife and I'll take the consequences.'

'Please, Pa, no! Think what it will be like for Melia and me if they arrest you for murder.'

'Oh, Janey, what have I done?' He sank down into the chair and covered his face in his hands.

'Look at me, Pa!' He raised his head, a lost look in his eyes. 'You have to go and fetch the doctor now. Tell him Ma had an accident that's all you need to say. I'll tell him you were out in the shed when it happened. Ma had one of her bad headaches, turned dizzy the way she does sometimes and fell.'

He looked at her hesitantly. 'Are you sure that's what you want me to do?'

'I don't want you to go to prison. They might hang you . . .' She saw the colour drain from his face. 'What happens to Melia and me then?'

'You might be better off without me. Alice would take you. If anything happens to me you go to my sister, Jane.'

'Nothing is going to happen to you, Pa. You weren't even in the room when it happened. Ma fell and hit her head . . .' She looked him in the eyes. 'Go and fetch the doctor and tell him what I said.'

'All right, Jane. I can't fight you. I'll do as you say.'

Jane brought him his coat, helping him on with it. She kissed his cheek and then pushed him towards the door. After he had gone she sat down on the sofa. Her legs had suddenly turned to jelly and she felt icy cold. She had just persuaded her father to cover up the murder of his wife, which made her an accessory to the fact if the truth ever came out.

'I am so very sorry,' Doctor Martin said as he finished his examination of Helen Shaw. 'She must have fallen heavily to have this kind of injury. You didn't see what happened?'

'I was just about to call my father in for his tea. I heard a sort of gasp and then a bang and when I turned she was just lying there.'

'I see – so you weren't in the room, John?'

'No . . . I . . .' John Shaw sank down on the lumpy sofa and covered his face with his hands. 'It was all my fault . . . I killed her . . .'

'You mustn't blame yourself, John. I know Charlie's birth pulled her down and she never truly got over it, but that doesn't make this your fault,' Doctor Martin said kindly. 'Mrs Shaw's headaches were becoming increasingly frequent. I asked her to let me admit her to the hospital for tests some months ago but she refused.'

John's head came up. 'Was she really ill? I mean . . . I sometimes thought the headaches might be imagination?'

'They were real enough. I believe she may have had a tumour pressing on her brain. I don't suppose she told you that sometimes her sight was affected?' John moved his head negatively. 'It was the reason that I thought there might be a growth in her brain – but I dare say the autopsy will tell us the truth.'

'Do you have to do that?'

'It is usual in sudden death these days. I know this is a terrible shock to you all . . .' Doctor Martin's gaze moved to Jane. 'I shall go home and arrange for an ambulance. It may mean a week or two before they let you have the funeral.'

'Thank you.' At the sound of voices outside the door, Jane got to her feet. 'That is my sister. I must tell her . . .' She glanced at her father, her expression compelling. 'See Doctor Martin to the door, Pa.'

'You've had a terrible shock, John,' Jane heard the doctor's

voice as she went out to the yard where Melia was still talking
to their neighbour.

'You'd better come in, love. The doctor is here.'

'Aggie told me. Is something wrong?'

'Is there anything I can do, Jane, love?' Aggie Bristow asked.
'I heard a bit of a commotion and then the doctor came.'

'You must have heard me calling for Pa when I found Ma,' Jane
curled her nails into her palms. 'She had a bad fall, Aggie . . . she
hit her head on the range and she's dead.'

'Lord have mercy!' Aggie crossed herself. 'I'm real sorry, Janey
love. If you need any help . . .'

'They need to do an examination at the hospital because it
was sudden.' Jane felt as if she would faint. The doctor had come
out of the house now and was getting into his gig. 'Perhaps for
the funeral . . .'

'Bless you, love. You've had a dreadful shock. Take your sister
inside and make a cup of tea. Put some whiskey in it. I've got a
drop if you're out of spirits.'

'Thank you. Pa might have some. I think he needs it . . .'

Jane pushed her sister ahead of her. She was desperate to get
away from Aggie's inquiring eyes. Her neighbour had obviously
heard the shouting before the accident. Jane could only hope that
she would accept her explanation. She had lied to the doctor. It
was too late to tell the truth now.

Jane sent Melia straight up to her room. They had covered her
mother's body with a sheet and Melia had burst into tears as she
saw it.

Jane saw that her father was drinking a glass of whiskey.

'Are you all right, Pa?'

His eyes met hers. 'You know what you've done, Jane – the
consequences if they decide it wasn't a funny turn that made her
fall?'

'All you have to do is hold your nerve, Pa. She felt ill, turned
faint and fell. If Doctor Martin is right it may be for the best. You
wouldn't want her to suffer more than she already has, would you?'

'No . . . if there is a growth it would have been a terrible way
to die, but I know what I did, Jane. I've done what you asked
for your sake and Melia's but don't ask me to pretend to myself.'

He walked to the door, opened it and went out. Jane wanted to call him back but she knew he couldn't bear to stay in the house with his wife's body. He would go to his shed and stay there until the ambulance had been.

Jane turned to look at where her mother's body lay. Tears stung her eyes and she felt a rush of regret and remorse. There had been a time when she had loved her mother so much but everything had gone wrong after Charlie was born.

'I am so sorry,' she said and the tears trickled down her cheeks. 'I didn't want you to die, Ma. I know we quarrelled but I wouldn't have deserted you . . .'

'You're not going to work this morning?' Melia looked at her in distress. 'You can't go and leave me here alone.'

'You should go to school, Melia. I have to work for a few hours but I'll be back to get lunch.'

'I'm not hungry. I don't know how you can just carry on as if nothing had happened.'

'I'm sorry Ma died but if the doctor is right about the headaches they were going to get much worse.'

'You didn't think like that when Charlie died.'

'I didn't want Ma to die, love. I'm going to work because we need the money. It will cost more than Pa earns to pay for the funeral.'

'Oh shut up! I can't bear to think about things like that – and I'm not staying here alone.'

'Where are you going?' Jane asked as she snatched up her coat.

'I'm going round with Aggie. I can't stay in this house. I can't!'

'I'll fetch you when I get back, but you'll have to go to school tomorrow. You can't miss lessons if you're going to pass that exam.'

'I don't care about the exam. I'm not sure if I want to go to college.' Melia went out, slamming the door behind her.

Jane woke as she heard the wind howling outside. Something was rattling. She wasn't sure what but it was an eerie sound. Shuddering, she jumped out of bed, pulled her shabby dressing robe on and went downstairs.

In the kitchen she found her father making a pot of tea. 'Couldn't you sleep – or did I wake you?'

'I heard something rattling outside.'

'I think it must be a loose gate somewhere. Would you like some tea?'

'Yes, please.' Jane sat down. 'Has anyone said anything to you at work?'

'I was told I could take a few days off if I liked but I would rather work.' He poured tea into a mug and gave it to her. 'I've put what I had in the firm's bank, Jane – but I can't replace the petty cash.'

'Maybe they aren't sure the five pounds was ever there – if no record exists they can't prove it.'

'If they think I've taken money they will let me go even if they can't prove anything.'

'But they would have to give you a reference, wouldn't they? I thought we might leave March – live somewhere else?'

'Perhaps . . .' He sipped his tea. 'I'm not sure what else I could do . . . I feel lost, Jane. Guilty. I keep thinking the tests will prove that I killed her . . . marks where I grabbed her throat. They will ask more questions. I am not sure I can go on lying.'

'You have to, Pa.'

'I won't let them blame you, Jane.' He gazed at her in silence for a moment, then, 'I know you did it to save me but if anything happens – you will find an insurance policy and letters from my sister in a brown suitcase under the bed. Take care of Melia. She will need you.'

'Nothing is going to happen to you, Pa.' Jane felt cold all over despite the hot tea and the warmth of the room. 'Everything will be fine, you'll see.'

'The autopsy confirmed what I thought,' Doctor Martin told Jane when he called some days later. 'They think she must have had a blackout and that is why she fell so hard. Had she not died as she did, she would have suffered terrible pain towards the end.'

'Poor Ma . . .' Jane felt a lump in her throat. 'Was it that thing in her brain that made her so bad tempered of late?'

'I imagine it contributed. Your mother was always a fire-eater, Jane – as I believe you may be at times. Have you forgiven me for telling you that Charlie's death was a happy release?'

'I wasn't angry with you, just at the world for letting it be.'

'Well, I must get on.' He rose to his feet. 'The undertaker will fetch your mother back – do you want her here or at the Chapel of Rest?'

'I think it best she goes there. Will we be able to have the funeral soon?'

'I imagine you can make the arrangements as soon as you are ready.' He looked awkward, then cleared his throat. 'If you are short of money I could lend you some, my dear.'

'I'll earn it somehow. I'll find another job.'

'You could do a few hours at the surgery, help keep it tidy, take notes that sort of thing . . .'

'You are very kind but that is the same as giving me the money. I'll find something else.'

'Well, I hope you get good news soon.'

'They told me I was being let go because they no longer trusted me,' John Shaw told his daughter that evening. 'They aren't going to call the police in, because they can't prove I've stolen money but they won't give me a reference either.'

'Oh, Pa . . .' Jane saw the defeat in his eyes. 'That is so unfair . . .'

'If I got what I deserved I should be in prison about to go on trial for murdering my wife.'

'You didn't intend to kill her. You struck her in anger and she fell.'

'It wasn't that simple, Jane. I regretted it almost as soon as I pushed her but in that moment I wanted her dead.'

'Doctor Martin told me it was a blessing. You saved her from a slow and painful death.'

'I suppose that makes things better but . . .' He shook his head as Jane put a plate on the table in front of him. 'I'm not hungry, love. I'll just go down to the shed and have a smoke.'

'You don't have to sit in that cold shed now, Pa.'

'Yes, I do. This is still your Ma's house and it always will be.'

'I heard you were cleaning at the Royal Arms,' Aggie told her when she popped round the day before the funeral. 'Why did you take a job like that, love? I could put a word in for you with my boss.'

'I don't have a reference, Aggie.'

'You've got me for a reference, Jane.' Aggie looked awkward. 'I'd have spoken to you before but I thought your Ma might object to your working in a pub.'

'Ma said things she didn't mean.'

'It doesn't worry me, love. I popped in a couple of times when you were away, just to see how she was like.'

'Ma thought I was selfish to go away and perhaps she was right. If I had stopped at home I wouldn't have been dismissed...'

'You haven't a selfish bone in your body,' Aggie said. 'Why don't you think about what I've said?'

'I am not sure. My father is upset at the moment, and Melia can't bear to be in the house. We might move away . . .'

'We should miss you if you did that, Jane. Mind you, it looks as if the war is inevitable. It's going to bring a lot of changes. My husband and your father are too old to join up, but there's a lot of young men who will.' Aggie stood up. 'Well, I shan't keep you. I dare say you've enough to do with the funeral tomorrow – but don't forget what I said about a job.'

Six

Jane sat dry-eyed throughout the service, feeling numb and guilty. God could see into people's hearts and minds. He knew exactly how her mother had died – and that she had persuaded her father to lie about it.

She followed the vicar and her father out to the graveyard. One or two of the neighbours had come to cluster about the open grave, watching as John Shaw threw a handful of earth on to the coffin.

When her father walked away, Jane stopped to ask a few people if they would like to come back for a cup of tea and a sandwich. She felt as if she were acting a role and half expected the sky to part and an angry god to strike her down.

Nothing happened, however, and she managed to keep her calm manner as she walked home and then welcomed the handful of curious neighbours who had come to see what sort of a spread they had put on for Helen Shaw.

'I am so very sorry, Jane,' Robert Hastings said when he took his leave later. 'I'll call one day soon – when is it convenient?'

'I work in the morning and again in the afternoon. Evenings would be best. Did you want to discuss Melia's future?'

'I was wondering about certain things.'

'I shall be here every night – unless I can find another job. Aggie told me there might be some bar work at the pub where she is employed.'

'Are you sure you want to do that?'

'I don't have a choice.' Jane bit her lip. 'My father has lost his job.'

'That is disgraceful.' Robert looked shocked. 'After all those years of dedicated service.'

'Yes, it was distressing . . .'

'What will you do?'

'I don't know. My wages at the moment won't even pay the rent let alone what we owe for the funeral. Pa may find something when he starts to look – or we may have to move away.'

'What will happen to Melia's schooling then?'

'I wish I could say she could continue but at the moment I am just not sure. She may have to take a job . . .'

'That would be a shame. Let me give this some thought, Jane. I might be able to help . . .'

Jane closed the door behind him. He had been the last to leave and Melia was already clearing the dirty plates and glasses. Her father had gone out earlier and they were alone.

'I suppose you heard all that?'

'Yes, I did. Pa told me it would be all right. I don't know what he meant.'

'Where did he go – to the shed?'

'I expect so. It's where he usually goes, isn't it?'

'Please don't look at me like that, Melia. I promised I would try to sort it out and I shall. You'll get your chance if we can find the money to keep you at school and then college, but I don't know where it is coming from at the moment.'

'I hate being poor. How shall we manage now that Pa has lost his job?'

'I'll find something. Aggie said she would put in a word for me with her boss.'

'It won't be enough. Aggie doesn't earn much and you won't either.'

'It is all I can do, Melia.'

'I don't want to be like you or father.' Melia stared at her miserably. 'I want to go to college and learn so that I can have a decent job.'

'Father had a decent job. He didn't earn enough but we managed to live better than many people.'

'Well, he shouldn't have lost it then!' Tears hovered on Melia's lashes. 'I'm going next door. I hate this place.'

Jane watched as her sister went out and slammed the door, leaving her with the washing up. She didn't mind even though her hands stung when she put them into the hot water. Melia was right. Jane didn't want to live here either. It would be better for all of them if her father would agree to move.

She looked at the clock. It was past seven, time she started to make dinner. She considered going down to the shed but decided to wait until the meal was ready. If he didn't come by then she would go and fetch him.

Jane glanced at the clock. An hour had passed since she started to reheat the stew. Where was he? He must know that everyone had gone by now. She hoped he wasn't going to say he didn't want anything again this evening. If he didn't start to eat his meals he would become ill.

She pulled on a jacket and walked to the shed. The weather that day had been mild for late February but there was a cold breeze now and Jane felt chilled.

There was no light in the shed. Her father must be sitting in the dark. She knew he was suffering because of what had happened. He couldn't forgive himself for what he had done, and Jane felt a pang of remorse as she realized that she had forced him to lie – but what else could she have done?

She paused outside the door then took a deep breath, opened it and went in. 'Pa, your supper is on . . .' The words caught in her throat as she saw the shadow above her and looked up. 'No! No, Pa . . . you mustn't . . . you shouldn't . . .' She gave a terrible scream of anguish as she realized that it was too late. Unable to bear his failure and the guilt of his wife's death, her father had come down here when she was busy with their guests and hanged himself.

If only she'd come sooner! If only she'd looked for him before she got the dinner ready she might have been in time to save him, but she hadn't dreamed he would do something like this.

'Pa . . .' she sobbed. 'Oh, Pa . . . why did you do it?'

Turning, Jane ran next door, not to Aggie's house where her sister was staying but the other side. She pounded frantically at the door in her distress. Tears were running down her face as her neighbour came to answer it.

'Jane, lass – what's the matter?'

'Oh, Mr Robson . . . please, can you come? It's my father. He's hung himself.'

Her neighbour swore and set off at a run. Jane lingered as Mrs Robson came to look at her, then she gave a sob and ran after him. Perhaps she was wrong. Mr Robson would get Pa down. He might still be alive . . .

Jane lay on Aggie's sofa listening to the sounds outside. There had been people coming and going: the police, doctor, ambulance and most of the people from the other houses in the street. Everyone was curious, their faces shocked, eyes staring at Jane with pity as she waited while they cut her father down and pronounced him dead. It was when the ambulance took him away that Aggie finally persuaded her to come into her house.

'You can't stay there alone tonight, Jane, love – and Melia is upstairs in bed. She was in such a state that the doctor gave her something to make her sleep . . .'

'Thank goodness she didn't find him!' Jane was shivering. She had wept as they cut her father down and she saw the protruding tongue and his face gone purple and black.

She struggled to block out the terrible picture, but she knew it would never go away. His face would haunt her. She would never forget it, never forgive herself.

'I am so sorry, Pa,' she whispered into the darkness. 'So very sorry.'

It was quiet outside at last. Jane knew she wasn't going to sleep. She had too much on her mind, too much to reproach herself for to be able to rest. This tragedy was all her fault. Her father couldn't bear the knowledge that he had killed his wife. She ought to have let him confess, because forcing him to lie had made him wretched. If he had pleaded provocation, he might have been let off with a prison sentence. He might still be alive.

'I am so sorry,' she whispered. 'So very sorry . . .'

'Don't go back there yet,' Aggie begged when Jane announced she was going to get some things from the cottage the next day. 'Why don't you leave things the way they are until another day?'

'I have to go through Pa's things. See what I can rescue from this mess.'

'I doubt he had much of any worth.'

'I'm sure he didn't but he told me there were some letters and things in a suitcase under his bed. I need to find them – and I should clear up. I left the dinner on the table last night.'

'You'll make yourself ill if you don't slow down. I can't imagine what got into you – going to work before it was light this morning.'

'I promised I would work my notice if I wanted to leave and I shall. Besides, we both need some clothes. I'm going to clean the house and then give notice. Someone can clear the house once I've got all we need.'

'You might get a nice few bob from that. Your ma had a few good things – that Crown Derby teapot and some candlesticks, and the American wall clock in the hall. The junk shop should give you a pound or two for that, Jane.'

'You can have the teapot and the candlesticks. You've done a lot for Melia and we'll need to stay with you for a while – just until we leave for London.'

'This is all a bit quick, isn't it? Your Pa isn't buried yet and there may be an inquest . . .'

'Perhaps I should keep the house for a bit longer. I'll take Melia to my aunt's house and come back.' She put on her jacket. 'The sooner I contact my aunt the better. I'm not frightened of the house the way Melia is.'

'I don't think there's much that scares you, Jane.'

Jane smiled, turned and went out. Her father had known what he intended when he'd told her about that suitcase. She needed to fetch it and she needed to sort the house out. Her father had bills to pay and there would be his funeral to find the money for now. She wasn't sure if they would let her bury him in church. He had committed suicide and that was against the laws of God and man – and that meant no insurance!

She was frowning as she went into the kitchen. The plates of congealing stew almost turned her stomach. She scooped them up, taking them out into the yard and calling to one of the dogs that was lurking about in the street.

Jane went upstairs and took her own clothes and Melia's from the wardrobes, shoving them into her father's old portmanteau and a suitcase she knew was her mother's. She reached under the bed and slid the suitcase out. It was a small one and could only contain papers or trinkets. Tucking it under her arm, she carried everything downstairs. The kitchen fire had gone out and it felt cold. She shivered as in her imagination she heard a shuffling sound and heard a voice call to her from upstairs.

'Jane, come and help me . . .'

It was a trick of her imagination. Aggie was right! She ought to have waited for a few days.

'Did you find what you wanted?' Aggie asked when she came downstairs to her kitchen and found Jane poring over the contents of the small case. 'Are the letters from your aunt still there?'

'Yes, they are. Aunt Alice asked Pa to visit several times and to bring his children. She doesn't mention my mother at all. Perhaps they didn't get on.'

'That might be why your father never went home. He was a devoted husband.'

'Yes, he was . . .' Jane's eyes filled with tears. 'Whatever she said or did . . .' *Except for that last time when his temper had broken.* 'He would never let us say a bad word about her.'

'Well, nor should you, Jane. Your Ma was your Ma and if she was so ill it was no wonder she got irritable sometimes.'

'Yes . . .' Jane held back the words that hovered on her lips. 'My aunt's name is Mrs Alice James and she lives in Hampstead.'

'Hampstead? That's a good area, Jane. Do you think she is well off?'

'I don't know but I'm going to write to her and post the letter on my way to work this afternoon. If she says we can go to her, I'll take Melia and then come back to see to things here.'

'So you're going back to that place again?'

'I'm giving in my notice this evening but if Ernie is rude or unpleasant I shan't go back again.'

'You want to be careful of that one,' Aggie warned. 'It isn't just the work that puts women off working for him, you know.'

'I hate the way he looks at me but so far that is all he has done – and he paid me for a week so I owe him this anyway.'

'Well, just be careful. I wouldn't touch that man with a barge pole!'

'He gave me a job when no one else would. Besides, I'm going to need every penny I can get to pay for Melia's schooling.'

Ernie glared at her and then deliberately spat on the floor she had just finished scrubbing.

'So yer're no different from the rest of them, can't do an honest day's work.'

'I'll work my notice. I told you it was only for the time being when I came. I shall be leaving as soon as I get things settled here.'

'Runnin' away are yer? Coward like yer Pa – can't face up to what yer've done?'

'What do you mean?'

'Got the push from his job and then topped hisself. Stands to reason there 'as ter be a reason – 'ad his fingers in the till, did he?'

'My father was let go because they considered him redundant. He did nothing dishonest so just mind what you say or I'll sue you for slander.'

'Mebbe I know a bit more than you think. Mebbe I 'ad a letter askin' ter check what I give yer old man ter settle me account.' Ernie leered at her and came round the corner of the bar. 'Yer better be nice to me, Janey, or I might be the one doin' a bit of suing . . .'

'Don't you dare touch me!' Suddenly, she couldn't take any more. She picked up her bucket of dirty water and swung it in his direction, the water going all over him. She was tempted to laugh as she saw the shock in his face but then decided that the best thing to do was run.

She ran until she was out of breath, then slowed down as she reached the end of her street. That just served him right! She wouldn't dare to go back there again, so she was breaking her word in the end but he deserved it.

Jane was doing the washing up after supper when someone knocked at Aggie's back door. Aggie went to open it and invited the visitor inside.

'It is Mr Hastings come to see you, Jane,' she said. 'I'm going up to Melia. If she has left her supper again I am fetching the doctor to her in the morning.'

Aggie went out, leaving Jane alone with the visitor. She wiped her hands on the towel and turned to look at him.

'Melia has been crying and she says her head hurts. I hadn't got the heart to send her to school.'

'Melia has been through a terrible time recently. You have too, Jane. I came to ask if there is anything I can do for you? I am not sure what to say about your father – I am so very sorry that you were the one to find him.'

'It wasn't pleasant. I expect I shall get over it in time.' She lifted her head, meeting his look of sympathy but refusing to let it touch her. 'It's just as well you came. We are going away. Neither of us wants to live in the cottage and Aggie can't have us here forever. Besides, I think it is best to make a fresh start.'

'Are you sure that is what you want to do? Melia was doing so well in school.'

'She can go to a new school where no one knows that her father killed himself. I think that is the reason why she wouldn't get up this morning. She can't face the curious stares.'

'Your father was grieving. He took his life when the balance of his mind was disturbed.'

'That is what they will say at the inquest but it doesn't answer questions. People want to know why. Even Aggie is curious but there is nothing I can tell them.'

'I didn't come to pry, Jane – and I don't listen to gossip. I just thought perhaps I could help, but I see that you've made up your mind.'

'Yes, I have. I gave up my job at the pub. I can't go back there and I couldn't find work before this . . . it is for the best.'

'Perhaps it is.' Robert hesitated then held his hand out. 'I wish you better luck in your new life, Jane. If there is ever anything I can do for you please let me know.'

'Goodbye, Robert. I am sorry it has worked out this way.'

'Yes, so am I.' For a moment regret flickered in his eyes. 'Goodbye, Jane.'

Jane was silent as he left. She had liked Robert Hastings. It hurt to say goodbye.

Aggie looked at her when she came downstairs a few minutes later. 'Gone already has he? What did he want?'

'Just to ask if we were all right. I told him we were leaving soon and he wished me luck.'

'Humph . . .' Aggie grunted. 'I think he was fond of you, Jane. I hoped he might persuade you to stay, ask you to marry him perhaps. You could have looked after his mother but I suppose he can't afford to get married. Although, he'll need someone to move in with her once the war starts.'

'Maybe it won't. I know the papers are full of it but it hasn't happened yet.'

'It will any day now. You wait and see . . .'

Two days later, in the middle of the morning, Jane opened the back door to a woman she knew at once was her father's sister. For a moment they looked at each other in silence and then Alice James nodded her head.

'You're Jane. Your father sent me a school photograph once. You were a lot younger then but I would have known you anywhere. May I come in? Is your neighbour home?'

'Aggie has gone to the market to do her shopping. She persuaded Melia to go with her but they won't be long. I've been baking. Would you like a piece of Victoria sponge and a cup of tea?'

'Are you a good cook, Jane? I know your mother used to be. It was a pity she became an invalid. I always thought she put her illness on to spite John but it seems she was ill – at the end anyway.'

'Yes, she was, far more so than we guessed.' Jane led her aunt into the large warm kitchen, which still smelled of baking and spices. 'You obviously didn't like her – was that the reason my father left his home and would have nothing to do with the family?'

'No. Helen was a selfish little madam and sharp tempered – but I didn't dislike her. John left for reasons of his own and if he didn't tell you anything perhaps I shouldn't.'

'Ma said he must have done something bad for his father to disown him?'

'He quarrelled with his father and he knocked him down. John hardly ever lost his temper but he did that day – struck his father so hard that it broke his jaw. My father would never speak of John again. They both thought I didn't know the reason for their argument – but I knew what was behind it.'

'You won't tell me why they quarrelled?'

'Perhaps when we know each other better.' Alice glanced round. 'I like to see a kitchen spotless. Is this your work?'

'Aggie has to work and she won't take anything for our keep so I've done my best to pay in other ways.'

'Pay and be paid that's my motto,' Alice said approvingly. 'You want to come and live with me – is that right?'

'Yes, please. Melia will go to school somewhere near you and

then go on to teaching college. She had a chance for a free scholarship but I'm not sure she will get it when she moves on. I'll
find the money to send her somehow.'

'I've enough money to pay for her school and to send her to
college,' Alice said. 'I'm a widow now and my husband left me
comfortably off. Besides, there's a bit of family money.'

'I shall still go to work.'

'That is your decision, Jane. I've got a small business. You can
help me with that if you wish.'

'You will take us then?'

'Yes, of course. Did you imagine I would leave you to walk the
streets? I shall expect proper behaviour. I've always been respectable
and there's been enough scandal over your father's suicide. You are
a good girl, Jane? I don't approve of loose behaviour.'

'I shall not let you down, Mrs James. Nor will Melia. She is
upset at the moment but all she wants is to study hard and go
to college.'

'Melia is young enough to mould as I want her but you're
older. I hope you don't have any secrets that could come back
to haunt us?'

'I was accused of taking a brooch by my employer but I swear
I didn't touch it.'

Alice made a tutting sound. 'That is unfortunate but hopefully
it won't matter. You won't need a reference if you work for me.
However, I meant man trouble. You haven't been silly with a man
I hope?'

'I've never had a boyfriend. I wouldn't do anything like that
anyway.'

'I can see we shall get on well together, Jane. You are honest and
I like that.' She ate a piece of Jane's sponge. 'This is good. Do you
want to pack your things? We can catch a train this afternoon.'

'I'm not coming immediately. I have to sell Ma's things and
clean the cottage right through before I give the key back.'

'Very well. It is the proper way to do things. I shall take Melia
with me and you can follow in a few days.'

'I shall be as quick as I can – but I have to see to Pa's funeral.
Unless you want to do it?'

'No.' Alice spoke hastily. 'The less my friends and customers
know about this unpleasant business the better. I doubt they will

let you bury him in consecrated ground but you must do what you can for your father. I'll give you some money to do it properly – then you can come to me when it's over.'

'I wish you were coming.' Melia clung to her. 'I hate leaving you here.'

'But you are happy to go with her – aren't you?'

'She seems nice and she says I can go to college. I don't even have to win a scholarship unless one is offered.'

'I did what I thought was right, Melia – and I'll join you as soon as I can.'

Melia hugged her tightly. 'Aunt Alice has a teashop. She says you are going to work for her. You will like that, won't you?'

'Yes . . . Yes, I shall, Melia. I suppose that was why she was pleased I could cook.'

'I'd better go down. I don't want to keep her waiting. You will come soon?'

'Yes, of course I shall,' Jane said and gave her a little push away. 'Aunt Alice has a nice house with four bedrooms. You'll be able to choose which one you want.'

'I'll leave the best for you, Janey. I know how much you've done for us all.'

Jane's eyes suddenly filled with tears as her sister went downstairs. She followed Melia down to the kitchen, bidding her aunt and sister farewell with a forced smile.

'Well, you've made your bed, Jane,' Aggie said as the door closed behind them. 'I hope it isn't too hard for you to lie in it.'

'What do you mean? Melia likes Aunt Alice.'

'Did you?'

'I'm not sure. She said some things that made me wonder if she is very strict, but Melia wants to go to college and I think my aunt will make sure that she does.'

'Oh yes, I could see they got on together. Your aunt will like that – a niece in college. It's you that will have to pay the price. If I were you, Jane, I'd stick to your guns and find a job for yourself.'

'I'll see how it goes. I'm going next door. I want to start clearing out Ma's things.'

'Do you want some help?'

Jane hesitated and then shook her head. 'Thank you but I'll be all right now, Aggie. I'm over the worst and it won't take me long to find what I need. Once I have all the clothes and personal stuff out of the way I'm going to let someone clear the furniture, and then I'll scrub it from top to bottom before I give the key back.'

Jane cleared her father's things first. Anything of any value had been in his suitcase; his papers, some gold cufflinks and a silver watch. The rest was just clothes and old shoes, most of which she thought would be best thrown away.

She tossed the rags into a heap and packed the clothes she was giving to charity, then, drawing a deep breath, she went into her mother's room. The chill seemed to strike into her bones and she worked swiftly. Her mother had some decent clothes, a lot of them good quality and bought years before. Had Aunt Alice not offered them a home Jane might have tried to sell them, but somehow she felt her mother would prefer her clothes to be burned under the copper.

Bundling them up in armfuls, Jane took them to the head of the stairs and threw them down. When the cupboard and chests were empty of clothes she ran downstairs and took them into the scullery, putting them in the grate under the copper and adding paper and wood so that they would burn well and heat some water.

While the water was heating, she returned to her mother's room and looked at the things she had kept. Her mother had a few items of jewellery; some of it costume stuff but also one or two good things. Jane's father had probably bought the gold brooch and bangle for her when they were young and things were better between them.

Jane gathered the things together and walked downstairs. Everything she wanted was on the kitchen table ready to be taken next door. She went through to the scullery and tipped the hot water into a zinc bath that was kept hanging on the wall. Undressing, she climbed in and sat, then slid right down and dipped her head under.

It was lovely to have a good soak and wash her hair. She hadn't wanted to bother at Aggie's because she felt awkward about putting her friend to extra trouble, but here there was no one to disturb her. She closed her eyes and let herself relax in the warm water.

Suddenly, tears began to slide down her face. Pictures of her childhood were running through her mind. She was remembering the good times . . . the day at Hunstanton when Melia was just a baby and her father had taken her for a ride on the donkeys. Her mother had been wearing a green dress . . . a dress she had just burned under the copper.

Jane got out of the bath and wrapped a towel around her. There were a few things she hadn't managed to squeeze under the copper before she set light to her mother's things. Perhaps the green dress hadn't been burned.

She hunted feverishly through them but it had gone. She had carelessly thrust everything into the fire and the few rags left belonged to her father.

'Ma, I'm sorry . . . your lovely dress. I'm so sorry for everything . . .'

Sinking to her knees, Jane sobbed as if her heart would break. Her mother had been so bad tempered for such a long time; she had forgotten how good it had been when she was a child, before things started to go wrong.

'Ma, I'm so sorry . . . so sorry. I burned your dress and you'd kept it to remember that day.'

The sound of knocking at the door roused Jane from her fit of remorse. She pulled on her shabby old dressing gown and walked through to the kitchen. She opened the door, rubbing the tears from her cheeks, her wet hair hanging about her face in limp strands.

'I decided to have a . . .' Jane's voice died away as she saw who was standing there. 'I thought it was my neighbour. I wouldn't have answered like this if . . .' Her cheeks were burning as she saw the way he looked at her. 'I didn't expect you, Mr Heron.'

'Aren't you going to invite me in, Jane? I've come a long way to see you.'

'I'm not dressed . . .'

'I'll wait while you put some clothes on.'

'Come into the kitchen. Take a seat while I make myself presentable.'

David followed her inside. His eyes seemed to search her face. 'You look as if you've been crying?'

'I have been clearing my parents' things out. It upset me more than I anticipated.'

'Yes, I imagine it would. To lose them both like that must have been very distressing.'

'Yes, it was.' She pulled at her dressing gown, aware of its shabbiness. 'Please wait here. I shan't be a moment.'

Jane hurried into the scullery and scrambled hastily into the clothes she had taken off earlier. She buttoned her dress to the neck but she couldn't do much about her wet hair, except rub at it with a towel as she returned to the kitchen. David was sitting on the sofa, his long legs crossed and looking perfectly at home.

'I'm sorry about the mess – and my appearance . . .'

'You look beautiful to me. You always have, Jane.'

'Thank you . . .' Jane looked at him uneasily, feeling somehow vulnerable. 'Why have you come?'

'I wanted to bring you this . . .' David took an envelope from his jacket pocket. 'The letter is an apology from my sister. The brooch was not stolen. I had sent it to the jeweller for repair. Maria isn't good at apologizing but I made her write this and the money she owes you is there too. Mrs Buller has given you a reference in case you need one.'

'Oh . . . thank you. It isn't very nice being accused of theft – and it isn't easy to find a good job without a reference.' Jane felt sharp regret. Had she been given her wages at the time her father could have repaid his debt. He might still be alive.

'It was a damned insult. I'm not surprised you told Maria a few home truths, Jane.'

'Perhaps I shouldn't have done that . . .' Jane sat down on the sofa next to him. 'How is Ned? I have been worried about him. He must hate me for leaving him.'

'No, he doesn't hate you, Jane – though I am afraid he hates his mother. I took him to his new school early, and I had to order new clothes for him in London. Then I had to report back to my unit for some training – but I have a weekend free now. I wondered if you would like to visit Ned?'

'Could I? Where is he? Is it far?'

'I have my car. I could take you – if you would permit me?'

'How long would it take us? I have things I need to do . . .'

'I promise to bring you back safely.' He looked amused. 'I'm not asking you to have an illicit weekend with me, Jane. Don't you trust me?'

'Should I?'

'Probably not – but I promise to be good. It will mean one night at a guesthouse . . . separate rooms, of course.'

Jane was silent for a moment, then inclined her head. 'Can you give me an hour to pack my things?'

'Yes, of course. I have been told I need a haircut. If I don't want the regimental barber to make a mess of it I had better see to it. I'll leave you and come back in an hour . . .' His smile was warm, encouraging. 'Ned will be thrilled to see you. He is expecting me to take him to tea but he doesn't know I have a special treat for him.'

It was late in the evening when they finally arrived at the hotel. Jane had thought it would be a small guesthouse and was startled to discover that it was a private country house which had been converted into an exclusive hotel.

'Isn't this expensive?' she asked as David took their bags from the boot of his car.

'Don't worry, Jane. I get special rates. I know the owner and he lets me have rooms cheap. Besides, I am paying.'

'I would prefer to pay my own way.' She felt uncomfortable because she could never have afforded to stay at such an exclusive hotel.

'We shan't argue about it now,' David said. 'Enjoy yourself, please. I am trying to make up for what Maria did to you.'

'Oh . . . thank you,' Jane blushed. 'It wasn't your fault.'

'I know but she is my sister and she treated you shamefully.'

'You know she sent me ten pounds? That is more than I was owed.'

'I told her you could sue for unfair dismissal.'

Jane understood that it was his influence that had moved Maria Stratton to apologize and pay her extra.

She didn't say anything more about it, because David was checking in at the desk. Her heart raced for a moment but quietened as she heard the receptionist tell him that their rooms were ready. They followed the porter into a lift and were whizzed up to the top floor. The door to Jane's room was unlocked first. She walked in feeling uneasy, because she wasn't used to such luxury.

David followed her in and glanced round. The room had a

comfortable chair, writing table and single chair as well as the bed, wardrobe and dressing chest.

'You've got a good view of the gardens from here,' he said. 'Will it do?'

'Of course. It is wonderful – much better than I'm used to.'

'You are worth far more, Jane. Perhaps one day . . .' His expression made her heart race and she took a step back. His hand moved towards her and then dropped. 'You are right. This is not the time to make promises. Change and come down to dinner. They have a dance on this evening – do you dance?'

'Not very well. I've only been to church hall things. I don't have a proper dress.'

'Then we'll just have dinner and give it a miss.'

David left and Jane began to unpack her things. She had packed her best dress and a skirt and blouse. The dress would do for dinner, even though it was hardly good enough for a place like this.

She suddenly saw a door that didn't seem to lead to the hall or the bathroom and tried it. The lock stayed shut. Perhaps it was an unused door that didn't go anywhere. There was no key so it couldn't be opened, which meant that it wasn't important.

Half an hour later, Jane had dressed. She had let her hair down and knew she looked the best she could. Besides, what did it matter if the other guests thought she looked dowdy?

Her heart beat rapidly as she walked down the stairs. David was waiting for her in the small lounge near the dining room.

'You look very nice, Jane. Shall we go into dinner?'

'Yes. I'm hungry.'

'Good. Order whatever you like, Jane. Everything is top notch here.' His gaze went over her. 'I'm hungry too – especially now that I have such a pretty companion.'

'I'm not pretty.'

'No, the word doesn't do you justice. Beautiful would be a better one.'

Seven

Jane stretched and woke, slowly becoming aware of her surroundings. She was lying in one of the most comfortable beds she had ever known in a room that was unfamiliar and luxurious.

'I could get used to this,' she murmured and then laughed. It wasn't going to happen again!

David had been a perfect gentleman the previous evening. They ate a lovely meal together and then took a little walk in the hotel gardens before he escorted her to her door and said goodnight.

Jane had expected he might try to kiss her but he hadn't, even though the look she'd seen in his eyes had seemed to burn into her.

Men like David did not marry girls like Jane.

Jane reminded herself sharply as she had a bath in a shining white porcelain tub with hot and cold running water.

Afterwards, Jane dressed in a skirt and blouse and went down to the dining room for breakfast. There was no sign of David so she ordered, and ate bacon and egg followed by toast and marmalade and a pot of tea. After her meal she called at the reception desk and asked where she might find Mr Heron.

'I believe he went riding, Miss Shaw. He left a note for you.'

Jane opened the letter as she returned to her room. David would see her at lunch and then they would visit the school to fetch Ned out for tea.

Jane decided to go for a walk in the grounds of the hotel. It was such a lovely day and she was enjoying herself.

Later, she found a newspaper abandoned by one of the other guests and read about the government telling Germany it would honour the Treaty of 1839. She looked up as she became aware of someone watching her. She smiled at David as he came to sit next to her.

'Have you been enjoying yourself, Jane?'

'It is wonderful here. I didn't know you could stay in places like this, so peaceful and quiet.'

'You are so easy to please.' He leaned towards her and took her hand, lifting it to his lips. 'Shall we have a drink before lunch? You like sherry, don't you?'

'I suppose I do . . .' Jane accompanied him to the bar.

David ordered a glass of sherry for her and a double whiskey for himself. He drank that straight down and then ordered another, which he took into the dining room.

'Do you like white or red wine?'

'I don't think I've ever had red.'

'There is a first time for everything. It will go well with the roast beef, which you must have because it is excellent.'

'I was thinking just something light . . .'

'Nonsense. You will have some wine and the beef – and finish that sherry.'

The sherry was not as sweet as Jane liked but she couldn't waste it, because he had spent good money buying it for her. She didn't much like the wine he ordered either, because it tasted musky and dry on her tongue, but she drank it for the same reason. However, she would not let him pour her a second.

Jane refused pudding too. 'If I have any more I shan't eat anything at tea and that might upset Ned.'

'Go up and change into a dress then,' David said. 'Did you bring another?'

'Just the one I wore last night.'

'That will do then. We shall take Ned to a special teashop for his treat – and we might go on the river for a while.'

Jane nodded and ran upstairs. David Heron had been drinking steadily since he came back from riding. He wasn't drunk but she didn't think he was quite sober either.

'Jane!' Ned yelled in delight when he saw her and rushed to put his arms about her waist. 'Uncle David said he might have a surprise for me next time he came but he didn't say it would be you.'

'Are you pleased to see me?'

'You know I am.' His look became accusing. 'You went away and didn't tell me . . .'

'I left a letter for you. If your uncle hadn't brought me here today I should have come as soon as I could. A lot of things have happened since I saw you.'

'You lost your mother and your father. Uncle David warned me not to say – but you told me we could say anything to each other, didn't you?'

'You must never be afraid to tell me anything, Ned.' Jane took his hand and squeezed it. 'We don't want to talk about sad things today. Your uncle is taking us to tea and we might go on the river in a rowing boat – if you would like that?'

'Can we really?' Ned smiled at her, holding tight to her hand. 'Do you remember the day we had a picnic by the stream?'

'Yes, of course. How could I forget?'

Ned clung to Jane for a few minutes at the school gates. He hadn't wanted his treat to end and it was past seven o'clock when they finally said goodbye.

'You will come again soon?' he asked, a hint of tears in his eyes.

'Yes, of course. On my own next time, I promise.'

'You'd better or I'll send you a frog in my letters!'

'No, you won't. You'd better go in now or your teachers might be cross.'

She turned to David as Ned disappeared inside, after waving to her at the door. 'He had such a good time. Thank you for bringing me. I shall treasure this memory.'

'It isn't over yet. I thought we might drive a part of the way back to Cambridgeshire this evening and then stop for a meal somewhere.'

'I couldn't eat another thing. I had such a good tea.'

'It's too late to drive all the way back to Cambridgeshire tonight. I suppose we could stay here for one more night.'

'Did you book two nights?'

'I was vague when I made the booking. I said I would let them know. Don't worry, Jane. I am sure they won't throw us out.'

'We could find somewhere else – somewhere cheaper.'

'Oh, I think I can manage one more night of luxury.'

'I would like to pay for myself.'

'I don't think so. Don't argue, Jane. We don't want to spoil things.' David took a small silver flask from his pocket and drank some of the contents. 'And don't look at me like that please. I'm not drunk.'

'I didn't say anything.'

'You thought it.'

'I'm sorry if I looked disapproving. It isn't my place.'

'Why not? Damn it, you're not a servant now!'

It was wiser not to argue. David's mood seemed to have turned sullen. She wasn't sure how to answer him so she was silent as he drove them back to the hotel. He drove very fast at one time swerving to miss a rabbit that ran into the narrow lane, almost putting them in the ditch. He slowed down afterwards, but it didn't improve his mood.

'I'm going for a walk,' he said when he parked the car outside the hotel. 'If you want dinner order it in your room or go down alone. I'm not in the mood.'

'I'm not hungry,' Jane said. 'Have I done something wrong?'

'Of course not. Don't be stupid.'

Jane felt as if he had slapped her face. She hurried straight up to her room. She'd had such a wonderful time and then suddenly it had all gone wrong.

Jane was dreaming, tossing restlessly on the pillow. She could see her father's face as it had looked as they cut him down, his protruding eyes and his tongue. The dream was so real that she cried out in terror, then woke suddenly, sitting up in alarm as someone touched her arm.

'Wake up, Jane. You are having a nightmare.'

Jane came out of the dream and looked at David in bewilderment. What was he doing in her bedroom? He was wearing just his pyjama bottoms, his hard, smooth chest completely bare.

'What are you doing? How did you get in here?'

'Through the connecting door. Didn't you wonder where the locked door went to, Jane? This is a suite. I could have walked in on you at any time but I didn't . . .'

Jane sat up, hugging the bedclothes to her. 'Why have you come now?'

'You were crying out, Jane, having a nightmare. I thought you needed someone.'

'It was just a bad dream. Please go . . .'

'You have been crying again.' David sat on the edge of the bed. He reached out, brushing his fingers over her wet cheeks. 'You shouldn't cry, Janey. I'll make it all better for you . . .'

He pulled the covers back, his eyes moving over her with a hot, feverish glint that made her jerk back in fear. She tried to tug the covers back but he wrenched them away.

'Stop teasing me, Janey. You know this had to happen. When you agreed to come with me, I knew you wanted it as much as I do.'

'No!' Jane could smell the whiskey on his breath. She pushed him away as he bent over her, grabbing her nightgown, lifting it, tearing it from her. She tried to cross her arms over herself but he pulled them back, holding them above her head with one hand. 'Please don't do this . . . please don't hurt me . . .'

'You know it has to happen, Janey.' His voice was slurred, foolish. 'I want you and I always get what I want . . .' He bent over her, forcing his mouth on hers.

'No . . .' she opened her mouth to deny him but he thrust his tongue inside her mouth. She tried to pull her head away but then he was lying on top of her, crushing her into the bed. He still held both her hands by the wrists above her head with his right hand, his left moving down to part her legs.

Jane tried to protest but his tongue filled her mouth, choking her. She struggled to throw him off. He held her down by the power and weight of his body, and then she felt him lift himself. He was fumbling with his pyjama bottoms. As she bucked and tried to throw him off, he bit her bottom lip and then she felt the heat of his flesh, his thrusting penis pushing at her. He had got between her legs, forcing them wide. She tried to wriggle away but he suddenly put an arm across her throat making her gasp for air.

'Lie still and I won't hurt you,' he muttered thickly. 'It's too late to stop me now.'

'Please don't . . .' she cried but she had no breath to make the words. She felt him parting her legs even wider and then he was thrusting into her. He felt huge and she was dry, a virgin who had never been touched, never known what it felt like to have a man inside her. The pain as he tore her hymen would have made her scream if his tongue hadn't been inside her mouth. As it was the tears trickled down her cheeks silently as she just lay there and let him have his way.

It was over quite soon. Jane lay with her eyes shut. She felt his weight as he collapsed on her, then he grunted, rolled over and she was free of him. Her eyes remained closed, her cheeks wet with tears.

He leaned over her, touching her cheek.

'Look at me, Janey. Don't cry. I never meant to hurt you. I didn't know it was your first time.'

Jane opened her eyes then. 'Of course you knew. You must have known I wouldn't let anyone do that when I'm not married.'

'Why should I have known?' His sullen look reminded her of Ned when he'd done something wrong. 'You came with me. You must have understood what it was all about.'

'You promised you would behave. You promised me!'

'I did behave. I could have done this last night.'

'Why did you wait?' Jane asked bitterly. 'I thought you were so nice bringing me here – such a gentleman.'

'I meant to be good to you, Janey. You know I love you.'

'If you loved me you wouldn't have raped me.'

'It wasn't rape, Janey. Girls always get hurt the first time. Next time if you just relax and let me it won't be so bad.'

'There won't be a next time.' Jane got out of bed and headed for the bathroom. 'I'm going to clean myself up and then I'll call for a taxi to take me to the station.'

'I'll take you home tomorrow as I promised.' Jane looked at him scornfully. For a moment he held the look then had the grace to drop his eyes. 'I'm sorry. I had too much to drink and you looked at me in that reproachful way earlier. It made me angry . . .'

'Don't make excuses. You planned this from the start – didn't you?'

'I meant to do it better,' he said. 'Forgive me, Janey. I'll make it up to you. I'll buy you a present.'

'I don't want anything you can give me. If you come near me again I'll call for the manager and inform the police of what you've done.'

'Do you think they would believe you? Decent girls don't stay in expensive hotel suites with a man they hardly know, Jane.'

Jane gave him a look of disgust. 'No, they don't, do they? I should have known it was too good to be true.'

She went into the bathroom and locked the door. David banged on the door but she didn't answer him. After a while there was silence.

Jane climbed into the bath. She felt sick and ashamed. She should never have let David bring her to a place like this; she should have known there would be a price to pay.

When she went back into the bedroom David had gone. She saw the key to the adjoining door was on her side. Locking the door, she lay down on the bed. David was right. If she went to the police to complain of rape they would look at her as if she were a piece of dirt.

She had stayed in his suite. He had paid all the bills. What kind of a girl allowed a man she didn't know well to do that? Only the kind that was prepared to sleep with him to pay for her supper.

She was such a fool! Why had she agreed to come?

The answer was staring her in the face. She had liked David Heron a lot. Perhaps if he had come to her sober she might not have said no . . .

Jane left the hotel the next morning. She didn't see David but the girl at the reception told her the bill was paid. A part of her had hoped for a letter or some message but there was none. It seemed that he had taken her at her word and left her to find her own way home. It was a good thing she'd brought some of the money Mrs Stratton had paid her just in case. Jane paid the taxi at the station and queued to buy her train ticket. She heard a boy at the news-stand shouting about something and thought she heard the word war but wasn't sure.

Jane was wrapped in a cocoon of pain, too locked into her own misery to bother going to find out. When she was on the train and settled, she looked out of the window. There seemed to be a lot of people saying goodbye to each other, and several of the men were in uniform.

Three soldiers came into the carriage. They took their caps off and one of them looked at her hesitantly.

'Do you mind if we sit here, miss?'

'Of course not,' Jane replied. She would have preferred to be alone but they were entitled to a seat. In her state of numbed misery she hoped they wouldn't talk but the young soldier seemed to take her acquiescence as an invitation to make conversation.

'So it has happened at last then,' he said. Jane looked at him in a puzzled way. 'Haven't you heard? Germany fired the first shots and we've declared war . . .'

'I saw something in the paper yesterday but I didn't take much notice and I didn't realize war had been declared.' Jane felt cold all over. David Heron was in the army. Had he known it would happen so soon? Was that the reason he had drunk so much – or did he often get drunk? 'The papers have been talking about it for ages so I wasn't sure anything had changed.'

'They say it will be all over by Christmas,' one of the other young men chipped in. 'Can't see it myself. The Germans have been preparing for this for ages. We're the ones caught with our pants down.'

'Bill! Be careful what you say to a decent young lady.'

'Sorry, miss. I didn't mean to offend you.'

Jane shook her head. They believed she was decent but what would they think if they knew the truth?

Jane's skin crawled as she thought about what had happened to her. She wasn't decent any more. David Heron had ruined her. No one would want to marry her.

Her throat felt hot and tears burned behind her eyes. She had been such a fool, enjoying the treat of staying at a place like that and never giving a thought to the price she might have to pay. She should have known that she didn't belong there – that David Heron had brought her there for a good reason. Like an idiot she had taken his generosity at face value.

Well, she had paid the price for her foolishness and there was no changing what had happened. She remembered telling her aunt just recently that she hadn't been with a man. She could just imagine what Aunt Alice would say to her if she knew what Jane had done.

'So the funeral is over then,' Alice nodded her satisfaction. 'Now that you're here you can put all that stuff behind you and move on. Your sister is already settling in nicely. I'll take you to the teashop tomorrow and you can see what you feel. I thought you could help me with the cooking for a start and then you might like to have a go at the cash desk.'

'Thank you. I should enjoy helping you with the baking, aunt

– but I'm not certain I want to settle for working in the tea rooms. There will be lots of work for women now there's a war on. I might volunteer for something.'

Alice's face showed her disapproval. 'I hope you aren't thinking of factory work? That is so common, Jane. You would be much better off working for me.'

'I'm very grateful to you for taking Melia in. I shall contribute to her keep once I start earning some money, of course – but I need something more than working in a teashop.'

'Indeed?' Alice raised her brows. 'A week or two back you were scrubbing floors in a public house!'

'That was a temporary measure and there wasn't a war on. I would like to do something to help.'

'Well, I can't stop you, but I think you might show a little more willingness to help me.'

'I shall work for you until I find something useful I can do for the war effort.' Jane didn't want to offend her aunt but she'd had enough of being told what to do by people who imagined they owned her. Her period had started a few days after the visit to Ned, so that was one worry off her mind. It was time she started to live for herself. 'I'm sorry if this offends you, Aunt Alice, but I have to make my own way. I don't know what I want to do yet, but when I do I'll let you know . . .'

Jane saw the glint of anger in her aunt's eye. No doubt she had believed Jane would be only too grateful to fall into line. Perhaps she would have had she been the same girl who had gone to work for Maria Stratton, but she wasn't. She had grown up, changed, become a different person.

Eight

Jane picked up the newspaper that one of the customers had left behind, glancing at the headlines. The defeat at Mons was crushing. The Germans were much stronger than anyone had thought and the British and French troops were suffering appalling losses. Wounded men were being brought home and the hospitals were swamped. She scanned an article further down. The Queen was backing an appeal for women to go out to work and especially those women who were prepared to join the Volunteer Aid Detachment.

Jane felt the prick of tears as she saw pictures of wounded men coming home. For weeks they'd had nothing but jingoistic propaganda from the papers, articles urging men to join the army and fight. Now they were reporting the shambles that had seen the British army suffer a terrible defeat.

'Jane, haven't you finished clearing that table yet?' Aunt Alice's sharp voice broke into Jane's thoughts. 'We have customers waiting.'

'Yes, I've finished.' Jane picked up her tray and carried it through to the kitchen at the back. She didn't mind working in the tea rooms despite the fact that her aunt was a slave driver. However, she wanted to be doing something to help the war effort and now she knew what to do about it, because she had torn out the article she needed.

'You were a long time,' Alice said looking at her suspiciously. 'I hope you weren't flirting with those young men. I know they are soldiers and we should all respect them for what they are doing, but I won't have my girls flirting with the customers.'

'I promise you I wasn't. I was reading an article in the paper. It sounds as if everything is going wrong out there . . .'

'War is always a waste of good money if you ask me. I don't know why we had to get involved in the first place.'

'Pa said it was to do with treaties. Once the Russians were involved we more or less had to declare war.'

'Rubbish! I blame the government for the problems. If they knew they were going to get involved they should have been more prepared.'

'Yes, they should. We should all have known that it wasn't going to be as easy as sending a gunboat.'

'We have sold all the ginger cake and the almond tarts you made this morning,' Alice said dismissing the subject for one of more importance. 'Your baking seems to be popular, Jane. I think we are even busier since you started working for me.'

'I'm glad you're pleased.'

Jane let the opportunity pass. If she had her way she wouldn't be working in her aunt's kitchen for much longer.

'Is this the right queue for the nursing?' A pretty red-haired girl touched Jane on the arm. They were in the church hall and it was filled with chattering, nervous young women. Several desks were grouped at one end and every now and then the line moved forward. 'I put my name down at the door and they told me to get in the queue. I think a lot of girls want to help with the wounded but we shan't all get in.'

'I think they interview us and then decide where we are best suited.' Jane offered her hand. 'I'm Jane Shaw. I'm hoping they will take me as a nursing volunteer but they can send us anywhere – factories, farming, the war office, anything they like.'

'I know. My brothers have all joined the army.' The girl seemed pensive. 'I'm Sally Barnes. I've been working in a factory but I hated it. I've seen all those dreadful pictures of wounded men. They say the hospitals will be swamped if things get worse.'

'They won't let us nurse the men for ages, but we may get to give them a glass of water or run errands. I expect most of it will be scrubbing floors and emptying bedpans.'

Sally looked horrified. 'I was thinking I could hold their hands and give them something to make them feel better.'

'I couldn't make up my mind what I wanted to do but when I saw that the hospitals needed volunteers urgently I decided to sign on. I don't mind scrubbing floors if it helps.'

'Well, I suppose . . .' Sally frowned. 'My friend joined the army as an ambulance driver. I wish I could drive. I wouldn't mind doing that.'

'You should take lessons.' Jane turned her head, listening. 'Oh, that was my name. I'd better go. Good luck.'

'Thanks. Maybe I'll see you around . . .'

'Yes, perhaps.'

Jane hurried to the desk and looked at the bespectacled, grey-haired woman who had called her name. She held out her form and waited as the woman inspected it before looking up.

'Why do you want to join the nursing division?'

'Because I read in the paper that they were desperate for volunteers.'

'What do you imagine the job entails?'

'Helping the nurses, cleaning wards and bedpans – anything I'm told to do.'

That brought a nod of approval. 'How are your feet? Do you have a problem standing for long periods?'

'I work as a cook and serve tea but I've done other things – including scrubbing floors when I had to.'

'You sound exactly the sensible sort of woman we need.' The woman behind the desk stamped Jane's form. 'Take this to the desk at the end of the room – down there to your right. You will be given instructions where to report.'

'Does that mean I'm in?'

'We can't afford to turn down girls like you. I'm not sure some of this lot will be of much use but you certainly sound promising.'

'You have done what?' Alice was angry. 'I think that was very underhand of you, Jane – signing up without even telling me what you intended. What am I going to do without you?'

'You managed before I came.'

'I was hoping you would take over the baking from me in time,' her aunt said and glared at her. 'I wish that you had told me before you signed. I doubt if you can get out of it now.'

'I don't want to change my mind. The hospitals need girls like me, aunt – girls who are prepared to do anything they are asked. Some of the girls don't want to do the dirty jobs but I don't mind.'

'And you consider that more important than working for your own family?'

'If it gives the nurses more time to do their jobs – yes, I do.

I am sorry if that makes you cross, aunt – and I am not ungrateful for what you've done for us.'

'I think you are making a big mistake. This place could have been yours one day – yours and Amelia's.'

'Melia wants to go to college and teach. One day I'll do something more challenging. It might even be something to do with teaching, but for the moment I feel it is my duty to do what I can for our country.'

Her aunt's thin lips curved back in a sneer of derision. 'If you consider scrubbing floors war work you are easily satisfied. I doubt you will ever amount to much, Jane Shaw. You have too much of your father in you.'

'I would rather be like him than my mother.'

Alice smiled unpleasantly. 'Perhaps if you knew why he quarrelled with his father you might change your mind.'

'I wish you would tell me instead of hinting at things.'

'You really want to know?' Jane nodded. 'Your father took money from his own father to spend on your mother. When he was challenged he said it was owed him, then he knocked his father down and walked out on him.'

'I don't believe you. Pa wouldn't . . . he wouldn't . . .' Jane felt sick as she saw a look of triumph in the older woman's eyes. 'That isn't the whole truth. I don't believe you and I never shall. I was sorry I had let you down but I'm not now. As soon as I have enough money I'll send for Melia to come and live with me.'

'I don't think your sister will listen. She likes being with me – and she is sensible enough to know which side her bread is buttered. She can go to college if she wants, but she will never make as much money as she could from her own business. When I retire the business would have come to both of you but now it will be Melia's.' Alice's eyes narrowed with spite. 'If you leave like this I don't want you. Once you go that is it – don't ask to come back, because my answer will be no.'

'Why did you have to quarrel with Aunt Alice?' Melia asked, tears in her eyes. 'And why did you have to volunteer? I don't want you to go! You might have thought about me before you signed up!'

'You seemed happy here. You are, aren't you? I could find somewhere for you to live when I'm settled . . .'

'And move school again just when I'm getting used to everyone? I'm in a good school now and the teachers are pleased with me. If I work hard I should get a place in teaching college.'

'You still want to be a teacher then?'

'Yes, why wouldn't I?'

'Aunt Alice said something about you owning the teashop one day.'

'When she's dead,' Melia said. 'It doesn't mean I shall have to work there. Besides, you were the one she intended to run things for her.'

'I didn't fancy being tied to her apron strings for too long. I want to do my bit for the war effort and then we'll see.'

'Mr Hastings thought you should be a teacher too. You haven't thought of going to college, Jane?'

'I thought about it once but Ma needed me. It is too late now.'

'Mr Hastings said you could be a mature student. Or you could be a pupil teacher. I'm not sure how that works but I think it means you study as you work and take your degree later in life if you want to be a head or senior teacher.'

'Maybe I'll think about it after the war, Melia – but I've signed up for this. I couldn't get out of it if I wanted.'

'Oh . . .' Melia sniffed and then hugged her. 'I just wish you weren't going away. I shall see you again, shan't I?'

Jane's heart caught as she hugged her. 'Silly! Of course you will. I shall write to you and we'll meet sometimes. You can come and visit when I know where I'm going to be. At the moment I'm being sent for training. I don't know where they will send me once I've learned how to do what they need.'

Jane soon settled into the nurses' home, which was situated just a few miles outside London. There were a lot of girls like her and they came from all walks of life, some from poor families some from good homes.

Frances Milton was one of the first to introduce herself as they were shown to their living quarters the first day. Her accent told Jane that she was from a good family and she was wary for a few minutes, but Frances was such a friendly person that they were soon talking and laughing as if they had known each other for years.

'Daddy said he would disown me if I didn't do my bit,' Frances said. 'Mummy wasn't too happy when she knew I was going to be a VAD. She wanted me to do charity work; roll a few bandages and visit the patients at one of the homes she is setting up for the badly wounded to convalesce. Daddy said he is proud of me for wanting to do more so she couldn't stop me signing up. Besides, she has given up trying to find me a husband. I need to lose about two stone to have a chance but I'm always hungry.'

Jane smiled because her new friend was undoubtedly a big girl, though more solidly built than fat.

'You wait until they have you scrubbing floors and on your feet for twelve hours a day. You will lose some weight then.'

'I'll probably just eat more to keep my strength up – but you are already so slim. By that principle you will waste away to nothing.'

'I'm used to hard work and my appetite is pretty good. It's just that I don't seem to put on weight.'

'My father says it is all down to your metabolism,' a pretty girl with soft fair hair chimed in. 'I'm Rose Hylton. My father is a doctor at an Infirmary in the East End, and he deals with people's diets and things like that – he's an expert on nutrition and he says most people eat all the wrong stuff. Lots of stodge and fat when they should be having fruit and greens.'

'Most people can't afford a lot of fruit,' Jane said. 'We hardly ever had it at home, unless it was in season and we could either grow it in the garden or someone brought us a bag of windfalls to make apple pie.'

'Well, it didn't do you a lot of harm by the looks of it.' Rose grinned. 'What do you think about us three taking the beds right at the end of the dorm?'

'Yes, why not?' Frances agreed. 'Let's try to do everything together. It will be easier if we help each other to get through the training.'

'My feet are killing me!' Rose groaned as the three of them met just before lights out at the end of their first week. 'I thought I knew what hard work was but I'm exhausted.'

'It's the scrubbing that gets me,' Frances complained and looked at her hands, which were red and sore. 'My knees hurt and my back aches.' She lay back on her bed and closed her eyes. 'I wish I were dead.'

'You don't mean that,' Jane smiled. Scrubbing the floors at the hospital was easy compared to cleaning the Royal Arms. Besides, she liked being a part of the busy life of the hospital. 'Nurse Johnson let me help her take the water jugs round this morning. When you see the men . . .' her voice caught with emotion. 'Some of them have some terrible injuries and they are so brave. It just makes whatever we do worthwhile.'

'You were honoured. All I've been allowed to do apart from scrubbing is to empty bedpans.' Rose wrinkled her nose and sighed. 'I suppose it is what we expected but I want to help the patients.'

'We are helping them by giving the nurses more time to do their job.' Jane took her shoes off and rubbed at her feet through the thick stockings that were regulation wear, like the ugly uniforms that covered them from neck to ankles. 'It is hard work but I wouldn't go back to what I was doing if I was paid double.'

'We start lectures next week,' Frances said. 'We have to fit them in and still do the rest of it. We shall be on our feet for most of the day and half the night.'

'I can't wait to start the lectures,' Jane said, 'but I shall be glad to get to sleep. I'm almost asleep on my feet.'

'We get our first thirty-six hours off this weekend,' Rose announced when they had all scraped through the first month of training. 'Why don't we catch the train and go into town to a Music Hall?'

'I wish I could.' Frances threw her a look of apology. 'Mummy has a big dinner on and she made me promise I would go home as soon as I got leave.'

'Oh, well, you have to do what you have to do. What about you, Jane?'

'Yes, I should like that,' Jane agreed. She didn't have a home to go to, but she wasn't going to admit it. 'Where shall we stay?'

'We can stay at my house overnight and come back in the morning – if that is all right with you? My parents told me to bring my friends home.'

'I should like to meet them.' Jane felt a little uncomfortable because she wouldn't be able to return the favour, but perhaps she could make it up some other way. 'Yes, that would be lovely, thank you.'

'Mum will be pleased. I've told her about you, Jane – and Frances. She was thrilled that I had made such good friends. We'll do some shopping, have tea with her, get changed and go out for the evening, and come back here after breakfast. Unless you want to pop home for a bit?'

'My aunt won't expect to see me. I know my sister is all right because I had a letter a few days ago.'

She reached for her writing pad. She tried to write a few words every night before she went to bed. Ned had been thrilled to get her first letter from the hospital and his reply had been full of questions about the patients and what she was doing.

She smiled as she thought that today she would be able to tell him that one of the nurses had complimented her when she'd helped to strip the beds.

'Your corners are neat and tidy, just as Sister likes them, Shaw. I think I can leave you to finish off the empty beds yourself. We have a new influx of patients coming in shortly and I have a dressing to do.'

Jane had been thrilled to be given the responsibility. Making a bed might not seem important to outsiders, but Sister had an eagle eye and slipshod work resulted in it all having to be done again.

Her letters to her sister and Ned were filled with what went on with the hospital, but after this weekend she would be able to tell them about her visit to Rose's home. She was going shopping with Rose and she would be sure to buy something to send Ned; perhaps some postcards to add to his collection or a packet of toffee.

Jane needed some new shoes. They had all been provided with uniforms but most of the girls bought their own black button boots or heavy lace-up shoes for when they were on duty.

Rose was more interested in purchasing a pair of tan leather Cuban-heeled shoes for Sunday best. They visited half a dozen shops before they both found what they needed.

'We had better hurry or we shan't have time for tea with Mum,' Rose said looking at the little silver watch she had pinned to her lapel. 'We don't want to be late for the show this evening.'

'We might catch a bus . . .' Jane said. 'Look, it is at the stop . . .' She started to run, caught her heel on the uneven pavement and nearly fell, her parcel tumbling to the ground at the feet of a man in army uniform. 'Oh . . . thank you . . .' She looked up as his hand steadied her.

'Are you all right, miss?' he asked handing her the parcel.

'Yes, thanks to you. I wasn't looking where I was going. We wanted to catch the bus that just left.'

'Were you in a hurry?'

'Yes, a bit. We've been shopping and the time slipped away.'

'Where are you going? If it is Bermondsey way I can give you both a lift in my car.' He looked inquiringly at Rose and then smiled. 'I believe I know you – you are Rose Hylton, Doctor Hylton's daughter.'

'Yes, I am Rose – and this is my friend Jane Shaw.' Rose shifted her parcel under one arm and offered her hand. 'It is nice to see you, Captain Bedford. My father told me you had been given a medal for your work in France. You saved the lives of several men at Mons . . .'

'I did very little. Please do not make me out to be a hero. It was a bloodbath and we all did what we could. Would you like that lift? I am going your way.'

'Yes, thank you.' Rose glanced at Jane. 'Doctor Bedford is a friend of my father's. He used to be resident at the local hospital but he joined up when the war started and he has been out there working with the wounded at the sharp end.'

'A lot of the men talk about the treatment they get when they are first wounded,' Jane said. 'If it were not for doctors like you they would suffer a lot more than they do, I think.'

'You are in the VADs too, Miss Shaw?' His eyes were on her face, warm and approving.

'Yes. I joined the same day as Rose.'

'How do you find life at the hospital?'

'I enjoy helping wherever I can. It would be nice to do more to help the wounded men but they don't trust us with anything more than scrubbing a few bedpans just yet.'

'I feel for you girls, I really do,' he said and opened the door of a large, rather old-looking phaeton, waiting for the girls to tuck themselves inside the motorcar before going to turn the handle. Despite its disreputable appearance and the fact that it smelled slightly of wet dogs in the back, the engine started easily. 'We doctors get all the glory and you get the dirty jobs – but we couldn't do it without you and the nurses.'

'The doctors at the hospital don't even notice us.' Rose made a rueful grimace as he pulled into the traffic. The road was congested with cars, lorries and wagons pulled by horses. 'Sister thinks we are all morons and the nurses turn their noses up as if there were an unpleasant smell when we're around.'

Jane laughed. 'I agree about the doctors and Sister Nottingham certainly thinks we've only got half a brain between us – but some of the nurses have been helpful. Nurse Jennifer let me give one of the patients a glass of water yesterday.'

'Wonders will never cease!' Rose laughed. 'I mean how much training does it need to help someone drink a glass of water? If they are ill it stands to reason they can only sip a little at a time.'

'You should have taken up nursing before the war, Rose.' Doctor Bedford glanced at her in the driving mirror. 'What about you, Miss Shaw? Is it your ambition to become a nurse eventually?'

'I am certainly loving the experience but what I really want is to work with children. However, I should like to progress and be of real help while there's a war.'

'I don't think it will be over for a few years. You girls have plenty of time to learn.'

Jane thanked Captain Bedford when he delivered them to Rose's front door. She shook hands with him, approving his firm grip and pleasant manner.

'Richard is a hero whatever he says,' Rose confided as she led Jane into the house. The hall was narrow but the glass in the front door let in plenty of light. The whole house smelled of lavender polish and pot pourri, and was furnished with good quality furniture that probably belonged to the late Victorian period.

Rose's mother came bustling through to meet them. She greeted Rose with a hug, inspected Jane for a moment and then did the same for her. She smelled of rose water and her large bosom was comforting and maternal.

'Rose has told me what a wonderful worker you are. The nurses all think the world of you and that is recommendation enough for me. I shall be happy to give you a bed whenever you get up to town – with Rose or without her.'

'That is very generous of you,' Jane said, overwhelmed by such a welcome. 'We don't often get much free time and I like to share with my friends when we do – but thank you. If I'm ever stuck for a bed I'll remember.'

'Come and have tea the both of you. I've got crumpets and some strawberry jam I made this summer. I'm not sure if I shall be able to make so much next year, because I think we may find things like sugar are harder to find. However, I've put a couple of pots out for you girls to take back with you. Rose told me the food isn't all that good.'

'It's better than they get in the trenches. One of the men told me he has never eaten so well.' Jane laughed, as Mrs Hylton looked surprised. 'I think he came from the Northeast. Perhaps he has known what it is like to have bread and dripping for supper.'

'Have you known that, Jane?' Mrs Hylton's eyes were curious.

'My father was a clerk in a solicitor's office. He kept us decently clothed and there was usually enough to go round, but sometimes, when there were extras to pay for, like medicine, we had none left for food.'

'Henry hopes for the day when medicine and the doctor's fee will be provided by the government. Perhaps things will change after the war.'

'Yes, perhaps they will. If women get the vote they will know what needs to be done for the family.'

'Are you a Suffragette, Jane?'

'I've never been to a meeting, but I've read their views in the newspaper and I think I agree with a lot of what they say.'

'You should try to learn more, go to a few meetings if you can,' Mrs Hylton nodded her approval as Jane took a crumpet and began to spread it with butter. 'Put some jam on, Jane – or honey if you prefer. I belong to a group of ladies of a more moderate order. As a doctor's wife I have to be careful. My husband cannot afford to upset his paying customers. They fund his charity work at the Infirmary.'

'I know the papers condemn some of the more violent behaviour by Mrs Pankhurst's group and others, but it may be that she
needed to do something to make people aware.'

'Yes, indeed – but we cannot all chain ourselves to the railings
or no work would get done.' Mrs Hylton looked on benevolently
as the two young women tucked into the cake she had baked.
'You both look too thin – do they give you enough to eat at
that place?'

'We get plenty, Mum,' Rose said. 'Not as good as your food
but we manage, don't we, Jane?'

'This sponge is beautifully light.' Jane finished hers but refused
seconds. 'If supper is too awful we sometimes get someone to
fetch fish and chips from the village shop.'

'Oh, well, I suppose I don't need to worry about either of
you. You both look perfectly well . . .'

'You enjoyed the show, didn't you?' Rose hugged Jane's arm as
they came out of the theatre that evening. 'Was it your first time
at the Music Hall?'

'Yes. I've been to amateur dramatics at home and my aunt
took us to the theatre once to see a Shakespearean play – but
she didn't approve of Music Hall.'

'My parents took me for the first time when I was eleven. I've
been going ever since. Your aunt sounds a bit of a tartar?'

'I suppose she is in a way. She took us in after our parents
died but . . . she didn't like it because I joined the VADs. I'm not
welcome there any more.'

'That's a bit mean of her.' Rose looked shocked. 'Mum meant
it you know. You can stay at ours any time you want.'

'Your mother is very generous. You're lucky, Rose.'

'Yes, I know.' She smiled at her. 'It was great bumping into
Captain Bedford, wasn't it? Did you like him, Jane? I think he
was taken with you.'

'Oh no, I am sure he was just being polite.' Jane shut down
the silly fear that made her stomach tighten. 'Besides, I shan't see
him again. Didn't he tell us he was going back to the Front soon?'

'Yes, he did . . .' Rose was thoughtful. 'I heard they were asking
for volunteers amongst the nurses to go out there . . .'

'Nurse Jennifer is volunteering.'

'Do you think we shall get a chance to go?'

'Perhaps in a year or so – if they are desperate and if the war lasts that long.'

'It isn't going to end anytime soon. The papers kept telling us it would be over by Christmas but my father never did believe them. He thinks it will be a long struggle. I just hope we don't lose . . .'

'I haven't thought much about the outcome. I just hate the idea of all those men getting maimed and killed – on both sides. The Germans must be suffering heavy losses as well, Rose.' Jane's face was tight with emotion. 'If we did get the chance to go over there once we've finished our basic training, would you volunteer?'

'Would you?'

'Yes, I think I might.'

'Then I shall too. We'll stick together whatever happens and Frances too if she wants.'

'Would you like to stay for Christmas?' Frances asked Jane as they walked from the hospital to the nurses' accommodation a week or so later. 'I asked Rose as well but she is working over the holiday. I know you have three days off the same as me. My parents would be pleased to meet you.'

Jane had considered going up to London and staying with the Hylton family so that she could visit Melia, but didn't want to abuse their kindness by taking it for granted. She would send her sister some money and visit her another time.

On her shopping trips, she had found some good quality colouring pencils and a drawing pad for Ned; he was always short of paper and drawing materials so she knew that her present would please him. She had also purchased a box of special caramels, which he would enjoy. Jane would have liked to pop down and see him at the school before Christmas but it wasn't possible.

Glancing at Frances, who was waiting for her answer, she came to a decision. 'Yes, I should like to stay – if you are certain your mother won't mind?'

'She will love it. Honestly, Jane. Mummy is really pleased that I've made such good friends. We have a journey of two hours there and back, but Daddy will send a car for us and we'll have plenty of time to enjoy ourselves.'

'Then I should love to come. Is there anything I can bring? What sort of present would be suitable?'

'You don't have to bring anything – but if you want to, Mummy loves flowers. Especially those big round chrysanthemums you can get this time of the year.'

'I've seen them somewhere locally. It is a nursery just a mile or so from the hospital. I've got an hour off this afternoon. I think I'll pop down and order them today. Just to make sure that I don't leave it too late . . .'

Jane walked back to the hospital later that afternoon. It was cold now and she had a felt cloche hat pulled down over her ears, a thick scarf wound around her throat.

The sound of a car coming up behind her made Jane move to the grass verge and wait for it to pass. The lane leading to the hospital was narrow at this point and there had been one or two near accidents when it was dark. Dusk was beginning to fall now and Jane was taking no chances. She was surprised when the car halted after it had passed her and the driver got out to turn and look at her.

'Miss Shaw?' the man said. 'I thought it might be you. I am going to the hospital. Can I give you a lift back?'

'Captain Bedford . . .' Jane smiled as she walked to join him. 'Thank you. It isn't far but it is very cold. I've just been to order some flowers for Christmas.'

'The nursery is a fair walk on an afternoon like this . . .' He smiled at her. 'Rose's mother sent me with some parcels she didn't want to post, because they are too heavy. I had to come and see someone here at the Malchester Military so I was pleased to be of use.'

Jane hurried to the car. 'It is lovely to see you again. When did you come home?'

'I got back the day before yesterday. I accompanied some badly wounded soldiers to a military hospital in good old Blighty and I was glad to have a break for Christmas. I don't think the men will get much cheer over there.'

'We had a whip-round for parcels. Sister Nottingham has been organizing it for the past month. Some of us knitted socks and scarves when we had a spare moment, and we've bought cakes and biscuits in tins, packets of toffee to send out there.'

'What a lovely idea. I thought Sister was a bit of a tyrant?'

'Fancy you remembering.' Jane glanced at him as he released the brake. 'She is when it comes to work but she has a real feeling for the patients . . .'

'Yes, I expect she is a dedicated nurse. I dare say the patients have told her the kind of things they lack. It is hard for some of the poor blighters in those trenches. Your feet can be wet for hours and it's good to have some spare socks when you have the chance to change them.'

'The papers tell us some of it but it is hard to imagine what it is really like in the trenches. All that mud and the noise – and the rats!'

'If I were you I shouldn't even try. It is thinking of girls like you at home that keeps us all going . . .' He glanced in the rearview mirror. 'I thought about you, Jane. I wondered if you would spend a bit of time with me over the holiday?'

'I should have liked that but I've agreed to stay at Frances Milton's home for three days . . .' Jane saw his disappointment. 'I am on night shift this evening but tomorrow I have a few hours free. I could come for a drink at the local pub – if you like?'

'I should like that very much.' His face lit up. 'I hope you didn't mind my asking on such short acquaintance? These days there isn't time to do things the right way.'

'I'm glad you asked. I would love to hear more about your work out there. I'm just a raw skivvy at the moment but when I have a bit more experience I should like to work in one of the field hospitals or perhaps a clearing station.'

'You must be mad,' he said but there was a twinkle in his eye as the car halted in the hospital grounds. 'I'll pick you up outside the nurses' home at about seven tomorrow – will that be all right?'

'Yes, thank you. I shall look forward to it.'

Jane was smiling as she made her way through the grounds to the residential area. Because Captain Bedford had given her a lift she had time to grab a cup of tea and a bun before going on

duty. He was nice and he didn't make her feel nervous, but friendship was as much as she could offer.

For a moment she recalled the night David Heron had raped
her and felt sick with humiliation. She wasn't sure that she could
ever trust another man sufficiently to give her heart – or her
body.

Nine

'I wish I were coming with you and Frances,' Rose said looking a little envious as she watched Jane pack her case. 'Thanks for the pressie, and I hope you like what I've given you.'

'I am sure I shall.' Jane hugged her. 'I think you will have a good time on the wards singing carols and handing out presents to the men.'

'I was told it was good fun, which is why I volunteered to work over the holiday – but now I wish I could be with you two.'

'I'll tell you all about it. Maybe Frances will bring some goodies back with her to share with you.'

'I wasn't thinking of the food so much, though I bet it will be good – but I wanted to see where Frances lives. Someone told me it is posh, right out in the country.'

'Yes, I suppose that is why it is a longish drive.' Jane laughed. 'Frances will ask you again, Rose. Besides, her home couldn't be nicer than yours.'

Rose hugged her tight. 'Have a wonderful time and think of me slaving away on the wards!'

Jane was in awe when she caught her first sight of Frances's home. She had been prepared for something special but this was far beyond her expectation. The house had a main building of pale buttery stone and a wing at either side. It was built in the Georgian style and looked impressive in the pale wintry sunshine. The grounds were large and there was a park and a lake in the distance, the formal gardens composed of smooth lawns with box hedges enclosing rose gardens and beds of herbs or perennials.

'I was told it was posh,' Jane breathed ecstatically, 'but this is beautiful, Frances. You must love it very much?'

'We are lucky that the government hasn't taken it over yet for a convalescent home. Daddy would fight tooth and nail if they tried, of course, but he has offered them another smaller house so perhaps they won't ask.'

'It would be just too awful to have a house like this taken from you.'

'I'm glad you feel like that, Jane. Some people think we ought to give it up gladly.'

'Why should you?' Jane frowned. 'I know some of the girls are jealous because your family is wealthy but you don't flash your money around. You wear the same things we do and you don't complain the way a lot of them do when you're asked to work longer hours.'

'I know how lucky we are but Daddy does a lot of charity stuff and so does Mummy. I don't talk about it because it sounds patronizing, but honestly we couldn't help everyone even if we gave all we had away.'

'You don't need to apologize for what you have. I've been poor, Frances. I know what it is like to be without a shilling for the gas but I don't grudge other people what they have. I hope that one day I'll be able to earn enough money to live in a nice house and not worry about where the next meal is coming from, but for the moment I love what I'm doing.'

'I do too.' Frances smiled. 'I knew you felt that way or I wouldn't have asked you to stay.' She look self-conscious, then said shyly, 'If you would like to borrow any of my clothes while you're here you are welcome, Jane. Mummy said I should ask. I've got some I had when I was slimmer that would fit you with a little bit of alteration.'

'Thanks. I've brought a dress my aunt bought me for evenings and a couple of others, but if there's a special affair one evening I wouldn't mind borrowing from you.'

'You aren't offended because I asked?'

'We swap at the hospital, why not here?'

'I nearly didn't ask, Jane. I wouldn't offend you for the world.'

'Well, you didn't, so stop looking so anxious.'

'You'd better come and meet my mother.'

Jane followed her into the house. It was obvious that Mrs Milton suspected Frances's friend from the hospital might not have the right clothes for her dinner parties. She wondered if she would wish herself back at the hospital with Rose before the end of the visit.

★　★　★

Mrs Milton was a tall elegant lady with fair hair that she wore in a sleek pleat at the back of her head. She was wearing a blue cashmere twinset with a tweed skirt, and a double row of pearls at her neck. Jane thought her perfume sweet and flowery, a little overpowering.

'My daughter has told us so much about her friends. It is delightful to meet you at last, Jane. I may call you Jane, I hope?'

'Yes, of course, Mrs Milton.'

'It is Lady Milton actually, Jane – but my friends call me Mitsy and Sir Bartrum is usually Barty. He won't answer to anything else, hasn't for years. We don't stand on ceremony here in the country. I hope you will find your room comfortable. If there is anything else you need you should ring the bell and someone will come.'

'Thank you . . .' Jane couldn't imagine calling this woman by her first name and she was surprised that there was a title. Frances had certainly kept quiet about that one! She presented her flowers. 'Frances told me you love these.'

'Yes, I do, thank you – but you really shouldn't have brought anything.'

Jane felt a bit foolish and was relieved when Frances grabbed her arm and took her upstairs to the bedrooms.

'Don't let Mummy intimidate you. She is a bit daunting at first sight but she is nowhere near as snooty as some of her friends.'

'Will her friends be coming for Christmas?'

'To the Christmas Eve party but not on Christmas Day. Daddy insists that is for family – aunts, uncles, cousins; my brothers would normally be here but neither of them can get home this year.'

'I'm sorry about that, Fran. Your mother must miss them a lot?'

'I think Daddy is the one who worries the most. Mummy loves us all of course but she puts a brave face on things. Daddy is a big softie.'

'You love him very much, don't you?'

'Yes, I do.' Frances linked arms with her. 'Come on, I'll show you my room first and then we'll go to yours . . .'

Frances had kept most of her childhood books and toys and her room was crowded with clutter of all kinds, including stones and fir cones she had collected over the years. However, the furnishings were all good quality mahogany and the huge wardrobes contained more dresses than Jane could imagine one person wearing.

'Most of these were Mummy's idea and they just don't suit me.' Frances pulled out a dozen beautiful evening gowns and spread them on the bed. 'None of these are right for me. You can choose anything you like, Jane. If you pick some you like I'll get Maisie to alter them to fit.'

'Most of these are too grand for me but that grey silk is lovely. Could I try that on?'

'Of course you can. Bring it with you. I'll show you your room now. I asked for you to have the green room, because it has one of the best views.'

Jane had to agree as she looked out of the window. The view was of the lake in the distance, open grassland and also some beautiful trees in the park. There were several magnificent oaks, also an ancient cedar tree with branches that seemed to sweep close to the ground and a wonderful blue green foliage.

'This is lovely. It was good of your mother to put me here.'

'Mummy wanted you to be happy, Jane. She really is pleased to have you here – even if she doesn't show it much.'

Jane tried on the grey dress at Frances's insistence. The waist needed taking in and the hem would have to be shortened but otherwise it fitted well.

'That looks better on you than it ever did on me, even when it fitted me,' Frances said. 'I'll get it altered for you and you can wear it for the Christmas Eve party – if you want?'

'I would love to. It is generous of you to let me wear it.'

'You can keep it. I have far more than I need.'

'Well, it does suit me. I could give you something for it?'

'Just lend me some stockings next time I'm out.' Frances looked relieved. 'Wear what you like this evening, Jane. It is always informal my first night home.'

Jane wandered around the room after Frances left her. It was beautifully furnished but much less cluttered than her friend's; Jane's clothes had been unpacked and hung in the wardrobe, which looked empty compared with Frances's.

Jane selected a pretty yellow jumper and a grey skirt that she had bought when she was in London and hardly worn since. She took Frances at her word and decided to keep her dresses for Christmas.

When the bell sounded Jane found her way down the stairs to the hall below. She was trying to make up her mind where the dining room was when Lady Milton came downstairs wearing a long evening gown in a heavy dark blue material. Jane realized that she had made a mistake. She ought to have worn a dress! Her cheeks burned as she felt Lady Milton's gaze on her.

'How charming you look, my dear,' Lady Milton said. 'Frances told you that we would be informal this evening, of course. You must excuse me for dressing up. My maid put this out for me and I didn't like to disappoint her.'

'Would you like me to change? I do have dresses I could wear but I was keeping them for the Christmas party.'

'Certainly not. It is I who should change if anyone. Come along, Jane. We really must not keep Cook waiting . . .'

Jane allowed herself to be swept along by her hostess. To her relief when she entered the dining room she discovered that Frances was wearing a skirt and blouse and the elderly man who turned to look at her had on an old tweed jacket with patched elbows. He had blue eyes that sparkled and he came towards her with outstretched hands.

'Jane – welcome to our home,' he boomed and took the hands she instinctively offered, squeezing them heartily. 'It is good to meet you at last. My little girl has talked about nothing but Jane and Rose for weeks.'

Christmas Eve was a busy day for the girls. Jane and Frances were given the task of decorating the huge tree that had been brought in from the gardens.

'Daddy won't have it in until the morning of Christmas Eve,' Frances told her. 'Mummy has far too much to do getting ready for this evening. I usually decorate it with my brothers – but we can do it together this year.'

There were several boxes of delicate glass balls, candleholders and silver ribbons, which were tied to the branches and made into bows. The task was considerable and it took all the morning to get it just right.

Lady Milton approved their work just as the gong sounded

for luncheon. After the meal she gave her daughter two baskets that were to be delivered to the Vicarage.

'These are for the Vicar and his family – and these small parcels are for him to distribute at the village children's party later today. I usually have them to him before this but I haven't had the time this year because of all my committee work. I hope you and Jane won't mind taking them for me?'

'It will be a nice walk to the village,' Frances said. 'Jane likes to walk – don't you?'

'Yes, I do. I shall be happy to take one of the baskets.'

'Put your hats and scarves on,' Lady Milton advised. 'The sun is lovely but it will be very cold out. It was frosty earlier and I think it will freeze again this evening.'

Jane would have liked to stop longer with the Vicar and his family. She and Frances had helped him to pile presents under the small tree in the village hall. A long table was groaning under the weight of all the sausage rolls, iced buns and jellies that had been prepared for the children's treat.

'You would hardly think there was a war on would you?' she remarked to Frances as they walked back from the village later. 'I know they are beginning to feel the shortages of things like eggs and butter in London. Melia told me that Aunt Alice was worried whether she would be able to carry on making her best-selling cakes. She may have to substitute things like jam tarts and bread and butter puddings.'

'Mummy had them kill a pig for the Vicar to distribute this Christmas. If the Government bring in more restrictions she might not be able to do that next year . . .'

'Do you think we shall still be fighting a war next Christmas?'

'Daddy says it is going to be a long business. I know he has made lots of provisions just in case it drags on for years.'

Jane was thoughtful as she went back to her room to change for tea. If the war did drag on for a long time, and her aunt was forced to close the teashop, it might mean Melia would not get her wish to go to college.

She changed into a dark green wool afternoon dress and some black court shoes and tidied her hair, letting it hang loosely on her shoulders. Jane didn't have any jewellery. She had let Melia pick what she wanted of their mother's things and then sold the rest. She would have liked a small brooch to wear at the neck of her dress, but since she didn't have one she would have to manage without.

She went downstairs and headed for the drawing room. The sound of laughter told her that guests had arrived and were already gathered in the large room. Knowing that she looked the best she could, Jane stuck her head in the air and walked into the room. Frances beckoned to her and she crossed the floor to sit on a little sofa by her friend.

'You do look nice,' Frances said approvingly. 'I haven't seen that dress before.'

'Aunt Alice bought it for me. I don't wear it much.'

'Will you have some tea, Jane?'

She glanced at Lady Milton. 'Yes, please.'

'Do try one of the almond cakes, my dear. Frances, remember it is a special dinner this evening.'

'I wish she wouldn't remind me,' Frances said, a hot colour in her cheeks. 'I feel such a pig if I eat more than one cake but I'm starving.'

'So am I. It must have been the fresh air.' Jane grinned. 'I'm going to have two of those cakes while I've got the chance.' She took them from the maid who was offering plates round and winked as Frances followed suit. 'They will go down in one swallow. We're used to more substantial stuff at the canteen.'

'Roly-poly suet pudding with treacle,' Frances said relaxing. 'Mummy likes things to be small and delicious, which these are – but they don't fill you up.'

Jane glanced across the room as another guest entered. For a moment her heart stopped beating and she felt as if she couldn't breathe. She wanted to jump up and run away but her limbs wouldn't move. If she had thought for one moment that *he* would be a guest in this house for Christmas she would never have come.

'Is something wrong, Jane? You've gone white.' Frances looked at her in concern. 'Are you ill?'

Jane was tempted to lie, then pride came to her rescue. Why should she run away as if she had done something wrong? He was the one who had behaved despicably. David Heron was the one who ought to leave.

She raised her head, her gaze travelling to his face. He was aware of her and there was a slightly apprehensive expression on his face. He met her gaze for a moment and then his fell away.

'No, I'm not ill,' Jane replied belatedly to her friend's inquiry. 'I just saw someone I knew. I worked for Mr Heron's sister for a few months.'

'Captain Heron.' Frances looked at him and smiled. 'He was badly wounded in that awful defeat the troops suffered at Mons – do you remember the papers were full of it? He was shipped home and has been recovering since. He must be feeling better at last.'

David was studiously avoiding looking in her direction. Jane risked another glance and realized that he looked thinner and his face was pale. Now that Frances had told her, she could see that he had been ill.

'Jane . . .' David's voice reached her as she prepared to go upstairs a little later. 'May I speak to you please?

Jane turned reluctantly, waiting for him to come up to her. He took her arm and steered her from the hall into a small sitting room to the left. She shook his hand off.

'Don't you dare touch me! If I'd known you would be here I wouldn't have come, but I can't run away without upsetting Frances. I would be obliged if you would just leave me alone.'

'Please don't hate me, Jane – and don't think of leaving. If anyone leaves it must be me.'

'I see no reason to upset Lady Milton's arrangements. Just stay away from me.'

'You do hate me. I can't blame you.' His expression was contrite almost pleading. 'I'm sorry. I shan't ask you to forgive me. I can't forgive myself. I don't know what got into me that day . . .'

'You drank too much.'

'Yes, but it was more than that. I should explain but I can't . . .' David moved his hand as if to touch her but dropped it as she shrank back. 'You are quite safe. I promise I will never hurt you again.'

'You won't get the chance.'

'I would turn the clock back if I could. I really care about you, Jane.'

'Well, I don't care about you. You are nothing to me. Just leave me alone.'

'I understand how you feel.'

'Do you? I doubt it. You don't know the meaning of the word love. You just see what you want and take it.'

'I was wrong. I admit it and I beg your pardon. Perhaps one day I shall be able to make it up to you somehow.'

'I doubt that very much. If you will excuse me I must change for dinner.'

Jane walked past him and ran into the hall and up the stairs. She had known that there must be a confrontation as soon as she saw him. If he was really sorry he would do as she asked and stay away from her for the rest of the night.

Jane was shaking when she started to change for the evening. She had locked the door after her. David Heron would never walk in on her again unannounced!

The grey silk gown was waiting for her on the bed. Jane put it on, feeling pleased with the way it fitted her. She had decided that she would put her hair back from her face but leave it hanging loose. The dress would have looked better with a necklace of some kind but Jane did not possess one. However, just as she had finished doing her hair someone knocked at the door.

Jane approached it cautiously. 'Who is it?'

'It is the maid with your corsage, Miss Shaw.'

'Oh . . .' Jane unlocked the door and looked at the spray of pink roses the girl had brought her. 'Are they for me? How lovely. I wasn't expecting anything like this . . .'

'Lady Milton gives them to all the ladies staying with us,' the girl said. 'There is a little pin attached for you to fasten them to your dress if you wish.'

'Thank you. Yes, I shall.' Jane went to the mirror and fastened the small posy at the spot where the neckline dipped to reveal a glimpse of her breasts. The flowers were scented and delicate and took away the bareness that had made her feel she needed a necklace. Nothing more was required. Her gown was simple yet elegant and she felt confident as she went down to join the other guests.

A mixture of ladies and gentlemen were assembling in the drawing room when she entered. Some of the ladies were wearing magnificent jewels and their gowns were exquisite. Even Barty was wearing a smart black evening suit with a starched white shirt and black bow tie, a wide red silk cummerbund about his portly waist.

Frances was standing with her father and she beckoned Jane to join them. She was wearing a string of large creamy pearls around her neck and touched them reverently as Jane looked at her.

'Look what Daddy gave me, Jane. Aren't they lovely?'

'Beautiful. You look really lovely, Frances.'

'So do you, Jane. Daddy got these for you – I hope you like them?'

Jane hesitated and then took the small box. Opening it, she found a pair of gold earrings with pear-shaped drop pearls.

'These are lovely – but much too expensive. I can't possibly accept them.'

'We should like you to have them – they are from all of us,' Barty said. 'The earrings are a token of our affection, Jane. Please don't refuse us.'

'Oh . . .' Put like that Jane could hardly deny him. 'You are so generous, sir. I do not know how to thank you – all of you.'

'Wear them tonight,' Frances said. 'Put them on now, Jane. Give me the box and go to the mirror. They are exactly what you need.'

Jane gave her the box, which she set down on a little occasional table. She accompanied her to the mirror and clipped the earrings to the lobes of her ears.

'They are wonderful. I've never had anything like this – I'm not sure I ought to have taken them.'

'Daddy gives presents to everyone. He would be upset if you refused them – and they look well on you.'

Jane had to admit they did. 'Well, it is very kind of your father – all of you. I shall treasure them.'

'Good. I wanted you to have something nice.'

'You let me wear your dress.'

'It is yours now, Jane. Besides, it wouldn't fit me.'

Jane felt a little overwhelmed by their gifts but decided it was best just to accept rather than make a silly fuss. What seemed a huge gift to her was obviously nothing to someone as wealthy as Sir Bartrum.

She glanced round the room and saw that David Heron was

watching her. Something in his expression made her shiver. He had promised that he would never hurt her again but she didn't trust his word. The heat in his eyes seemed to burn into her, making her want to run away and hide.

Jane's chin went up. She wasn't going to run away!

It was an evening of music, fun and laughter. Some of the guests danced in the long gallery after dinner. There was a quartet playing and the chairs and tables had been pulled back to clear the floor. Jane watched for a while but when someone asked her to dance she shook her head. She wasn't sure that she could bear any man's hands on her, even though it was only a dance.

She wandered back into the drawing room. Card tables had been set up. Frances was playing whist with three of her mother's guests. Jane went over to the window and looked out at the night. The moon had disappeared behind some clouds and it was quite dark.

'Wouldn't you like to dance?'

'No thank you,' Jane replied without looking round. 'I am quite content to listen to the music and watch others.'

'You are too beautiful to sit on the sidelines like a wallflower.'

'I thank you for your concern but I would prefer it if you left me alone.'

'I thought about you when I was close to death. Would you have been glad if I'd died, Jane?'

She turned to look at him then. 'Perhaps I would have killed you that night if I could, but now . . . I feel nothing for you.'

'You are harsh, Janey.'

'I think I have the right to be harsh.'

'Yes, you do. I hope you will forgive me one day. I would like the chance to make it up to you.'

'Just how do you imagine you could do that? Can you give back what you took?'

'Surely it wasn't that bad? I would make you happy if you would let me.'

'Nothing you could do would make me happy – except to take yourself off and not bother me again.'

'Jane—' He broke off as Lady Milton approached.

'Jane my dear, do you play cards? We need another fourth at whist if you could sit in?'

'I'm not very good but I shall be happy to oblige.'

Jane followed her hostess to one of the tables and discovered that she was to partner Sir Barty himself. She did not look back but she sensed that David Heron was still watching her as she began to play.

Christmas Day was a much quieter affair. The family went to church in the morning, returning to a buffet lunch in the smaller dining room. Presents had been exchanged the previous evening so Jane was surprised to discover a small parcel on her dressing table when she went up to change for the evening. She opened it and discovered a gold cameo brooch, which was exactly what she would have chosen to wear with her afternoon dress if she could have afforded to buy such a trinket. She looked for a card but there was none.

When the maid brought Jane's dress, which had been sponged and pressed, she asked her if she knew where the parcel had come from.

'I believe it was delivered to the house some time this morning, miss. Is something wrong?'

'There was no card. I wondered who had sent it.'

'Perhaps it fell off, miss. I'll see if it is lying about anywhere.'

Jane pinned the brooch to her dress when she went down for dinner. Frances remarked on it and Jane told her that it had been left in her room but the card was missing.

'My name was written on the brown paper but there was no message.'

'The card must have got lost.' Frances arched her brows teasingly. 'You have a secret admirer, Jane.'

'It wasn't you or your family?'

'No. Mummy would have told me if she had given you something – the earrings were from us, Jane.'

'Yes, I know. It just seems so strange that there was no card.'

'I shouldn't worry. It was probably your aunt. You told me you had quarrelled with her so perhaps she sent the brooch but didn't want to send a card.'

'Yes, perhaps.'

It was a sensible explanation. Jane decided to put the mystery to the back of her mind. This was her last night so she might as well enjoy it.

The meal was excellent. There were only Sir Barty, Lady Milton, Frances, two elderly aunts and Jane at table; a much quieter affair than the Christmas Eve party but perhaps even more enjoyable from Jane's point of view.

They were about to leave the table for the drawing room when the butler brought in a small buff envelope on a silver tray. A silence fell over the company as they all realized the significance. No one would send a telegram on Christmas Day unless it was important. Barty took the envelope, glanced at his wife and then opened it.

'No!' He spoke the one word with such anguish that Frances gave a cry of fear and got up, running round the table to his side. As he looked at her the tears were running down his cheeks. 'It is John . . . dead . . .'

Lady Milton's face went deadly white. She sat silent and still, as if frozen, unable to move. Barty got up from the table and staggered a few steps down the room. He clutched at his right arm and made a muffled moaning sound before falling to the floor.

'Daddy!' Frances screamed. She stood looking at him, her face reflecting her terror and distress. 'Oh, Daddy . . .'

Jane rose to her feet. Her heart was pounding as she approached Barty. He was such a strange colour! She knelt down beside him, rolled him on to his back and felt for a pulse. She couldn't feel anything. He might already be dead, but there was just a small chance she could do something. Jane pushed a finger in his mouth, checking that he hadn't swallowed his tongue. Then she pinched his nose, placed her mouth over his and breathed into him. She repeated the action three times, then placed her hands on his chest and started pumping.

'What are you doing?' Lady Milton demanded, galvanized into speech by this strange behaviour. 'Stop it at once!'

'No, Mummy. Jane is giving him what the doctors call the kiss of life. I wouldn't know how to do it, but I've seen a doctor doing this . . .'

Lady Milton had risen to her feet. Her face reflected her suspicion and anger as Jane breathed into Barty's mouth once more.

'I really think . . .' she began and then the little miracle happened. Barty choked and the colour came back into his cheeks. 'Oh my God! Barty . . .'

Lady Milton rushed to her husband's side and knelt beside him. She glanced at Jane as his eyelids flickered.

'How did you know what to do? You aren't a nurse?'

'I've seen it done and I've read the manuals. I wasn't sure it was the right thing but he seemed to have stopped breathing. I thought it was worth trying.'

Barty opened his eyes but though his lips moved no words came out. He seemed to be pleading with his wife.

'Someone send for the doctor,' Lady Milton said. 'Frances, get the servants in here. Your father must be carried to his room. He is ill and needs to be in his bed.'

Jane wondered if it would be better not to move him until the doctor arrived but Lady Milton had taken over. She was in charge of the situation.

'That was wonderful . . .' one of the elderly aunts spoke to Jane. 'We owe you a debt of thanks, young lady.'

'I was just lucky it worked.'

Jane left the room feeling that she might be in the way.

Going up to her room, Jane started folding her things. She had an extra dress to pack and it wouldn't be easy to get it in to her small suitcase without crushing it. When the knock at her door came she was sitting in her dressing gown brushing her hair.

'Come in . . .' Jane turned feeling surprised as Lady Milton entered. She rose to her feet. 'Sir Barty . . .?'

'Is as well as can be expected. The doctor said he was lucky to be alive and that your prompt action undoubtedly saved him. I wanted to thank you. Frances had no idea what to do, though she has as much experience as you.'

'I saw it happen a couple of times at the hospital and I wanted to know more so I slipped into a lecture about first aid and I took some of the pamphlets to read.'

'We are fortunate that you bothered to discover the technique, Jane. Had you not learned it properly I should now be a widow.' Lady Milton seemed overcome with emotion. 'What may I do for you in return? I imagine you do not receive much for your work at the hospital?'

'Are you offering me money?' Jane felt cold all over. 'I don't want anything. Your family has already given me far too much this Christmas.'

'I didn't mean to insult you . . .' Lady Milton seemed stunned that her good intention had caused offence. 'Truly, I am very grateful. I just wanted to show my appreciation.'

'I may come from the working classes, but I did what I did instinctively. I would have done the same for anyone and I do not require payment.'

'You are very proud, Jane. You shouldn't let pride rule your heart, my dear. The last thing I wanted was to offend you.'

'I am not offended.' Jane was suddenly uncertain. 'I'm sorry if I reacted badly. I am fond of Frances and I wanted to help her father. To be offered payment . . .' She shook her head. 'May we just forget anything was said? I do want to continue as Frances's friend.'

'Of course.' Lady Milton's manner had reverted to her usual reserve. 'However, I have told Frances that she must ask for compassionate leave. I shall need her at home to help me with her father. He was extremely attached to his eldest son.'

'Yes, of course. I know you must both be upset but in time . . . Frances was so happy at the hospital . . .'

'You must allow me to know what is best for my family. Please visit us again when you have time.'

Jane stared at the door as it closed behind her. Her skin prickled and she felt embarrassed. Lady Milton had been emotional. She had wanted to show her appreciation, even though her offer had been misguided. Perhaps Jane was too proud.

'So you came back alone on the train?' Rose stared at Jane as she finished telling her what had happened on Christmas Day. 'Fancy you giving Frances's father the kiss of life. I know how to do it in theory but I am not certain I could.'

'If you had to you would.' Jane smiled at her. 'I wish you had been there, Rose. It is a beautiful house and Sir Barty is a lovely man. I hope he will get over this attack, but Frances says the doctor told her it may be a long time before he is on his feet again.'

'It is rotten for her having to take indefinite leave.'

'She was nearly in tears when we said goodbye. Her father means the world to her and she wants to look after him, but she will miss this a lot.'

Rose nodded. 'We might not all be together soon anyway. Sister Nottingham told me that some of us are being recommended as probationer nurses.'

'Are you sure?' Jane stared at her. 'If she told you, you must be on the list.'

'I think you are too. You've got to report to her first thing in the morning and I'm half an hour after you. She didn't say anything about Frances so she might not be on the list.'

Jane's heart raced. 'What will you do if she asks you to become a nurse probationer?'

'I shall jump at the chance. It doesn't mean an end to all the chores but it does mean that we shall have a chance to learn – and we'll get to do more on the wards.'

'I never expected to be more than a skivvy.'

'You're worth more than that,' Rose said and smiled at her. 'Captain Bedford left you something, Jane. It is in your locker. I put it there for safety.'

'Oh . . .' Jane bent down to open her locker and took out the small package inside. It was flat and soft and when she untied the strings she discovered a pretty blue silk scarf inside. The card wished her a happy Christmas and reminded her that she had promised to write. 'That is nice . . .' She thought for a moment, then took out the brooch she'd received mysteriously on Christmas Day. 'I thought he might have sent this but if he left the scarf for me . . . it couldn't have been him.'

'That is gorgeous.' Rose touched the brooch reverently. 'Don't you know who gave you this?'

'There was no card . . .'

Jane frowned as she replaced it in the box and put it in her locker. She had puzzled over the brooch but could not decide; it might have been Aunt Alice or . . . it might have come from David Heron.

It was the sort of thing he might give her thinking it made up for what he had done. The more she thought about it, the more she felt certain that the brooch must have come from David. The suspicion made her feel she did not want to wear it. If she was sure he had sent it she would find a way of returning it, but for the moment she would simply keep it safe.

★　★　★

'I expect you know what this is about, Miss Shaw?'

'Yes, Sister. Rose Hylton told me some of the girls are going to be taken on as nurse probationers.'

'We need more nurses. There are plenty of volunteers to scrub floors and run errands but we need girls capable of doing more. I realize that you volunteered for the duration of the war but nursing is a vocation. If you succeed you may find that it takes over your life.'

'Yes, Sister Nottingham. I imagine it might.'

'I have noticed that you do not waste your time flirting when you should be working. I believe you intelligent enough to pass the necessary examinations and your dedication is not in doubt. May I put your name down, Jane?'

'I am grateful for the chance. When I signed I was willing to do anything but it would be wonderful to do really worthwhile work.'

'Good. I think you are exactly what this profession needs – now and after the war is over.'

Ten

'I never knew that it was possible to ache in so many places all at once,' Rose said as she came off duty that night. 'Sometimes I think we must be mad to do this job.'

'You don't mean that.' Jane laughed. 'My feet hurt the worst but we've been on duty for eighteen hours with hardly a break. I've got a forty-eight hour pass coming up this weekend. What about you?'

'I volunteered for extra duty.' Rose groaned as she lay on her bed. 'I know I am a fool but our ward is snowed under with new admissions. Your patients are medical and you know that their next move is either home or a convalescent home, ours are surgical. Whenever something big happens on the Somme we get a huge influx.'

'Yes, I know, but you didn't have to volunteer, love.' Jane yawned and started to undress. 'I thought you might want to come to town with me. I've promised to meet Melia and take her shopping.'

'I should have loved to come.' Rose could hardly keep her eyes open. 'You will stay with Mum even if I'm not there?'

'Yes. I am fond of your mother. She has made me feel so welcome these past two years.'

'You've never been back to your aunt's?'

'No. I wrote to her that first Christmas but she returned the letter unopened.'

'You didn't tell me that?'

'It wasn't important. We were starting our training proper and I just put it out of my mind. Melia seems happy enough whenever I see her. Aunt Alice has managed to keep the teashop going by introducing different things so I haven't needed to worry about her.'

'We have exams coming up next month. If we pass they might let us go out there . . . if you still want to?'

'You know I do.' Jane took the pins from her hair and shook it free. Some of the nurses had cut their hair short because it was easier, but Jane liked hers the way she'd always worn it and was resisting the change. 'We do a good job here, Rose – but not all the girls want to go to the Front. Richard told me how bad it was in his last letter.'

'Have you had anything from him recently?'

'Not for a month. When I do I shall probably get three all at once. The post from over there is peculiar to say the least.'

'I know.' Rose's eyelids flickered. 'Sorry, I can't talk any more . . .'

Jane smiled as she got into bed. Rose was almost dead on her feet. All the nurses were working extra shifts, particularly those on the surgical wards. The war had been hard for the British soldiers and too many were dying out there in the trenches. In July 1916 fifty-eight thousand men had died in one day at the Somme. All the flag waving and jingoistic talk was over. It was spring 1917 now, and the reality was badly wounded men, over-flowing hospitals and no end to the bloodiest war anyone could ever remember.

Jane opened the door and stared at Richard in disbelief. She was so shocked that for a moment she couldn't speak, then the emotion swept over her and she rushed to hug him, drawing him into the house.

'Look who has come to visit,' she called as Mrs Hylton came through from the kitchen. 'Why didn't you let us know?'

'I sent you a letter a week ago. You will probably get it when I've gone back,' Richard grinned. 'I've seen Rose, Mrs Hylton. She told me Jane was here and sent her love.'

'That girl is always volunteering for extra work. She will wear herself out and then where shall we be.' Mrs Hylton came forward and kissed Richard's cheek. 'You look thinner. You must come for dinner. They aren't feeding you properly out there.'

'I eat like a horse. I just don't put on any weight.' Richard glanced at Jane. 'I was hoping we might go to the first house at the theatre and then dinner somewhere – if there is anywhere decent left to eat?'

'There are a few places,' Jane laughed. 'I should love that, Richard. I have the rest of the day free as it happens. Why don't we make the most of it?'

'You don't have any plans?'

'I took my sister shopping yesterday. It would be nice to walk in the park and have tea somewhere. Then come home and change before the evening.'

Richard looked at Mrs Hylton. 'Perhaps tomorrow for lunch?'

'Of course. You are always welcome. Get off the pair of you and enjoy yourselves.'

'Let's take a tram,' Richard suggested as they went out into the spring sunshine. 'They will be a thing of the past before long but I've always enjoyed them . . .'

They ate iced buns and drank tea from thick, slightly chipped cups in the park, then strolled past the small lake and watched the antics of the ducks and geese as people fed them on scraps of bread.

'Even in wartime people find a few crumbs for the birds.' Richard threw a piece of bun from his paper bag, laughing as two ducks squabbled over the delicate morsel. 'I've always enjoyed the parks in London. Some of the streets are dirty and noisy, and there's too much traffic – but you can find peace and quiet if you search for it.'

She tucked her arm through his. 'Let's go and find somewhere nice to have tea – and I'm paying.'

'Come into a fortune?' Richard teased. 'All right, I'm man enough to let a girl treat me occasionally.'

'It is just so lovely to have you here. How long do you have?'

'Two weeks. I have to go home for a while but then I'll find somewhere to stay near you. We might get the odd hour to slip off for a drink or something?'

'Yes, why not? I'll try to change duties so that we can have another day together – if you would like that?'

'You must know you're my best girl, Jane?'

The look in his eyes told her that he liked her a lot but she wasn't sure how she felt. At one time she'd believed that she could never trust or care for a man, but writing to Richard had somehow taken away the humiliation and pain of David Heron's betrayal.

'Am I? Your very best girl?'

'My only girl as it happens,' Richard said. 'I'm not going to make a thing of it, Jane, because neither of us are ready for marriage – but I am hoping you will make me a happy man one day.'

Jane's heart missed a beat. She squeezed his arm, gazing up at him for a moment. She wasn't ready to think about marriage just yet, though she knew she liked him more than any other man she had met recently.

'Ask me when the war is over.'

'That is my intention – but now you know.'

'Yes, now I know.'

Jane bought Richard a gold St Christopher. She gave it to him the evening she knew would be their last together.

'Keep it in your pocket and think of me sometimes when things seem awful,' she said as they walked back to the nurses' home after having a drink in the local pub. 'I shall be thinking of you, Richard. Perhaps we shall see more of each other if I pass my exams. They are sending some of us out to the Front to help in the field hospitals soon.'

'Are you sure you want to come? It is pretty rough, Jane. We don't often get the chance for a bath. Most of the men are crawling with lice when they get stood down for a rest – and the food is atrocious. The nurses have a lot to put up with, believe me.'

'I know but it doesn't stop me from wanting to do my bit. Rose and I have agreed to volunteer if we get the chance.'

'Well, let me know if you do come out. I'll try to get to see you and make sure they are treating you well.'

Jane hugged his arm. 'I'm tough you know. I shan't run home if things are difficult.'

'I know – but I would rather think of you here.'

'I shall be nearer to you.'

'Does that matter to you?'

'You know it does. I'm very fond of you, Richard.'

Richard hesitated then reached out, drawing her close. A shiver went through her and for a moment she froze.

'Is something wrong?'

'Something happened once – before I met you – but I am over it now. Please kiss me, Richard. I want you to . . .'

He bent his head, looking into her eyes for a moment before kissing her gently on the lips. Jane let him kiss her, but then, as he would have withdrawn, she held his head, her arms about his neck as she pressed her lips to his. This time Richard's kiss was hungry, demanding. He met her anxious gaze afterwards.

'I promise I'll never hurt you. I'll always stop if you tell me, Jane.'

'Yes, I know. I trust you, Richard – and I think I am growing to love you. I just need a little time.'

'We have plenty of time, my darling. I shall never ask for more than you want to give.'

Jane wept into her pillow that night at the nurses' home. A part of her wished that she had gone away with Richard so that they could really be together. A lot of the girls took a chance when their men came home on leave. One or two had been forced to leave because they had got into trouble, and once Sister discovered you were pregnant you had to go.

Rose had told Jane that she had done everything but have intercourse.

'Andrew wants to go all the way but I'm waiting for marriage,' she'd confided. 'He thinks I don't love him because I won't let him, but it isn't that, Jane. I don't want a baby. Andrew says we could get married but that means leaving the service. I'm not ready to give it up yet.'

'I feel that way too.'

Jane had been so sure when she'd talked about things with Rose, but now she couldn't help thinking that perhaps she had lost a chance to discover what making love could be like. David Heron had forced her. She had found the experience humiliating and painful, and for a long time she'd thought that she would never want any man to touch her – but that was before she'd discovered how good a relationship could be.

Richard's letters were such a joy to her. She seized on them with delight when they arrived and read them over and over. His last visit had shown her that perhaps she was almost ready for something more than just friendship.

Jane decided that she must put her regrets to one side. She had important exams coming up and then perhaps she would be one of the lucky ones allowed to volunteer for service at the Front. Before that, she intended to visit Ned. They had been out to tea together several times now and the bond between them had grown stronger.

★   ★   ★

'How do you think you've done?' Rose asked as they met for a cup of tea and a bun after their exams that morning. 'That second paper was horrendous. I'm sure I've failed.'

'I'm sure you haven't.' Jane grimaced. 'I just hope I shall scrape through.'

'You're sure to . . .' Rose broke off as one of the senior nurses approached them. 'Look up! What have we done now?'

'Nothing as far as I know but Sister Hall does look serious.'

'Miss Hylton. I am very sorry . . . a message has just come for you. I hate giving my nurses bad news . . .'

Rose got to her feet, her face pale. 'What's wrong? Am I in trouble?'

'We've had a call from your mother – it seems that your young man . . . he has been badly injured. He is in the Malchester and they are not sure if he will make it through the night. You are being given immediate leave.'

'Andrew . . .' Rose's face had drained of colour. Jane stood up, reaching for her hand. 'No . . . please, no . . .' Her hand shook as Jane held on tightly.

'Shall I come with you? I can get someone to take my shift . . .'

'No. It's all right, Jane. I can manage . . .' Rose looked as if she were walking through a bad dream. 'I'll talk to you when I know . . .'

'Yes, you go, love. I'll be thinking of you.'

Jane watched her friend walk away. Rose had her head up and her shoulders back, but Jane could imagine what she was going through.

Rose was away for a week. When she returned to work she looked pale and her eyes were dead. Word had filtered through that Andrew had died the first night. Rose had taken a few days off to get over things and Jane felt she had come back too soon.

'You should have taken longer. No one expected you back on duty so soon, love.'

'I would rather be here. I keep thinking about what happened on his last leave and wishing . . .' She faltered, almost breaking down, then lifted her head, her eyes bleak. 'I can't go back. I can't tell him I love him and want him – so I have to go forward.'

'Rose . . .' Jane put her arms about her, holding her as the tears finally broke. 'I know it hurts dreadfully. You did what you thought right . . .'

'I was wrong.' Rose pushed her back. 'I made a stupid mistake. Andrew was more important. I care about my nursing but I loved him.' She raised her tear-laden eyes to Jane. 'Don't make my mistake, Jane. If you get the chance do whatever Richard wants. Don't throw away happiness. You may never get another chance.'

'I shan't forget,' she whispered as Rose flung herself on the bed and sobbed. She sat beside her, stroking her hair. 'I love you. I'll always be here for you.'

Jane smiled as Ned ran towards her. He held out his arms and she caught him round the waist, swinging him off his feet. Ned laughed, obviously delighted to see her. His face lit up when she gave him her present. She had brought an expensive drawing pad and a box of watercolours, because she wouldn't be able to visit for his birthday.

'These are smashing,' Ned said and grinned at her as they made their way towards the teashop. 'I'm doing well at Art and English Literature but I'm near the bottom in Maths. I can add up and divide all right but I get lost in logarithms.'

'Never mind. I was no good at those either. I doubt if you'll ever need them, Ned. Have you thought about what you're going to do when you leave school? I know it won't be for ages yet but it's nice to have something planned.'

'I did think I should like to drive a train or join a circus,' he said, giving her a mischievous grin. 'No, don't look like that, Jane! I'll probably go into the army. Uncle David came to visit me last month. He has been awarded a medal for bravery.'

'Oh . . . that's lovely. You must be proud of him, Ned. Are you going home for the holidays?' Jane didn't particularly want to talk about David Heron.

'I told you in my letter that Sara was getting married?' Jane nodded. 'She says I can stay with her for a couple of weeks and then I might go to a friend's house . . .'

'You ought to go home for a few days at least.'

Ned shook his head. 'Uncle David told me the same thing but I'm not going. I'm never going home again.'

'Why do you hate your mother, Ned? It isn't just because she sacked me I hope?'

'No . . .' Ned looked hesitant.

Jane suddenly remembered Ned's belief that his mother had something to do with the death of his father, and she didn't think this was the right time to push him for an explanation.

'You're all right, though?'

'Yes. I'm all right here. You will come again when you can?'

'I may be too far away to come for a long time. I will try to write, but if you don't get a letter as often as before you mustn't think it is because I have forgotten you.'

'I wouldn't think that,' Ned said. 'I know you are learning to be a nurse. Are you going to nurse the wounded men over there?'

'I might one day.'

'You might see Uncle David. He will be going back to the fighting soon now that he is well again.'

'You mustn't be too upset.'

'I'm proud of him. I want to be just like him one day.'

Jane watched as Rose took a tray and chose food from the canteen counter. She was eating less and less and her uniform was beginning to look as if it would swallow her up. The temptation to urge her to eat more was strong, but Jane knew the reaction it would bring. Rose was grieving hard, throwing herself into work so that she could sleep at nights.

Jane carried her tray to the table her friend had chosen and sat down. Rose was pushing her food around the plate but not eating it.

'Have you seen the list? It is what we've been waiting for. I've put my name down. You should put yours down, Rose. I think quite a few are volunteering this time.'

'What's the point?' Rose stared moodily at her plate. 'It doesn't matter whether they pick me or someone else.'

'I thought you were keen on getting over there?'

'I was before . . .' Rose pushed her plate away. 'I don't really care any more. I wish I were dead.'

'You soon will be if you carry on the way you are,' Jane's tone was harsh. 'I never thought you were selfish, Rose Hylton. What about your mother? She is worrying herself sick over you and your brothers. Don't you care about how she feels?'

'Of course I do. You know I do . . .'

'Well, you haven't shown much sign of it. You've lost too much weight and your eyes are sinking into your head. If you don't pull yourself together you'll be no use as a nurse here or there! Besides, you promised to volunteer if I did! You're letting the side down.'

'Bitch . . .' Rose pushed her chair back. 'Some friend you are . . .'

She walked off, leaving Jane to stare after her. Jane sighed and shook her head. She had tried everything she knew to bring Rose out of her misery and she'd hoped a bit of straight talking might do it, but it looked as if she might just have lost her best friend.

Jane ate her food and then went back on duty. The doctor's round was half over. She noted that three of their patients were being sent home the next day, which was good news. Curtains had been drawn round the bed at the end of the ward. It was the double amputee that had been brought in a few weeks back. He hadn't seemed too well of late. She asked Sister what was going on.

'It looks as if we're going to lose him. His wound has turned septic and they think it has gone too far. There's nothing we can do but help him through . . .'

Jane's throat caught with tears. She felt helpless. She couldn't take the pain from their patient and she couldn't take Rose's pain away either. Tears would not save either of them – or the thousands of young men dying out there in France.

Jane was feeling drained when she got back to the dorm that night. The double amputee had died and the whole ward had been subdued. Death was so final and it seemed endless. For every man they could patch up and send home there was another they failed.

She stopped by her bed. There was a small package lying on the pillow. Frowning, Jane picked it up and opened the brown paper to discover a bar of Frys cream chocolate. She found a piece of paper underneath and realized the gift was from Rose.

Sorry, Rose had written. *I'm an idiot and you're my best friend. I put my name down before I went on duty.*

Jane sat on the edge of the bed, tears trickling down her cheeks. Her rebuke had got through to Rose after all. It wouldn't stop her friend grieving but it might mean that Rose could start to recover.

'Daddy died three weeks ago . . .' Frances looked at Jane and Rose as they sat in the canteen together a few days later. 'We had hoped that he was getting better. He seemed almost back to his old self and then he had another attack.'

'I'm so sorry.' Jane reached across to touch her hand 'You must miss him terribly?'

'Yes, I do. Mummy does too, though she is trying to carry on as if nothing had happened.'

'Will you come back to the service now?' Rose asked.

'No. I could never catch you two up and I don't feel like starting out all over again. Mummy wants me to help with her charity work and I suppose I shall. I would feel awful if I walked out on her.'

'It seems a bit of a waste of your training.' Rose was disapproving. 'You were so happy when you were with us. I can't understand why you are ready to settle for so much less.'

'Mummy is lonely and I can't hurt her.' Frances sighed. 'I should have loved to become a nurse like you two but I suppose I'll settle for living at home until I get married.'

'Are you going to marry?' Jane asked.

'Oh . . . I don't know . . .' Frances blushed. 'There is someone. He hasn't asked me yet but I've been seeing something of him . . .'

'Well, I wish you happy.' Jane touched her hand again. 'Keep in touch and ask us to the wedding.'

'Yes, if it happens . . .' Frances looked conscious. 'I think you know him, Jane – David Heron . . .'

'Oh . . .' She wasn't sure what to say, because she couldn't tell Frances that she would be making a big mistake by marrying a man like David Heron. 'How long have you been seeing him?'

'He called a few days after Daddy died. I've seen him a few times since then. I don't know for certain that he will ask me but I like him a lot.'

'Then I hope you will be happy.' Jane forced herself to smile.

'I'm glad you came today, Frances, because we are off tomorrow. If you'd left it any later you would have missed us.'

'Where are you going?' Frances frowned as neither of them spoke. 'You mean over there? I don't think I would want to go so close to the fighting . . .'

'Why shouldn't we be exposed to some danger? The soldiers don't have a choice.' Rose stood up. 'I have some things to do, Jane. Bye, Frances. Have a lovely life.'

Frances watched her leave. 'What did I say?'

'Her boyfriend died of his wounds a few months back.'

'I didn't know. You didn't say anything in your letters, Jane.'

'I'm sorry. I should have told you, Frances.'

'You didn't know if you would ever see me again. I'm sorry I upset Rose – but you are still my friend, aren't you, Jane?'

'Yes, of course. I hope you will be happy whatever you do.'

'I'm not sure anything will come of it. It is probably all on my side.'

'You will find someone else. It is good of you to consider your mother whatever Rose thinks.'

'She likes you, Jane. She told me you are welcome to stay whenever you like.'

'I should have liked to come but there isn't time before we leave. Perhaps when we come back?'

'Yes, I should like that.' Frances got to her feet. 'I suppose I ought to be going if I want to catch my train.' She held out her hand. 'Good luck.'

'Silly!' Jane put her arms about her. 'I know I haven't visited since that Christmas but there was never time. I promise I shall come one day.'

'I do miss you.' Frances swallowed hard. 'I never have any fun these days . . .'

'I know how you feel.' Jane felt sympathy. Rose thought she had taken the easy way out, but Frances had given up so much to do what she thought of as her duty. 'I really hope things work out for you with David.'

They were nearing their destination at last. You could hear the sound of the guns booming in the distance, bringing home the reality that they were close to a war zone. After a short but unpleasant journey by sea they had disembarked near Calais and then been sorted into groups with their kit. Some of the nurses and new recruits were herded on to packed trains like sardines, others told to wait for the lorries that would take them to their postings. Jane and Rose were amongst the group of nurses and soldiers awaiting transportation by lorry.

'Are you feeling any better now?' Rose asked as Jane sat on her kit bag and sipped at a paper cup of water. 'I felt a bit sick on the ship but you were really ill.'

'I didn't know it was possible to feel so sick.' Jane grimaced and emptied the last drops on the grass. A soldier bent down and took the cup, placing it in the top of his kit bag.

'Feel any better, love? It's rough on you nurses the first time. I'm used to it now. This is my third posting. I've just got back from a spell of leave in Blighty.'

'I'm feeling much better now we're on dry land.' Jane smiled and got to her feet as the lorry arrived.

The driver's mate jumped down and opened up the flap at the back. Everyone started to make a move. The soldier who had given Jane a cup of water, picked up her kit bag and tossed it into the back for her, then gave her a hand up. Another soldier had done the same for Rose and two more nurses who were being sent to the same field hospital. Inside they all huddled together on the floor.

The girls weren't saying much, because it was all strange and new, and a bit scary now that they were actually here. The men were making jokes and passing sweets and cigarettes amongst themselves. One of them offered a toffee to Jane. She thanked him but shook her head. Everyone carried their own rations and it wasn't easy to come by sweets out here. The men going up to the Front would live on basic food for weeks and the only treats they were likely to get would be from food parcels sent out by relatives or the Red Cross.

It was a bumpy ride in the back of the lorry and the further they went the more rutted the roads seemed to become. The girls held on to each other as the vehicle lurched sideways.

'It's the craters,' one of the soldiers explained as Jane was flung against him. 'Sometimes they bomb ammunition lorries on their way up to the front and it blows the road to hell.'

One of the nurses gave a cry of alarm, looking around as if she expected a German plane to bomb them at any minute.

'Shut up, you idiot,' another soldier said. 'You're frightening the angels.'

'Angels?' Rose turned to him. 'Do you mean us?'

'That's what we call you nurses. You're all bloomin' angels to come out here when you don't have ter.'

'Why shouldn't we? You don't get much choice.'

'We're expendable, bloody cannon fodder that's us,' the private said gloomily. 'When the captain says go, it's over the top, keep yer 'ead down and pray for us poor sods. If yer quick enough yer can dodge the big guns but the bloody shrapnel will get yer or a sniper's bullet – ain't much difference. And if yer really in fer it you'll get a dose of the gas.'

'Don't take no notice of him, miss. He's a gloomy blighter,' the helpful soldier grinned at Jane. 'I'm Robin Holder and I've done two tours of six months each already. It's a doddle if you know what you're doing.'

'I'm sure it isn't easy . . .' Jane broke off as they heard the whine of a plane overhead and everyone looked at each other uneasily. One of the soldiers crawled to the back of the lorry and lifted the flap to look out. He dropped it, grinning from ear to ear.

'It's one of ours seeing us home safe,' he said and there was a collective sigh of relief.

Jane had sort of known they could be in danger, but the realization that her nursing career could have ended right there if the plane had been an enemy came home to her with a jolt.

The steady booming of guns in the distance was getting louder. One particularly loud bang made Jane jump. Robin Holder smiled at her.

'That's Big Bertha. She's a noisy devil but if you can still hear her, the buggers didn't get you.'

'That's one way of looking at it,' Rose said and grabbed Jane's arm with a grin. 'Looks as if we're in for an interesting time . . .'

They weren't really as close as it seemed. The girls were briefed when they arrived at camp and were given a swift tour of the hospital and the various facilities. It was literally a field hospital, the next in line after the clearing stations and just a collection of tents in a field sheltered by some dense woods.

'The front line is beyond those trees,' a senior nurse explained. 'We have the seriously wounded in the larger tent there – they are the men that we want to patch up and send back through the lines to be shipped home. The smaller tent is for the fatal injuries. We do what we can to ease their suffering and help them die, but if they are taken there it's because the doctors consider there is no hope.'

'Poor devils. Surely they all deserve a chance?' A third year nurse called Jean Stubbs spoke up.

'You'll understand when you see your first case of fatal,' the senior nurse assured her. 'I'm Staff Nurse Dorothy Martin and I felt the same as you when I first came out. You'll get used to it in time.' Her gaze narrowed. 'The tents over there are for the doctors and senior army personnel. The nurses' accommodation is grouped together in the far corner. And that long tent over there is the canteen. Nurses and serving men share, but take turns. You sleep six to a tent so you newbies will probably be split up into pairs. We like to put you in with experienced nurses so that you can ask questions.' Her eyes travelled from one face to another. 'Any questions you want to ask?'

'Yes – where are the lavatories? I need to go.'

'It's pretty basic. Don't expect running water. The men's lavatory is over there, though most of them just disappear into the woods because they can't stand the smell of the latrines. We have a tent with partitions and you get to sit down. The smell can be awful when the weather is hot. The men on latrine duty do the best they can to clear the night soil but you've been warned.'

'I didn't realize it was that bad,' Jean muttered.

'This is the front line. The men have it even worse. Stuck in those trenches for days and weeks on end. At least we have plentiful water supplies and we can have a wash, though you won't get a bath until you're back at headquarters on stand down. Even then you'll have to queue for your turn. The men bathe in old wine vats and the last in line gets pretty dirty water. We're a bit luckier but it isn't the Ritz. You should have had all this information before you volunteered. It is too late to complain now.'

The girls were shown the two tents where they would be

living for their tour of duty. Rose and Jane moved as one, leaving Jean and Sheila to take the other tent. When they went inside, a young nurse was sitting on a bed. She smiled and stood up.

'I'm Vera Smith. I've been out here for nine months. I volunteered to stay on when I should have gone home. I imagine you're feeling a bit numb at the moment. Everything is a shock when you first come out. Those two beds are the empty ones. You are expected to keep your corners to hospital standards. It sounds mad the way things are, but we get an inspection every now and then to make sure we aren't becoming lax, so don't let the rest of us down.'

'We shan't do that,' Rose said sounding more cheerful than she had for weeks. 'I know everything is a bit basic but at least we're doing something worthwhile.'

'The men call us angels,' Vera told her. 'I suppose they are all hoping if the worst happens they end up in Heaven rather than the other place.'

'We've had a pep talk from Nurse Dorothy Martin.'

'She scares the new recruits. It isn't as bad as all that most of the time. Better for us than the men in the trenches anyway.'

'Anything must be better than that,' Jane sat down on one of the beds. 'I was warned it was pretty rough out here.' She bounced experimentally. 'This isn't too bad.'

'You will get used to it. The days when mail arrives are good and it's nice when you can send a batch of men back through the lines knowing you've done your best.'

'What happens to those who don't make it?'

'They get buried, sometimes in the woods, sometimes where they fall so I've heard, others just go missing. The parson usually says a few words but it happens too often to make a big thing of it.'

Jane nodded. Vera was making it all sound ordinary but she wasn't sure she could ever get used to seeing men die in agony.

Eleven

'I've got a three day pass,' Richard said gazing anxiously at Jane's face. 'You look so tired. If you could get time off we might go somewhere right away from all this, be together. Just walk, eat and sleep . . .'

'Do you think we could find a little time for other things?' Jane teased, her tiredness seeming to fade away as she took his hand. 'I've got two days off and I could probably swing a third if I ask Sister nicely.'

'We've hardly had any time since you got here. Things have been too hectic for either of us to think of anything but work.'

'I can hardly believe that I've been here nearly six months.' Jane held his hand to her cheek. They didn't often have time to talk like this. Richard's visits were usually fleeting; a snatched moment or two between delivering wounded patients and a return to the forward placement. He was attached to a clearing station, right at the sharp end, his life in as much danger as the men he treated. 'I'd love to come away with you, Richard. I wanted to ask what your plans are. Sister said they would probably send me home for a couple of weeks nearer Christmas but she would like to have me back next year – if I am prepared to come.'

'It depends on how you feel about things. I've been told I've done my share. They want me to work in a special burns hospital back home. It seems that I have a lot of experience to share and they think I'm needed there rather than here. You know what the mustard gas does to the men. I wasn't sure how you felt, Jane. I would like to do another six months out here before they put me out to grass.'

'It is not exactly putting you out to grass. The work they are offering you is important, Richard.'

'But is it as important as what I'm doing here?' Richard shook his head. 'I don't have time to talk now. I'll pick you up tomorrow evening and we'll go off somewhere. Just drive until we find a nice place to stay.' He leaned forward to kiss her, then arched his eyebrows. 'One room or two?'

'You don't need to ask.' Jane put a hand at each side of his face, kissing him softly on the mouth. 'I love you, Richard. I want to be with you. I've wanted it for a long time now but we haven't had a chance . . . not to do things properly.'

'That is the only way as far as I am concerned.' Richard trailed his fingers down her cheek. 'I wanted to wait for the right moment. At one time I thought when the war was over but . . . I'm looking forward to a little bit of heaven with you, my dearest one.'

Jane watched as he got into his staff car and set off. Their time together was always precious, even if it was only to touch hands or snatch a quick cup of tea together. Even so it was more than they might have got if she hadn't taken the opportunity to come out here – and it made the heartache and hardship worthwhile.

Smelly lavatories and being unable to have a bath for weeks was the easiest part in Jane's opinion. She hated it when she got lice in her hair but she wasn't the only one. All the nurses had picked it up from the men they nursed at one time or another; they helped each other by using fine-tooth combs to get rid of the sticky eggs and used the special shampoos they were given to get their hair clean. It meant they smelled awful a lot of the time but it was just one of those things and you got used to it. Seeing the terrible injuries that some of the men suffered was harder to bear.

Back in England they had seen what Jane thought were terrible wounds but she hadn't known then how much worse it could be. Men were brought in with half their faces blown away, with severed limbs that leaked blood and twitched horribly – and with wounds to their stomachs that looked impossible to survive even for a moment. Some of them lingered too long; their screams of agony sending shivers down the spine of any who heard them. Jane understood now why they had the tent for those with no hope. None of the nurses really wanted to be assigned to those duties, because instead of nursing your patient and hoping to see an improvement, all you longed for was to see them breathe their last so that they were no longer in pain. Especially when the supplies of morphine were running low and had to be rationed.

'It's the fault of the stupid government,' Rose raged when she came off a particularly bad shift one night. 'Don't they know what we're going through out here? They started this damned thing. They should make certain we have sufficient medical supplies.'

'Richard said that they were short of ammunition at the front for a while,' Jane told her. 'I don't know whether a ship was sunk with essential supplies on board or whether it was just a mix up. I suppose the powers that be are doing their best.'

'Well, it isn't good enough,' Rose snapped. Her temper was getting shorter these days and she laughed less than she had once. 'I'm going to join the Suffragette movement after the war. I'm bloody sure women could do a hell of a lot better than the fools we've got now.'

'It has been warm today, like spring even though it is November,' Jane said as she slid into Richard's car the next evening. He wasn't driving the staff car but a battered old roadster that he sometimes borrowed from a friend. 'Where are we going?'

Richard leaned over to kiss her softly on the mouth. 'I thought somewhere quiet. We could have gone to the coast or a town but I thought of a place I know in the country. The last time I was there you would hardly have known there was a war on.'

'Sounds wonderful.' Jane snuggled down into her seat and sighed. 'It will be nice to forget for a while.'

Forgetting was out of the question for the first few hours. They drove past ruined houses, deserted farms and the ruins of a beautiful church. Here and there huge craters appeared in the road, all evidence of the bombardment from the air that this part of France was receiving. The Germans had wreaked havoc on the French towns and cities, and the people had suffered many hardships. For a while the Germans had looked like overrunning the whole country but things were gradually improving for the people and the Allies. An offensive had been going on at Ypres for the past few months, which had seen gains, though there had recently been a defeat at Passchendaele.

Jane deliberately shut out all thoughts of the war and its consequences. She didn't often have the chance to get away from the hospital, and even back at headquarters the feeling was still oppressive and sometimes depressing. This was her first chance to go away with Richard. They had kissed and touched a few times but always in the back of his car, and Richard refused to take their loving all the way in such a furtive manner.

'This is so lovely,' Jane said as they pulled up in the courtyard of the ancient chateau. 'When you said a guesthouse – well, I had no idea it would be like this, Richard.'

'I wanted it to be a surprise and I was a little worried that it might not have survived. I thought it might have received a visit from the Germans but it is untouched.'

The last rays of the evening sun were turning the creamy stone walls to rose. From a dovecote over the gates the sound of cooing added to the general atmosphere of peace and tranquillity. They were just far enough away from the front line to not hear the guns.

'It isn't as big as some of the great chateaux but it is pretty and the owners are very friendly. I sent a telegram to reserve our room – in the name of Captain and Mrs Bedford.' Richard handed her a small box. 'It isn't a wedding ring but wear it on your left finger, darling, and we shan't shock Madame Desailly.'

Jane extracted the pretty friendship ring of gold; it had a small ruby set in the hold of clasped hands and fitted her finger perfectly.

'It is beautiful, Richard.'

'It is a promise,' he told her and leaned forward to kiss her on the lips. 'As soon as we can manage some home leave together we'll get married, Jane. I know the rules say that the nurses shouldn't be married but they are so desperate for good nurses that I'm sure we can wangle it somehow.'

Jane nodded her agreement. 'I know one or two of the girls have married and kept it quiet. If Sister knows she doesn't say anything, because she doesn't want to lose them. Some of the newbies can't stand it and ask to go home before they've been out here five minutes.'

'That happened to one of the girls you came out with, didn't it?'

'Jean Stubbs. She hated it from day one and asked to be sent home as soon as she could be replaced.'

Richard picked up their cases and led the way inside the house. Jane was immediately aware of the scent of roses and lavender. She saw that there were bowls of dried petals and lavender spikes set on various tables. The soft furnishings had a look of faded grandeur and it was clear that nothing had been replaced in a long time, but everywhere was comfortable, neat and clean.

After the dirt and discomfort of the camp this was indeed a little bit of heaven on earth. All the furniture was gilded and belonged to a past age; elegant and evocative of a world that no longer existed.

Richard was talking easily to a lady wearing a dark blue dress. She had black hair coiled sleekly back, pearl drop earrings and several beautiful diamond rings on her fingers. After embracing Richard warmly, she came to Jane and did the same, welcoming her to the chateau.

'We are happy to have you stay with us,' she said. 'We in France know what you suffer for us.' Her eyes seemed to smile at Jane. 'There is plenty of hot water, Madame. I think you would enjoy a nice bath – no?'

'Yes, thank you. That would be heaven.'

Jane's heart beat wildly as they followed the young bellboy upstairs to their room. It was large, comfortably furnished and again smelled of flowers. There was a vase of what looked like delicate wild flowers on the dressing table. Walking over to the window, Jane saw that they had a wonderful view of a vineyard that seemed to stretch for as far as the eye could see.

'What a beautiful sight,' Jane said and turned with a smile.

'Beautiful,' Richard agreed but his eyes were on her. He walked towards her. 'Madame says we can have supper downstairs or here in our room – what shall we do?'

'Let's have it here. We can look out at the vineyard as we eat . . .'

Richard stroked her face. 'I would rather look at you, darling Jane. I've been thinking of this for weeks.'

'Only weeks?' she teased. 'I haven't stopped thinking of being with you since you were in England last time . . .'

Richard smiled and drew her to him. His kiss was hungry, demanding and yet tender.

'I love you so much . . . so very much.'

'I love you too.' Jane slid her hands up over his shoulders. 'I don't think I am very hungry, but first of all I think I should like that bath our kind hostess offered us . . .'

'Would you mind if I shared it with you?'

Jane gazed into his eyes and then smiled. 'I think I should like that,' she whispered. 'I should like that very much . . .'

Jane sighed as she woke and turned, nestling into the warm body that lay beside her. She thought Richard was still asleep and buried her face against his neck. He smelled so good and tasted lovely; she could still taste him on her lips.

Richard's loving had been generous, sweet and tender, thrilling her, bringing her to a slow building climax that took her by complete surprise. She hadn't expected to feel anything as lovely as she had, as she clung to him gasping and crying his name.

They had made love three times during the night, and each time it had seemed even better as their confidence grew and they learned to please and to laugh. It was, Jane thought, the laughter that made it so special.

'Happy, my love?'

Richard's question surprised her. She had thought he was sleeping. Curving into him, she kissed his throat and stroked his chest, her fingers appreciating the curls of hair that threaded down past his navel.

'Happier than I could have ever imagined – you?'

'The same.' He crushed her to him, his mouth seeking hers. She could feel the immediate response of his body, his heated manhood hard against her thigh, his hand beginning to stroke down the arch of her back. She gasped, instantly ready, wanting to feel him inside her again, deep, deep inside her silken moistness. 'Love you so much . . . so much . . .'

Jane surrendered to his need of her, finding exquisite pleasure as he slid inside her once more. He filled her completely and in every way; their bodies fit like two halves of one whole.

Jane wished that their escape to heaven could last forever. Everything seemed to be perfect, the sun shining as they walked through the peaceful countryside. They took picnic baskets and ate in the sunshine by the side of a gentle stream. If it was hot they abandoned their shoes and paddled in the water, the sandy bottom squeezing through their toes.

'I could stay here forever,' Jane murmured as they lay dreaming in the warmth of a summer day. She leaned over, tickling his face with a long stem of grass. He reached up and pulled her down, kissed her and then rolled her beneath him to kiss her again. 'I love you so much, Richard. I feel so lucky.'

Richard smiled down at her. 'I'm glad we've had this time together, Jane. It will give us both something to remember when things become unbearable.'

The war had intruded again. Here behind the lines of British and French troops, they had tried hard to shut it out but the shadow was always there, hovering like a menacing cloud.

'I keep thinking it must end soon but nothing seems to change. We see the same things happening day after day.'

'It's stalemate again for the moment but things will change eventually. They have to!' Richard looked grim as he sat forward, clasping his knees. 'These few days have made me see that I have too much to lose. I am going to tell my C.O. that this is my last tour of duty out here. We'll go home and get married, Jane. I'll find somewhere for us near the hospital they want me to work in and you can carry on working for a while if you wish. Strictly speaking you should resign but I can probably swing it so that you can carry on until we start a family.' His gaze was tender, loving. 'You've done your bit out here, darling.'

'Yes, I suppose I have. Rose is coming back after she has home leave but it's purely voluntary.'

Richard stood up, offering her his hand. 'Let's go back to our room. We don't have much time left.'

Jane took his hand. As she got to her feet she felt suddenly cold and shivered.

'Are you cold?' Richard put his jacket round her shoulders. 'It is a bit cooler.'

Jane hugged his jacket to her, not because she was cold but because it smelled of him and she found it comforting. She couldn't explain that her shiver had been because she'd had a sudden, horrible feeling that their lovely time together was over.

Jane clung to Richard when they said goodbye. She had always been able to let him go with a smile previously, but now she knew how good it was to wake up beside him

'I've only got a few weeks of this tour left,' Richard told her, smiling and brushing his thumb over her bottom lip. 'I'll let them know that I am ready to take the job at home and they may release me a little earlier. I'll write or come and see you as soon as I know anything.'

'Yes, of course.' Jane released him and stood back, making herself smile. Richard had his work to do and so did she. 'I'll speak to Sister, tell her that I want to go home when I've finished my time here. It may be a week or so after you but that will give you a chance to find somewhere for us to live.'

'We'll see what we can sort out.' Richard kissed her briefly on the mouth. 'You would be surprised how easily rules can be bent if you know the right people.'

Jane watched as he drove away. She shivered, feeling cold all over again. It was so silly but something was telling her that her few lovely days with Richard were all she would ever have.

'Was it good?' Rose asked when they met in the canteen that evening. 'You look as if you've spent some time in the sun?'

'We did a lot of walking and lying in the sun. The weather was so lovely for the time of year, but our hostess told me it often is here. It would do you good to get a few days off away from here, Rose.'

'I don't have anyone to take me away to a beautiful chateau,' Rose teased. The shadows were still in her eyes but she was doing her best to be cheerful. 'I'm going home for a couple of weeks soon. I told Sister I would rather just carry on but she put her foot down. She said I have to take a rest or I shan't be any good to her or anyone else.'

'I know I feel much better for having a few days off.' Jane hesitated, then, 'We are going to be married, Rose. Richard has been offered an important post back home. He has decided to take it and I'm going too so that we can get married.'

'Are you giving up nursing?'

'Not until I'm forced. Richard says he may be able to swing it so that I can carry on in some capacity.' Jane smiled. 'I wanted to do my bit for the war effort and I've enjoyed the experience, but it was never my first choice. I shall carry on for a while if I can but being Richard's wife and the mother of his children is more important to me.'

'So it should be.' Rose smothered a yawn. 'If Andrew were still here I would do the same but he isn't. There's nothing else for me, Jane. I know everyone thinks I'll find someone else but I shan't.'

Jane looked at her with sympathy. 'I'm so sorry, Rose. There's nothing adequate I can say.'

'Whatever anyone says, it doesn't change anything. I had my chance and let it slip through my fingers. So now I don't let myself think about anything but nursing.'

'What will you do when the war is over? Will you stay in nursing?'

'I haven't the faintest idea.' Rose drank her coffee. 'I'm going to bed. I am on again at six in the morning . . .'

'I shall be very sorry to lose you, Nurse Shaw,' Sister Evans told her. 'You've been one of our very best nurses. However, I understand that you want to be with your fiancé. Doctor Bedford is a hero for most of us and you both deserve happiness.'

'Thank you.' Jane shook her hand. 'Richard is coming here tomorrow morning. I am working until late afternoon but then we shall be off. I want to thank you for being such a tower of strength to us all, Sister.'

'If only that were true.' Sister Evans grimaced. 'Well, good luck, Jane. If I don't see you before you leave have a wonderful life.'

'I am sure I shall.'

Jane was smiling as she left the Sister's station. She took off her cap as she walked back to the tent she shared with Rose and the others. Rose had switched duty that evening so that they could have a last drink together. When she got back to the tent, Jane discovered that half a dozen of the nurses were waiting for her. They showered her with homemade paper confetti and someone blew a whistle.

'Here comes the bride!' Sally Marsh said. 'We've bought you some presents, Jane. Then we are taking you to the pub.'

'You shouldn't have done all this,' Jane said as she saw the cake someone had obviously been sent in a parcel from home and the glasses of sherry. 'I wasn't expecting anything at all . . .'

She had actually been looking forward to a quiet chat with Rose but her friends had other ideas. First of all she had to open her gifts, which ranged from a small bottle of French perfume to a pair of silk stockings and some silver spoons in a leather case.

After Jane had opened her presents and eaten a slice of cake, she was escorted down to the local pub. When they got there she discovered that some of the other nurses and doctors were there waiting to celebrate with her.

She was surprised at how pleased everyone seemed for her and felt a little overwhelmed by their kindness. She hadn't imagined she was this popular. If she had accepted all the drinks they wanted to buy for her she would have ended up tipsy but after a second sherry she stuck to lemonade.

Someone was playing a piano. Soldiers and nurses crowded round to join in the singing of songs made popular by the war.

'Aba, daba, daba, daba, dab, said the chimpie to the monkey . . .' Jane joined in a favourite with all the others. Then one of the soldiers sang the *Roses of Picardy*; his voice was pure and beautiful and he was greeted by rapturous applause. After that, everyone sang a rousing *Land of Hope and Glory* and *Pack Up Your Troubles*; the atmosphere rapidly descending into a slightly rowdy affair that made the girls decide to leave.

It was almost curfew when they got back to camp. Rose looked dead on her feet.

'I'm glad I'm not on until late afternoon,' she yawned sleepily. 'We had better say goodbye now, Jane. I shall probably still be asleep when you go on duty and I shall be on the ward when you leave.'

'It isn't goodbye.' Jane hugged her. 'It was fun tonight but I wouldn't have minded having more time with you. You will keep in touch?'

'Yes, of course.' Rose returned the hug. 'Sorry, I'm dead on my feet.'

Jane watched as her friend tumbled into bed still half dressed. Rose was sound asleep as she undressed more slowly and slipped into bed. She was happy about her decision to leave and marry Richard, but she would miss the friends she had made here, especially Rose.

Jane spent some time saying goodbye to the patients before she came off duty the following afternoon. She had a lump in her throat as she held hands and kissed one or two on the cheek. The men were always so grateful whatever you did for them, and it made her tearful as some of them told her how much they would miss her.

She finally tore herself away and returned to her tent to change out of uniform and finish her packing. Richard had told her he would meet her outside the canteen. Glancing at the little silver watch she wore on the lapel of her jacket, Jane saw that he should have arrived by now. She had just picked up her case when one of the nurses entered the tent.

'You're here . . .' she looked uncomfortable. 'Sister Evans sent me to see if I could find you, Jane. She wants a word with you . . .'

'I was just about to meet Richard. You couldn't pretend you didn't find me I suppose?'

'I think you should see her.'

'Why – is something wrong?' Jane shivered, her skin breaking out in goose pimples all over.

'It isn't up to me to tell you. I'm so sorry, Jane.'

Jane felt sick as she saw the pity in the nurse's face. They didn't know each other well and for Janet Smith to look at her that way meant something serious had happened. She left her suitcase and coat on the bed and went out of the tent. She could see that several ambulances had come in with wounded men. As she passed them one of the drivers stared at her so strangely that Jane broke out in a sweat. She started to run, her heart beating frantically.

Entering the tent where Sister Evans had her little office, Jane saw that the senior nurse was in conversation with an army officer. She hesitated, not wanting to intrude, and then Sister Evans turned and saw her. She said something in a low voice to the officer who moved away to the far side to speak to someone else.

'Jane,' Sister Evans came to her. 'I am so dreadfully sorry, my dear. I can't tell you how much grief this causes me – but there is no way I can make it easier for you . . .'

'It's Richard isn't it? Something has happened to him?'

'He got here early this morning. He was talking with the doctors when the call came through that they urgently needed some volunteers to go up to the Front and bring back a convoy of severely wounded men.'

'Richard volunteered?' The icy feeling was seeping through her body. 'It is what he would do of course.'

'Doctor Bedford . . . and Nurse Hylton,' Sister Evans said. 'Rose heard what was happening and volunteered. When the convoy was fired on she refused to abandon the patients, and when the lorry was hit from the air, Captain Bedford stayed with her. They carried a couple of patients to the side of the road and went back to try and get a third out . . . the engine was on fire by this time and the lorry exploded. Neither of them could have known much about it.'

'Rose too . . .' Jane's throat was closing, tears running down her cheeks. Something had told her Richard would never leave France with her, but she hadn't dreamed that her best friend would be with him when he died. 'Both of them . . .'

'I know this is a terrible shock for you,' Sister Evans said. 'You should sit down for a moment. You look very pale.'

'No, I'm all right . . .' Jane said and then fainted.

She came round as someone bent over her, waving a bottle of something sharp and acrid under her nose. Her head was aching and she felt sick as she struggled to sit up.

'I'm so sorry. I don't know why . . .' The officer helped her to her feet, looking at her anxiously. 'How are you, Miss Shaw? I am so terribly sorry to be the bearer of bad news. Richard should never have volunteered. He should have left it to others . . .'

'Richard wasn't like that,' Jane said. She still felt woozy and was grateful to sit down when someone offered a chair. 'Rose always volunteered for everything. She never thought of anything but work . . .' She stifled a sob. 'She is with Andrew now. I think it was what she wanted. She wouldn't have cared what happened to her if there was a patient in danger, but Richard . . .' Her sobs choked her as she bent her head, covering her face with her hands. 'Richard . . . it isn't fair. He shouldn't have been a damned hero. He shouldn't . . .'

'You are in shock, Jane. Drink this!' Sister Evans thrust a glass into her hands. 'Drink it all. It will steady you.'

Jane obeyed. The brandy was strong and stung her throat but she got it down. A feeling of numbness was replacing the shock.

'I don't know what to do . . .' She stared at Sister Evans, lost and bewildered. 'I was going to be with Richard . . .'

'You will accompany a shipment of wounded going home. Staff Nurse Skipton will be in charge of the operation and you will do as she tells you. You will accompany the patients to the hospital in England. After that you will take the leave due to you – and then . . . I can't tell you what to do with the rest of your life, Jane. In a few weeks the pain will ease a little and then you can decide where your future lies.'

'Yes, Sister. Thank you. I shall report to Sister Skipton now.'

'It will do in the morning.' Sister Evans looked at her sadly. 'Why don't you have a lie down or sleep for a while?'

Jane got to her feet. She didn't think the pain of losing the man she loved and her best friend would ever ease but she was grateful for Sister Evans's intervention. She needed direction because otherwise she might have crawled into a hole and never come out again. At least she had something she must do. She needn't think about Richard or Rose for the moment. Sister Skipton would tell her what to do and she would follow orders.

When she was back in England she would start to think about what had happened. Nothing would be the same again. She would never laugh with Rose again and she would never feel Richard's lips on hers or his arms about her.

She wasn't sure how she was going to live. The future was like a long black tunnel. She couldn't think about tomorrow or the next day. All she could manage was to put one foot in front of the other.

'We are all very sorry, Jane.' Sister Nottingham arched her hands in the steeple position, looking at her thoughtfully. 'Are you certain you wish to continue nursing immediately?'

Jane turned the friendship ring on her finger. 'I've had two weeks off. I've seen my sister a few times but Melia doesn't understand how I feel. She knows that I was going to be married but she hadn't met Richard – and she is about to go to college. Besides, I can't afford to live anywhere but the nurses' home for long.'

'You don't have family you could visit?'

'Melia lived with our aunt. I should not be welcome there.'

'In that case I suppose you would be better off at work. I don't like to see you so pale, Jane. However, if you wish to return to us I shall not deny you. Goodness knows, we can do with all the trained nurses we have.' Sister Nottingham hesitated. 'Have you thought of going back out there?'

'No, I don't think I could – not just yet anyway. It isn't that I'm afraid of getting killed. I just can't think about it . . .' Jane's voice quavered. 'We had planned to return to England. Richard had been offered an important position at a hospital in Portsmouth.'

'Yes, I know. We were all very proud of Doctor Bedford. He was a hero, Jane. You can feel proud of him – and of Rose Hylton too.'

'Yes, I am proud – and angry, with them both. Neither of them had to be there that day. The doctors and nurses were told to take cover but they wouldn't abandon the patients.'

'Would you have expected either of them to leave helpless men to die if by an action of theirs some might be saved?'

'No, I wouldn't – but I wish they had.'

'You are grieving and you are angry, but in their place you would have done the same.'

'Would I?'

'I am sure of it.' Sister looked thoughtful. 'Perhaps anger is the best way for you, Jane. You may report to Ward Seven in the morning.'

Jane stood up. 'Thank you, Sister. I shan't let you down.'

'I am sure you won't.' Sister Nottingham rose from her chair and came round the desk as Jane took a step forward, clutching at the desk to steady herself. 'Are you faint? I thought you looked unwell. Please visit your doctor this afternoon, Jane. If you are ill I shall insist that you take some time off.'

'I don't feel ill – just a bit sick sometimes and I've been dizzy a couple of times, that's all.'

Sister Nottingham's gaze narrowed. 'Have you considered that you may be pregnant?'

'Pregnant?' Jane stared at her. 'No, I hadn't . . .' Her cheeks felt warm as she saw the speculation in the older woman's arms. 'I suppose . . .' she broke off in embarrassment.

'You were to have been married, Jane. I shall not censure you but you know that it makes a difference, don't you? If you are pregnant you will not be able to stay with us. I am prepared to turn a blind eye for a while, just until you find somewhere to live and a job – unless . . .'

Jane didn't understand for a moment, then she shook her head. 'If I am having Richard's child I shall keep it.'

'Yes, of course. It will be difficult but you will not be the first war casualty to be caught in this situation, my dear. I suggest you visit the doctor at once. You need not tell me the result, but if it is positive you know what you have to do . . .'

Twelve

Jane bent over the toilet, as she was sick for the second time that morning. She was feeling wretched and looked at herself in the mirror as she got to her feet and rinsed her mouth with water from the tap. She could no longer doubt that she was having a baby. The doctor had confirmed it after an examination.

'You are about two months gone, Miss Shaw,' he told her. 'Everything seems normal and you are in good health.' He hesitated for a moment, then, 'I could recommend somewhere for you to stay for the birth. It is a Salvation Army home for unmarried mothers. They don't force you to give up the child, though they do recommend adoption.'

'I don't want that for my baby.'

'As I said, these people do not force you, unlike some of the more religious houses. Will the father marry you?'

'We were to have been married. He was killed trying to drag wounded men from a burning lorry in France.'

The doctor looked stunned. 'Forgive me. I didn't mean to preach — but you must know that many people will think the worst.'

'Yes, I am aware that some will think I am a scarlet woman.' Jane looked at him proudly. 'I shall think about what you've said — but I'm not ready yet. I hope to work for a few months and I need to find a room somewhere.'

'I imagine you can find a room for the moment, but once the child is born you will find it more difficult to secure decent lodgings, especially . . .'

'If the mother is unmarried.' Jane nodded. 'I do understand. I shall have to think what to do . . .'

'Well, if you need help please come to me. I am certain I could find you a place with the Salvation Army.'

'Thank you. I shall remember that . . .'

Jane looked at herself in the mirror as she got ready for work. She didn't show at all yet. How long could she do her job and get away with it? She would have to leave before Sister Nottingham was forced to sack her. Finding rewarding work wasn't going to be easy. She wasn't too proud to take on cleaning if she had to, but she wouldn't be able to manage really hard work for long.

Thoughts of Aunt Alice's tea-rooms crossed her mind. Something like that, perhaps working in the kitchen, would be ideal. She wasn't sure if anyone would want to take her on once they knew she was having a child.

Jane had a little money put by and she still had a couple of things from her father that she could sell if she was forced. She would manage somehow until the child was born, even if it meant going to the Sally Army home to have the baby. Afterwards, she could find someone to have the child while she went to work.

Jane thought about her friend Aggie Bristow. She had kept in touch with her until recently, but hadn't felt like writing after Richard was killed. Jane knew that Aggie would look after her baby while Jane worked. Living in a small community like March would mean she would be pointed at and condemned for being an unmarried mother, but what was her alternative?

Jane was coming off duty a few days later when she saw some male patients in the rest room. They were drinking beer from bottles and making rather a lot of noise. Sister would create merry hell if she saw them, because they were not allowed to consume alcohol in the hospital.

'Keep the noise down a bit, boys,' Jane said, poking her head in at the door. 'Sister will put you all on a charge if she hears you.'

'Here's the lovely ice queen come to smack our bums,' one of the men responded cheerfully. 'You can smack mine anytime, gorgeous.'

Did they think she was cold? It was true she didn't smile much these days.

'I've warned you,' she said preparing to leave again. 'On your own head be it . . .'

Her throat felt tight as she turned away. In France the soldiers had called her an angel, here they thought she was an ice queen. She fought the desire to weep.

'Jane . . .' a voice behind her made her stop and turn as a man came limping up to her. 'I thought it was you. Hang on a minute. I can't move very fast these days.'

'Captain Heron . . .' Jane was shocked as she saw that he had a livid scar at the right temple. He was on crutches, his right foot bound in heavy bandages and he looked as if he had been ill for a while. 'I am sorry. Were you in the rest room? I didn't see you.'

'Those idiots! They shouldn't have spoken to you like that. Fowler is a loud mouthed lout and I told him so.'

'He was probably drunk. You're not allowed alcohol in the hospital. Sister will be furious if they don't quieten down.'

'Serves them right . . .' David broke off and coughed; a deep wracking cough that shook his body. He wiped his mouth. Jane caught sight of a spot of blood. 'Sorry. It happens when I get over excited . . .'

'Is it shrapnel damage?'

'Apparently a piece is lodged somewhere near my lungs, there's another in my head so they tell me. One of these days one of them is going to move and . . .' He drew a finger across his throat. 'Curtains.'

Jane's throat caught. He didn't deserve this! No one did. 'I am so sorry. Have they tried to operate?'

'We are having discussions. I might not survive the operation. My lungs aren't much good either.'

'Does your wife know?'

'I don't have a wife. The only girl I ever wanted to marry hates me.'

'I thought you and Frances . . .'

'In her dreams. Frances is a little too well proportioned for my taste.'

'Don't be unkind. Frances is a friend.'

'She is a perfectly nice girl but I don't fancy her. Besides, I've only ever wanted to marry you, Jane.'

'You weren't interested in marriage.'

'I admit that I was just out for some fun at first but I soon realized my mistake. I would have married you − put it right, Jane.'

'Don't be silly. There's nothing to put right. I've forgotten about that . . .'

'Have you? I never have. Do you still hate me, Jane?'

They had reached the gardens. 'You shouldn't come any further. It is freezing out this evening.'

'I asked you a question, Jane.'

'No, I don't hate you. I stopped hating you a long time ago.'

'You feel nothing for me?'

'There's no sense in this, David. Please go back inside. You probably should be resting.'

'What does it matter? I have no reason to live.'

'Stop feeling so bloody sorry for yourself! Richard would trade places with you any day.'

'You were going to marry Richard Bedford. I was sorry to hear that he died, Jane. I wish it had been me instead. I would have changed places with him for your sake.'

'Please don't be silly. I shouldn't have said that to you just now. I'm sorry – and you shouldn't give up. Men live with shrapnel inside them. It doesn't necessarily mean you will die because—' she broke off as his eyes avoided hers.

'I don't care one way or the other.' He glanced at her for a moment. 'Marry me, Jane. Let me give you the things I always wanted to give you. I'm not dependent on my sister now. My grandmother died and left me her house and some money. I've no one else to give them to . . .'

'I can't do that, David. Please stay where you are and don't follow me outside. If you take care of yourself you may have a while yet. Ask Frances to marry you. She loves you.'

Jane opened the letter from Mrs Hylton the next morning. It was sincere and filled with concern for her.

> *I know why you haven't visited, Jane, but we would really love to see you. We miss Rose so much but we are proud of the way she died and we know how much she loved you. She told me that if it hadn't been for you she couldn't have carried on after Andrew died . . .*
>
> *Please come and see us when you can. It would really help the loneliness if you could visit now and then . . .*

Jane felt the lump in her throat as she finished reading Mrs Hylton's letter for the second time. She had written to Rose's mother but in her first tearing grief she hadn't been able to visit. However, that was selfish. She would write to her again and then visit as soon as she left her job at the hospital. Mrs Hylton might be able to tell her where she could find a place to stay or find work.

There was no sense clinging to her job when she knew the time was almost up. Jane decided that she would speak to Sister Nottingham the next day and give her notice in for the end of the week.

'I shall be sorry to lose you, Jane,' the senior nurse looked at her sadly. 'If you are ever in trouble please come to me privately and I'll do what I can for you. I wish I could tell you your job would be here after the birth but it is not in my power.'

'I know. Richard spoke of my carrying on after we were married but it might not have happened.'

'That is a slightly different matter. There is a school of thought that says we should allow married women to return to work after their families are grown up. I agree that a lot of good workers are lost to us for no good reason, but I don't have much say in these things.' She sighed and offered her hand. 'Take care of yourself, Jane. I am sorry things worked out this way.'

'It isn't your fault. I wouldn't change anything if I could.'

'You can work your notice and we'll say nothing of your reasons for leaving.'

'Thank you − for everything.'

Jane left her office and went back on the ward. One of the nurses stared at her but dropped her eyes as soon as Jane returned the stare. She was sure that some of the other nurses had begun to suspect her secret. It was a good thing she had not tried to carry on until the last moment.

By the end of her shift, Jane was feeling terribly tired. Standing took its toll on her and her feet ached, as did her back. What she would be like by the time her confinement arrived she hardly dare think. She had thought of trying to find work in a pub, either behind the bar or cleaning tables but she wasn't sure she would be able to do it for long.

'Jane . . .' She turned her head as she heard his voice. He was walking with a stick instead of crutches and seemed to be moving a little easier. 'I thought it was you.'

'Captain Heron. How are you? Have you heard from Ned recently?'

'I think he had the measles but he is getting over it now.' His gaze narrowed, intent on her face. 'Someone told me you are leaving at the end of the week?'

'News travels fast . . .' Jane hesitated. 'I don't have much choice. I've broken one of the cardinal rules.'

'What do you mean?' David looked puzzled. 'What stupid rule means you have to leave? You're a damned good nurse. Everyone says so.'

Jane sighed. 'I would prefer you kept it to yourself – but I'm pregnant. I'm having Richard's baby.'

'You . . .' The colour left his face. 'Damn him! He should have taken more care of you.'

'Stop it!' Jane was angry. 'It isn't your business. I'm glad. Do you hear me? I'm glad . . .'

She turned and walked off. He didn't call out to her. She knew he was shocked and angry. It was nothing to do with him. She wished she hadn't told him. He would have known soon anyway. You could never keep anything secret at the hospital for long. But the look in his eyes told her he wouldn't bother her again. He was angry that she was carrying Richard's baby.

'Jane, it is so lovely to see you.' Mrs Hylton opened her arms and embraced her. 'I am thrilled you have come to us. I hope you are going to stay for a long time?'

'I should like to stay for a while, but you may not want me to when you hear my news . . .'

'I cannot think of any reason I would not want to have you in my house, Jane.'

'I am having Richard's baby . . .'

For a moment Mrs Hylton stared at her in silence, and then the tears began to run down her face. 'My dearest Jane, how positively wonderful. Richard would be so happy if he knew. I am sure he does know. I like to think of him in heaven looking after my Rose. He was such a lovely man. You must be pleased?'

'Yes, I am. I thought I had lost him for good but now I have his baby and that is very precious to me.'

'I should think so, my love. Have you made plans for the future?'

'I need to find somewhere to live and a job. I have been told that the Sally Army might take me in while I have the baby, but I'm not ready for that so I shall wait until I can't work any longer.'

'And why should you go to a place like that?' Mrs Hylton looked indignant. 'Why can't you have your baby here with us? My husband will look after you and I shall be glad of the company. If you can find a nice little job that suits you, I shan't stop you going to work for a few months, but after that you will stay at home and let me look after you.'

'You are so kind . . . I don't know what to say. People will talk and . . .' she stopped as Mrs Hylton put a finger to her own lips.

'If they wish to talk they may, but they won't say anything bad about you in my hearing – or they will wish they hadn't. You were going to marry Richard. Perhaps some would say you should have waited but look what happened. You would have lost everything. Now you have Richard's child and I believe that is more important than a little gossip.'

'It may be more than a little . . .'

'Oh, we are more liberal in my circles these days. I dare say in a village people still point the finger, but my friends understand. There is a war on and these things happen, Jane. I want you to stay with us until you feel able to move on – perhaps when the child is able to go to nursery school and you can find a decent job.'

'I don't know how to thank you. There are no words . . .'

Mrs Hylton beamed at her. 'You don't have to say anything. I've been grieving so hard for Rose. This will help me to face the world again – and I've always loved babies.'

Jane felt tears sting her eyes. 'I miss Rose too. She was the best friend I ever had. No one will ever be like Rose . . .'

'It's as if she is watching us,' Mrs Hylton blinked hard. 'She brought you to me, Jane. I know she did . . .'

'Yes, perhaps she did. I was feeling low when your letter came. I was just going to ask if I could stay a few days, but I would love to stay longer – at least until after the baby is born.'

'You can stay until you are ready to move on . . .'

'The first thing I need to do is find a job!' Jane lifted her head, a gleam of determination in her eyes. She felt positive for the first time in weeks! She was carrying Richard's baby. A part of him was still with her and the future seemed brighter.

Jane walked slowly that summer afternoon. The weather had turned warmer this past week, the sun bringing people out to throng the streets as they shopped for whatever they could find in the shops. Trams were clattering in the distance, a delivery boy ringing his bell to warn of his presence as he raced by on his bicycle, and the voice of a man selling papers competed with the general noise of the London traffic.

Stopping to buy a paper, Jane saw that the new Allied tactics had got the enemy on the run at last, and in big black headlines there was more about the dreadful killing of the Czar and his family in a cellar.

Jane hardly noticed the noise of the traffic. She was used to it now, and liked to stop and look at the beautiful creations in the milliners on her way home from work. Life was as good as it could be for her. She had fallen into a job much sooner than she had imagined possible. Mrs Hylton had introduced her to the owner of a small bookshop on the corner of Oxford Street. He was an elderly gentleman, who liked to spend his time at auction sales buying second-hand books, and he had snapped up the chance to take her on for three days a week.

It was an easy job for Jane, dusting, sorting piles of books and serving the occasional customer. They didn't really get many customers, but Jane knew the real sales were done in the back room out of sight. Mr Bletchly dealt in precious manuscripts and first editions; the books on sale in the shop were just a by-product of his trade.

Jane was smiling to herself as she thought about the lady who had bought a rather battered copy of Jane Austen's *Pride and Prejudice* that morning. She had swooped on it with evident delight and carried off her treasure for tuppence.

'I do not know what you can find to smile at. I find your situation disgusting!'

The sharp note of accusation startled Jane. She swung round to find herself facing her aunt, who had clearly been shopping nearby and was carrying several parcels. For a moment she was so surprised that she could hardly speak. She had never imagined that she would meet her aunt in the street like this – or that she would stop and speak to her. Jane placed her gloved hands protectively over her stomach, knowing her condition was obvious to anyone who looked at her.

Recovering, she took a step forward, 'Aunt Alice. Forgive me, I didn't see you. Are you well?'

The older woman's lip curled in scorn. 'I am well enough but it was a shock to see you. Melia has told me that you . . . well, I was very upset when I learned that you had become a fallen woman. You are many things, Jane, but I am surprised that you flaunt your sin so openly. I have instructed Melia to have nothing to do with you.'

'Melia loves me. I hope I shall see her often.'

'If she associates with you, she may stay away from my house. I will not have our name made a byword, Jane. You may flaunt your disgrace, but if Melia cares for me she will not visit you – or see you again.'

'You can't mean that? You can't be so unfair? Please, Aunt Alice . . . Melia is my sister. You can't forbid her to see me again.'

'Melia will either do as I tell her – or she can forget becoming a teacher at my expense.'

'You wouldn't . . .'

'You may think me unjust but I offered you a home despite what your father had done. You chose to bite the hand that fed you. Well, you have made your bed and you may lie in it. Good day to you.'

Jane closed her eyes. The viciousness of her aunt's attack was so unexpected that it made her feel sick. If she had gone to Aunt Alice's house she would have been prepared for anger and rejection but she had not even attempted reconciliation. To be set on in the street like this was upsetting and uncalled for – and the threat against Melia's future was despicable.

Tears were trickling down Jane's face as she stumbled towards the tram stop. Everything seemed a blur and she hardly knew what she did as a man in rough working clothes helped her on to the tram.

'There you are, missus,' he said kindly. 'Feeling a bit under the weather, are you? Get yourself home and put the kettle on. By the looks of you, you haven't much longer to go . . .'

Jane mumbled her thanks. Strangers were kind. What made her aunt so cruel and vicious? Surely it wasn't just because she had refused to work in her teashop?

Jane stared out of the window without really seeing anything. Instinct prompted her to get off at the right stop. She walked slowly back to Mrs Hylton's house dazed and with a vague sense of feeling unwell. Her baby wasn't due for another three weeks or so but her back had been aching for most of the day. If Mr Bletchly had been in the shop she might have gone home early. Had she done so she wouldn't have seen her aunt.

She wasn't going to allow Aunt Alice to upset her! Reasserting her pride, Jane walked through the passage to the back of the house and went in at the kitchen door. The pain struck her as she took off her coat and hung it on the peg, making her double over for a moment.

'Jane – is that you, my dear?' Mrs Hylton called to her from the sitting room. 'There is someone to see you, my love . . .'

Jane had to catch her breath before she could move. She wondered who her visitor could be. Hardly anyone knew she was living here. She had written to Sister Nottingham to tell her that she was with Rose's mother but . . . walking into the little front parlour Jane saw the man sitting at the table. She gasped in surprise. He was the last person she had expected to see!

'Jane . . .' David rose to his feet. He was wearing a pinstripe suit and a white shirt with a dark tie. 'I hope you don't mind my calling out of the—' he broke off as she gave a little cry and then staggered, clutching at a chair to steady herself. 'Jane . . . are you ill?'

'I think it may be the baby . . .'

Mrs Hylton came to her at once. 'Jane my dear. It is a little soon for the baby. We were not expecting anything to happen for a few weeks yet.'

'I know . . .' Jane bit her lower lip. 'Perhaps it is a false alarm but it hurts rather a lot . . .' She tried and failed to stop herself crying out as another pain struck her in the back. 'I think it must be coming early . . .'

'You haven't had a fall?' Mrs Hylton questioned. 'You look very pale, my love. Can you walk upstairs?'

'I had a shock,' Jane said and crossed her arms over herself as the pain whipped through her. 'My aunt . . . we met in the street . . . she wasn't very nice . . .'

'That stupid woman, upsetting you at a time like this,' Mrs Hylton looked angry. 'I think you should lie down. If you could possibly help her upstairs, Captain Heron?'

'He isn't well enough . . .' Jane protested as David came to put his arm about her. 'Please don't hurt yourself . . .'

'I'm stronger than I was. Let me help you, Jane. I can't carry you, but I'm strong enough to support you if you lean on me.'

'Go with him, Jane. I'll telephone for my husband. I doubt if anything will happen yet but he will come to you as soon as he can . . .'

Jane felt too ill to resist. She let David put his arm about her waist, accepting his help gratefully as he slowly walked her up the stairs and into her room. When she was sitting on the edge of the bed he hovered uncertainly, then looked down at her.

'What can I do for you, Jane?'

'Just leave her to me, sir,' Mrs Hylton said coming in behind them. 'You may wait in the parlour downstairs until I come if you wish – or call back later to see how she is . . .'

'I'll wait,' David said and moved towards the door. 'I'll be downstairs if I am needed.'

'No, Pa, please don't . . .' Jane cried, as she tossed and turned, her body arching with the tearing pain. 'Please don't leave us . . . we need you . . .'

Her cheeks were stained with tears as the memories crowded in on her and she saw her father's face when they cut him down, his protruding tongue and eyes.

'Please . . .'

Jane did not know what she said. She had long since stopped thinking. Pain was everything, filling her world, blotting out all but the vivid pictures that filled her mind.

'Richard . . . please don't be dead. Why did you have to volunteer? Rose . . . I need you . . . I need you so . . . Richard, why did you leave me?'

'You have to push harder,' Mrs Hylton urged. 'Come on, Jane.

This isn't like you. You must try. I know it hurts but you must think of your baby.'

Jane didn't answer. She was lost in a haze of pain.

'How is she?' David asked when Mrs Hylton came down to the kitchen to fetch more hot water. 'Is it usual for a woman to have so much pain?'

'Some do, some are luckier,' Mrs Hylton replied, looking anxious. 'My husband says the baby has to be turned or it will never come. If he can't do it he must cut her.' She shook her head sorrowfully. 'She was to be married to Captain Bedford you know. I am not sure she has the will to live.'

'Do you mean Richard Bedford?' She nodded. 'He saved my life once.' David walked towards the door, halting as she called after him.

'Where are you going?'

'Jane needs me. The least I can do is to try and save Bedford's child . . .'

'But . . . I'm not sure. Jane hasn't mentioned you to me. It isn't proper for a man to be there, except the doctor . . .'

'I love Jane. Please let me try something.'

Mrs Hylton hesitated, then inclined her head. 'She is getting weaker. She needs to fight – to push harder.'

'Let me try. If it doesn't work I'll go away and not trouble you again.'

David was thoughtful as he walked upstairs. He wasn't vain enough to imagine that Jane would try for his sake but she might for the man she loved. She was screaming again. His expression hardened to grim determination. She wasn't going to die if he could prevent it. Jane might hate him, but he loved her and he would do his best to force her to live.

'Push a little harder, Jane,' Doctor Hylton urged. 'The head is the right way now and I think the child will come if you try . . .'

Jane sighed. What was the use of trying? She had no one to care whether she lived or died, no family left to her. The baby had been important once but she had forgotten everything but the pain.

'Let me die . . .' the whisper was barely audible. 'No reason to live . . .'

'Don't you want our baby, Jane? I never thought you were a quitter. Come on; stop this self-pity and push. Push for our baby – and me. Damn you, push!'

'Richard . . . is that you?' Jane's eyelids flickered but she was too weak to open them and see his face. 'I thought . . .' Tears trickled down her cheeks. 'I want our baby . . . but I am so tired . . . so very tired . . .'

Hands were gripping hers. They felt strong and compelling. She clung to the hands, crushing them without being aware of what she did. 'Push for Richard, Jane. Push for our baby.'

'Our baby . . .' Jane's hands clung to the strong hands that gave her comfort. She pushed harder with the last little bit of strength she had and felt a pain worse than any before it as the child suddenly came out of her in a slither of slime and blood. 'Richard . . .' She screamed his name and then heard a wailing sound. 'Our baby . . .' A sob of relief and exhaustion broke from her as she sank back against the pillows. 'Oh, Richard . . .'

'She will be all right now, sir. Leave her to us. You can come another day to visit.'

'Yes, I shall,' David said. 'I will call tomorrow if I may?'

'I am sure she will be very pleased to see you, sir.'

'It may be best if you don't tell her I was here while she gave birth . . .'

'Yes, sir. I shall leave you to tell her what you think best.'

'Don't bother to come down, Mrs Hylton. I can see myself out.'

Jane woke to see that it was a beautiful day. The sun was shining in through the window, striking showers of colour from a cut-glass vase on the dressing table. The vase was filled with yellow roses, their sweet perfume invading the room.

'They are so beautiful,' Jane said as Mrs Hylton came in carrying a tray with a pot of tea and a plate with scrambled eggs and toast. 'Thank you so much.'

'Captain Heron brought them for you. He called to see how you were yesterday, but you were sleeping a lot and I didn't think you would want visitors?'

'No, I was feeling exhausted, but I am better this morning.' Jane pushed herself up against the pillows, looking at the food.

'That smells good. I feel so lazy lying here and making you look after me.'

'It is no trouble to me.' Mrs Hylton turned her head as a whimpering cry came from the cot. 'I expect she will want her feed soon – but you must eat first. You need to build your strength up if you want to feed her yourself?'

'Yes, I do. She is perfect, isn't she? A bit small but perfect . . .' Jane glanced towards the cot where her daughter lay staring up at the ceiling. 'I would like to call her Rosie – if that is all right with you.'

Mrs Hylton smiled, blinking hard. 'I was going to ask you about that. My Rose would be thrilled – and I'm delighted, Jane.' She deposited the tray on Jane's lap. 'I'll nurse her for a while. Just until you've had your breakfast.'

Jane dipped a fork into the light and fluffy eggs. She sighed with pleasure as she ate. 'This is so good. I can't remember much of what happened when Rosie was coming. It all seems vague and distant now.'

'We were afraid we might lose you, Jane. You had a terrible time because she wasn't turned the right way. Mr Hylton says it was because she came too soon.' She looked angry. 'If I ever see that aunt of yours I shall give her a piece of my mind. Upsetting you like that!'

'I was shocked and upset, because she said Melia can't see me again – if she wants to continue at college.'

'If Melia has any sense she will stand up to her now and put a stop to this nonsense.'

'Melia wants to be a teacher so much. If my aunt refuses to fund her she will be devastated.'

Mrs Hylton made a tutting sound. 'Disgraceful! I don't know how that woman can sleep at night!'

Jane smiled and then finished her tea, pushing her tray away. 'I dare say she has her reasons for what she does. I'll take Rosie now. I'm sure she is hungry.'

Mrs Hylton put the baby into her arms. 'She is a little beauty. I thought we were going to lose you both until . . .' she broke off and shook her head. 'You came through it and that's all that matters.'

'You said until . . .' Jane wrinkled her brow. 'It seemed to me that I was ready to give up because I was just too tired and then . . . I thought it was Richard who held my hands but it couldn't have been.' Her gaze flicked to the vase of beautiful flowers. 'Was it David Heron?'

'I wasn't going to tell you. I thought you might be embarrassed to know he was here – but I think he saved your life. You were ready to give up. You wouldn't try and then he . . .'

'Told me he was Richard. He forced me to try.' Jane looked down at the softly flushed face of her daughter. 'If he hadn't, I might not have been here to feed her.'

'We were afraid of it.' Mrs Hylton hesitated. 'Captain Heron seemed quite determined that you were not going to die.'

'Yes, it would seem so . . .' Jane patted the child's back as Rosie burped. 'I am grateful for what he did. If he calls again please ask him to come up and see me.'

Jane glanced at herself in the little hand-mirror. Mrs Hylton had helped her to tidy her hair, which was sadly in need of a wash, and she was wearing a pale blue bed-jacket over her nightgown. She sat back against her pillows, her mouth a little dry as she waited for her visitor.

'Jane . . .' David seemed apprehensive as he looked round the edge of the door. 'Mrs Hylton said you asked to see me?'

'Please come in.'

'Are you very angry with me for lying to you?' He walked into the room. 'I knew you would try for him. Richard Bedford was a hero. I don't blame you for loving him.'

'I hated him for being a hero for a while.' Jane looked at him steadily. 'But I still loved him. Can you understand that, David – loving and hating someone at the same time?'

'Yes.' David moved closer to the bed. 'It is the way I feel about my sister. I love her for the way she was once and I hate her because . . .' He shook his head. 'She doesn't matter. Will you forgive me?'

'You saved my life and my daughter's,' Jane said. 'If I had died she might have too. Why did you do it, David?'

'Richard Bedford saved my life at the start of the war. The least I could do was to help his child into the world.'

'That wasn't your only reason, was it?'

'Promise not to get upset?' Jane nodded. 'I couldn't stand the sound of your screaming. I love you, Jane. I know you don't believe me – but I always have.'

Jane didn't answer immediately. For a moment it was so quiet that you could have heard a pin drop and then Rosie snuffled in her sleep.

'I really have forgiven you. I'll never forget what you've done for me, David.'

'You don't hate me?' He moved closer as Jane shook her head. 'Do you think . . .' David drew a deep breath. 'Mrs Hylton told me what your aunt said to you . . . what she threatened. I have money of my own now. A relative left me a considerable sum and a house in Norfolk. It isn't a huge fortune but it is enough. I could afford to send Melia to college and look after you and the little one. Ned would be happy if I married you. I worry about him, because he can't forgive his mother and his sister doesn't really want him living with her. If we were married he would have a home with us whenever he needed it.'

'David, I . . .' Her look reproached him. 'That is blackmail. You know I love Ned.'

'Don't turn me down without a hearing.' David avoided her eyes. 'I'm not sure how long I've got. They've told me it could be a few years if I'm lucky; it might be much sooner if the shrapnel in my brain moves. I would like a chance to make life good for you, Jane. If you could bear to give me another chance I'd like to spend what time I have with you.'

'I feel something for you. It might have been love if you hadn't . . .' Jane broke off as she saw the hurt in his face. 'I loved Richard so much. At the moment I am not sure how much I have left to give you.'

David surged towards the bed and sat down on the edge, reaching for her hand. 'I wouldn't ask for much. I'm not even sure it could be a proper marriage, because my body may take a long time to get back to normal. Even if I can't make love to you, I want to be with you – to give you all the things I meant to give you. When I got drunk that day I made the biggest mistake of my life.'

'Why did you do it?'

'I can't explain. I had something on my mind – something I

found deeply disturbing. When I had a few drinks you looked at me in a certain way; it made me angry for some reason. I knew the war was imminent and I wanted you. I suppose I just lost my head. You can't know how much I regretted what I did afterwards.'

'I liked you a lot. If you had come to me and been sober . . .' Jane sighed. 'We can't change the past. Everyone does things they regret. My father did something once and ended up ruining his life . . .'

'I thought about suicide. I wanted to die in the first weeks of the war but it didn't happen because a bloody hero came along and saved my life . . .' David laughed harshly. 'I've wished myself dead but now I'm glad I'm alive. If I can make you safe for the rest of your life I shall have done something worthwhile.' His eyes beseeched her. 'Please marry me, Jane. I want it more than anything in the world.'

Jane studied his face. He was sincere – and it would solve her problems. She would never want for money again. Melia could go to college even if Aunt Alice turned nasty and Jane could bring up her child, as Richard would have wanted.

'I'm not saying no . . .' Jane held his hand. 'I need to think it over, David. You are offering me more than I have any right to expect but you may not get much in return.'

'It will be enough for me to be near you – to have the privilege of caring for you and Rosie.'

'You can accept the child of another man?'

'I am unlikely to have children of my own, Jane. My wounds are such that it probably won't happen. I may not even be able to be a proper man . . .'

'Oh, David, I am so sorry.' Her fingers tightened about his. 'You shouldn't give up hope – unless it is physical?'

'It isn't lack of wedding tackle.' He grinned at her. 'Just general ill health and mental trauma.'

'And you are certain that you want this marriage?'

'More certain than I've ever been. When you were close to death, I couldn't bear it.' David's face reflected his fear and distress. 'I just want to look after you.'

'Give me three days and then come to see me again. I should feel able to get up by then . . .' She laughed as she saw his expression. 'I know the doctors say I should stay in bed for two weeks but I've never taken orders well. In three days I shall have my answer for you.'

He nodded, then leaned forward and kissed her cheek. She could feel his intensity, the suppressed excitement he was trying not to show, and in her heart she already knew what her answer must be.

Thirteen

'You are certain this is what you want to do, love?' Mrs Hylton looked at Jane. In her expensive pale grey silk dress, she was beautiful, a little pale but serene, the creamy pearls David had given her about her throat. 'You know you are welcome to stay with us?'

'Yes, I know.' Jane smiled and kissed her cheek. 'You have been wonderful to me – a good friend. When you took me in I had nothing and I didn't know what to do. Now the future is bright, for Melia and Rosie, as well as me. David will look after us all.'

'You're not in love with him, are you?'

'In love?' Jane shook her head. 'David knows how I feel. I like him. We get on well and I am grateful. I am going to try hard to make a good life for us all . . . He just wants a chance and I think in time . . . I am willing to take the chance and so is he.'

Jane came out of the Registrar's Office to be greeted with a shower of confetti from Melia, a very grown up Ned in his smart suit and highly polished shoes, and the two army officers David had invited. Mrs Hylton was smiling, her husband organizing the taxis that were to take them to the restaurant for lunch.

'Are you truly my aunt now?' Ned asked as he threw more confetti over Jane. 'Can I come and stay when I'm on holiday from school?'

'Yes, of course you can, my darling,' Jane said and gave him a hug. 'You will always have a home with me now.'

'David said I could visit when I like but I wasn't sure.' Ned looked a little shy. 'You've got a baby now, haven't you?'

'Rosie is beautiful. You will love her and she will love having a big cousin to look after her.'

Ned nodded and moved away as Mrs Hylton came up to Jane to wish her luck.

'You mustn't worry about Rosie tonight, Jane. She is being

looked after and she won't miss her mother for one night. You
and Captain Heron will have at least one night to yourselves.'

Jane hadn't told Mrs Hylton that it wouldn't be a proper
wedding night. David had taken a suite at their hotel and Jane
wasn't sure what to expect. She had gone into this marriage
expecting very little from it other than the material benefits he
had offered.

'Jane . . .' Melia took her arm, holding her back for a moment
as they moved towards the cabs. 'I need to talk to you please.'

'Can it wait until we get to the hotel?'

'Yes, I expect so.' Melia bit her lip and then smiled. 'Be happy,
Jane. I am so pleased you've found someone to love.'

'I am happy.' Jane glanced towards her husband. For a while
she had hated him but that was all in the past. He had promised
to be good to her and she believed he would do his best to make
her happy. She would try to be a good wife. 'Is something wrong,
Melia? Is it Aunt Alice?' Melia nodded. 'What has she said to you
now?'

'I'll tell you later.'

'She says she is ill, Jane. She says I can do my training and she
will pay for it but she needs me to come home once I've got
my qualifications. She won't ask me to work in the shop or look
after her – she can pay people to do that, but she wants me to
live with her, to be there at night and keep her company as her
illness gains a hold.' Melia looked at Jane unhappily. 'I would
rather come to you once I leave college but . . . she has been
good to me.'

'I know it is a difficult decision for you. I shan't put any pressure on you but I do want to see you sometimes.'

'She won't try to stop me. She has apologized about what she
said to you that day, because she knows I would never agree to
it. If it were a straight choice between the two of you, I would
come to you, Jane.'

'You mustn't feel that you are being torn between us. You can
come whenever you wish and you have a home with us after
you leave college. David is making you a present of some money
so you can pay for your own expenses if you have to.'

'It is very good of him, but Aunt Alice wouldn't do that to

me. She cares about me, Jane. I've asked her why she was so mean to you but she won't tell me.'

'It doesn't matter. As long as she doesn't harm you, I don't mind that she dislikes me.'

'I will find out one day,' Melia vowed, a determined look in her eye.

Jane was thoughtful as she parted from her sister. It seemed that Melia had a mind of her own, and she was able to wring concessions from their aunt. Her decision to make her home with Aunt Alice had done away with one of the reasons for Jane's marriage.

She hugged Ned before they parted. Mr Hylton had promised to give him a bed for the night and they were going to drive him back to school in the morning.

'Is everything all right?' David asked as they drove to the hotel where they would stay for the night. 'What did Melia want? She looked serious.'

Jane could smell the fresh scent of his cologne mixed with the tang of leather from the cab upholstery. It was the smell of wealth . . . money. For a moment panic rose in her like a menacing tide, threatening to engulf her. Had she sold herself for the safety David's money could buy?

'Melia says Aunt Alice has conceded on everything but wants Melia to make her home with her when she leaves college. She has told her that she will carry on seeing me, but she says our aunt is ill and she can't desert her.'

'Do you think it is true – about the illness?'

'I'm not sure. Melia believes her and it seems they get on well. It is just me my aunt hates.'

'Perhaps she just doesn't approve of you?'

'It is more than that but it doesn't matter.' Jane smiled at him as her sense of panic receded. David had changed. He cared about her. 'The money you gave Melia makes her independent. Perhaps that is why my aunt caved in. She knows she can't force her to do anything now so she is using persuasion.'

'Emotional blackmail?' David frowned. 'I think that is the worst kind. Maria uses it at times.'

'Your sister didn't come to the wedding. Was she very angry because you were marrying me?'

'I didn't ask her. We seldom see each other these days.'

'Did you quarrel with her?'

'Not really . . .' David looked at a point somewhere beyond
Jane's shoulder. 'I knew she wouldn't come if I asked so I didn't
bother.'

'I hope you won't be estranged from your family because of
me?'

'Ned will visit us sometimes. Sara is married and Angela spends
most of her time with her. I think she will join one of the
women's divisions soon or just get married. I don't know her
that well. Ned is the only one I keep in touch with these days.'

'He looked so grown up at the wedding. I think he was brave
to come all the way to London on the train by himself.'

'He is growing up into a proper young man; give him a few
more years and he will be a gentleman. You did that for him,
Jane.'

'Me? Nonsense! I am certain he is being taught all he needs
to know at that school.'

'Yes, the school teaches him how to be a gentleman – but you
were the one who taught him what it means and made him want
it.' David leaned towards her, brushing his lips over hers. 'You've
been good for this family, Jane.'

'I am going to try to be the kind of wife you want, David.'

'And what kind of wife do you think I need?'

'I'll try not to let you down – in front of your friends or in
any other way.'

'All I ask is that you be yourself – and try to forgive me. If I
thought that you loved me just a tiny bit I could die happy.'

Jane felt icy cold. She touched his hand, then curled her fingers
about it as the dread seeped through her. 'Please don't talk about
dying, David. The past is forgotten. All I want is for us to be
happy as a family . . . to make a good life for us all: Rosie, Ned,
Melia, you and me.'

David gripped her hand so hard that she almost winced. 'You
will never know how much I want that, Jane. I pray that I'll have
a few years to look after you and Rosie – to show you how
much I love you.'

Jane leaned forward to brush her lips over his. 'We won't think
of death. There has been too much of that, too many men dying

out there in the trenches. We will take each day as it comes, make the most of it.'

'It's enough for me to be with you . . .'

David tangled his hands in her hair, kissing her with a hungry passion that took her breath away; then he moved back, a rueful expression in his eyes.

'I wish I could go back to the beginning. I threw away my chance and wasted so much time. It may never happen the way I want, Jane – but at least I can take care of you, make up for what I did . . .'

David came to say goodnight when Jane had undressed that night. He still walked with a limp but in every other way he looked normal. Her heart took a flying leap because she thought he was going to make love to her. In that moment she discovered that she would have welcomed him to her bed. The bad memories had all gone, erased by Richard's tenderness and love. He had taught her to enjoy passion, to give herself freely.

As David drew her into his arms, Jane let herself relax against him, her lips soft beneath his as he kissed her lingeringly and with a hunger that shook his body. She felt her own surging response and immediate disappointment as he released her, his fingertips stroking her cheek.

'Thank you, my darling,' he said in a voice husky with regret. 'You didn't reject me. I hardly dared to ask so much of you and yet you gave it willingly. I wish with all my heart that we could be man and wife in truth this night, but it isn't possible.'

'It will happen.' Jane cupped his cheek with the palm of her hand, compassion and a dawning respect and affection in her heart. 'You gave so much for your country, David. People talk of Richard being a hero but you are a hero – all the men who fought and suffered, and go on doing it even yet – you are all heroes.'

'Sweet Jane. Would it shock you if I said the bloody country could go to the devil if I could have my time with you again? If I could just hold you and love you . . .' He broke off, turning away from her. 'Forgive me. We agreed not to dwell on the future.'

'There is nothing to forgive. Your body needs time to heal, my love. In time and with patience we may—'

He swung round, his eyes blazing with sudden heat. 'Do you truly care – just a little?'

'I believe I always did in my heart – but, yes, I do. I want this marriage to work.'

'You didn't marry me just for Melia, Ned and Rosie's sake?'

'I shan't lie to you. They were a part of it, a big part of it at the start – but I do care, David.'

'Do you love me as much as *him*?'

'That isn't fair . . .' Jane moved away. 'Don't ask me to compare. I am learning to love you. I shall always feel something for Richard . . . but that was different.'

'I know. I shouldn't have asked. Goodnight, Jane. Sweet dreams.'

Jane watched as he walked into the next room. Her heart ached for his pain. David wanted to turn back time. He wanted her to give him something she couldn't give. Richard had been her lover. He was Rosie's father. Nothing could change that and Jane did not want to change it.

She felt a mixture of love and compassion for the man she had married. Perhaps if it became a proper marriage one day the memories of Richard would fade, but for the moment they remained bright and vivid in her mind.

Rosie was whimpering as Mrs Hylton placed her in Jane's arms the next day, but she stopped as she caught the smell of her mother and burped, blowing a bubble of contentment, her eyes wide and inquiring.

'She took her bottle well this morning,' Mrs Hylton said. 'She isn't hungry, Jane – but I think she missed you.'

'I missed her,' Jane bent her head to kiss the child. 'Thank you so much for looking after her – and for all you've done for me.'

'You are very welcome, my love – and don't forget we shall always be pleased to see you.'

'I'll bring Rosie sometimes . . .' Jane promised and waved as they pulled out into the traffic.

'She doesn't really like me, does she?' David spoke without looking at her. 'She probably doesn't think I'm good enough for you – and she is right.'

'That is rubbish. She was fond of Richard. I met him through the family; they knew him long before I did.'

'Richard Bedford the hero . . .' there was a mixture of sarcasm, anger and jealousy in his voice. 'She thinks I shall let you down – hurt you. That is why she told you that you could run back there if you regret what you've done.'

'I don't regret it, David. I shan't.' Jane glanced at him, noticing the nerve jumping in his throat. She dropped her voice to a whisper, 'Be careful, Ned is listening. Please don't torture yourself. I went into this with my eyes open. Our marriage can be good if we make it so. It is up to us.'

'I shall be the one to ruin it if anyone does.' David grinned suddenly, looking more like his old self. 'My bloody pride. Do you remember the day we played cricket and you caught me out? I wasn't satisfied until I caught you twice.'

'We're alike in some ways. I can be proud and stubborn too.'

'I know. It is one of the things I love about you.' He glanced at the child. 'She is beautiful. I'm not surprised you adore her. We'll make a good life for her, Jane. Together for as long as I live. Afterwards, you'll be all right. I've made sure of that. No one will be able to take anything from you.'

'Don't think about it. I want you to live – for all our sakes.'

'This is wonderful.' They had dropped Ned off the previous day, stayed at a hotel over night and then driven the rest of the way without stopping. 'This part of Hunstanton is lovely, really lovely. It must have been all countryside until the Victorians came along and built their villas at the front. We're far enough away from the town to make it feel as if we're still in the country but with views to the sea.'

She was standing at the edge of the cliffs looking down at the sea. The breeze was cool on her face but the sun was warm for the time of year. It really felt like spring though it was still early.

'This is what the locals call Old Hunstanton. At one time it was all owned by one important family – all this and the whole of what is now the town,' David told her. He had come to stand at her side as she looked down. The sea was a long way out exposing wet, muddy-looking sand and rocks, which were covered with green weed and dotted with little pools left behind by the tide. To the right of them was a bank of dark green trees that clung to the coast in a misty smudge. 'The house belonged to my grandmother. I visited her often when I was young. I used to love coming here alone. My parents couldn't spare the time to come with me and Maria never wanted to visit the old lady. I spent hours on that beach hunting for crabs. My grandfather took me to Heacham or Snettisham and we dug for cockles in the sand. Grandmother cooked them in a huge saucepan and we ate them warm from the shells. Sometimes we dug for lugworm when the tide was out and then we took the boat out and went fishing.'

Jane turned to look at him, seeing the way his eyes lit and his face relaxed into a smile. She had forgotten he could look like this and her heart caught with love. Perhaps it wasn't the love she had felt for Richard, but it was a warm, satisfying feeling that made her happy.

'It sounds an ideal way to spend your childhood. Were you fond of your grandparents?'

'Yes. Particularly my grandmother. She stood by me after my parents died. I couldn't have finished my education if Grandmother hadn't made sacrifices for my sake. My father was in debt when he died. None of us knew but it all came out afterwards.' David frowned. 'I think that was why Maria married Stratton. She had been used to money . . . being spoiled. He was much older and she wasn't in love with him.'

'I got the impression from Nanny that their marriage never worked?'

'Stratton was jealous – madly so at times. He suspected she was having an affair. He blamed me for encouraging her.' David's lip curled. 'I did my best to keep her on the level but of course no one believed that, because I was a little wild at times. I had affairs, got into money difficulties . . . Grandmother might have helped me. I wouldn't ask her. Maria lent me money but I paid her back. Grandmother left me this house and all her property and savings – twenty-five thousand pounds in all. It isn't a fortune, Jane. I have invested some of it in a fishing business; supplying prawns and shellfish to shops and market stalls, which should bring in a good income. I'm a sleeping partner so I don't have to do much and that gives me a chance to try to make a living at what I really want to do . . .'

'What is that?'

David looked oddly shy. 'After I was given an honourable discharge, I decided that I want to write poetry and articles. I've had a couple of articles published in a country magazine. They were about Norfolk, about the history and heritage of our villages and famous people; Lord Nelson was born not far from here. I write about the wildlife too. We get flocks of geese flying in over the winter months. I've taken some photographs to accompany the articles and the editors were enthusiastic.'

'What a wonderful way to make a living.' Jane was intrigued. 'Will you let me see?'

'I have the first published article in my things. I'll show you later. The money isn't enough to live on, of course – but with the income from the shellfish business it should be enough. I shan't be living the wild life I did once.' He gave her a rueful smile. 'I may have overstated my financial position when I asked you to marry me. I hope you don't feel cheated?'

'I feel relieved. I'm not that interested in money, David – just enough to live comfortably and keep a roof over our heads. Besides, twenty-five thousand pounds *is* a fortune to me.'

'I know things weren't easy for you as far as money was concerned before the war . . .' He reached out for her hand. 'There was a time when my father had many times that in the bank but he made bad investments. Maria is much richer than I am, as you probably know? However, the bulk of Stratton's fortune was left in trust for his son.'

'I guessed your sister's husband left her a lot of money – but it isn't everything, David.' She looked at him thoughtfully. 'I hope Ned doesn't come into his money too soon?'

'His father made sure of that, don't you worry. He didn't trust Maria.' David touched her cheek. 'Money means nothing at all if you don't have someone to love. I don't envy Maria. I have more than she has ever had.' He smiled at her. 'I can hardly believe you are here with me. Come and look at the house, Jane. You will probably want to change some of it, because Grandmother didn't like modern things . . .'

Jane looked at the front of the house. It was built of some kind of sandy red brick with a sloping roof and small windows criss-crossed with lead; some of the bricks looked as if they were crusted with salt blown in from the sea. The front of the house faced towards the sea and there was a wide sweep of stubby grass, which led to the top of the cliffs. A little iron fence with a gate separated the garden from what was a public walkway. At the moment the rose bushes looked bedraggled, their branches needing to be pruned, the beds of lavender still giving off their wonderful perfume.

The wind blowing in from the sea had turned colder despite the sun they'd had earlier. David unlocked the front door and pushed it open for her. As he did so, an elderly woman came hobbling out from a room at the back. Jane gave a cry of pleasure as she saw her.

'Nanny! I didn't expect to see you here!' She looked at David, seeking confirmation. 'David . . .?'

'Nanny was living in the workhouse, Jane. She hated it there and we have six bedrooms here. I thought you might need help with Rosie?'

'What a wonderful surprise.' Jane was thrilled by his thought-fulness. 'Nanny dearest, it would be so much help to me if you could look after her sometimes.'

Nanny bent over the child in her pram. Then she looked at Jane, tears in her eyes.

'Madam let me go after Ned went to school. I stayed with my sister in Heacham for a while but she died three months ago and I couldn't manage to pay for food and rent alone. I was forced into the workhouse and thought I should die there, but then Captain Heron came to see me.'

'Ned told me you had written to him,' David said. 'When Jane said she would marry me I thought this arrangement might suit you both?'

'It was a wonderful idea.' Jane put her arms about his waist and kissed him.

David nodded as Nanny picked the baby up. 'There's no sense in letting a good nanny go to waste – is there?'

'Shall I take her upstairs, Madam?'

'Yes, please, Nanny – and it's Jane to you, same as always. I'll come up in a little and see how Rosie is settling in.' She turned to David as the door closed behind the elderly woman. 'That was so thoughtful of you – in more than one way.'

'I hated to see her in that wretched place, Jane. She would

have been dead before much longer. She didn't always approve of me, but I couldn't leave her there. I would have found her a cottage of her own, but then you promised to marry me and I knew you liked her.'

'Yes, I did – I do.' Jane went to put her arms about him. 'Thank you for bringing me to this lovely place – and for what you've done for Nanny. She will be a help to us and she can live out her days here.'

'I'm glad it pleased you,' David said and kissed her. He took her hand. 'Do you want to see the rest of the house? It isn't huge but I think you will like it.'

'I am sure I shall love it. I've always wanted to live in a house like this, David.' She gazed up at him. 'I think we shall be happy here – just as your grandmother was.'

'I love you, Jane. All I want is to make you happy.'

Jane's heart caught as she saw how tired he looked. She knew he had pushed himself these past days, keeping up the pretence that he was completely well again.

'You mustn't tire yourself too much, David.'

'No, I shan't . . .' His eyes were soft as he seemed to drink in the sight of her. 'I want to live, Jane. I want to live for as long as I can.'

Fourteen

Jane opened her letter and gave a cry of surprise and pleasure. David looked up from his newspaper, which was filled with stories about the famine sweeping much of central Europe and the aftermath of the bloodiest war in history. It was 1919 now and even though the German fleet had surrendered in November 1918, the papers were still reporting widespread unrest and gloom.

'Well, then, are you going to tell me?' he asked with an indulgent smile.

'This letter is from Melia. She says that Aunt Alice is going to a nursing home in Devon for three weeks to recover from a bout of illness and that means she can spend three weeks with us. She is coming the second week in July – which is just two weeks away. Ned will be here too. We shall all be together as a family, David.'

'If the weather is good we shall be able to have picnics on the beach and play cricket. We might be able to hire a boat for a sea trip to look at the seals.'

Jane was thoughtful. 'Will the rhododendrons be over do you think? Ned said he would like to have a look at the woods at Sandringham if they were still out.'

'They are at their best in May but the woods are still lovely. We could ride out that way and have lunch at a pub somewhere.'

'You won't mind? They won't interfere with your work too much?'

'Of course not. I have a stock of good pictures now, Jane. Plenty of material to use for my articles.' David rose to his feet. 'I'm going to Wells today. I want to take some pictures of the harbour and the woods – would you like to come for a ride?'

'Yes, I think I should.' Jane got to her feet. 'Rosie had a bit of tummy trouble yesterday and she will want to sleep today so I'll leave her with Nanny.'

David looked at his watch. 'Twenty minutes all right?'

'I can be ready in fifteen.' She started clearing the dishes on to a tray, disappearing through the door to the kitchen.

Jane enjoyed the days when David took her exploring with him. They visited many of the little villages and beaches, driving slowly on twisting, narrow roads that were barely wide enough for two vehicles to pass.

The villages often had odd sounding names, and some were so tiny they hardly existed, but they had a quaint charm that fascinated her, making these days an adventure.

It was such a lovely day when they set out for Wells that morning. The sun was high in an azure sky, the countryside alive with colour as they caught glimpses of gardens filled with flowers. The scents of roses and lavender blended with a tangy saltiness from the sea. At times the coast was hidden from their view, but at others they caught glimpses of a sea that reflected the perfect blue above. Flat sandy beaches and rocks where the white horses played endlessly, sending up crests of brown froth.

Approaching Wells, they skirted the Church Marshes, where the medieval harbour stretched beyond the thriving town. She stood on the harbour wall looking out at the muddy channels to the whelk sheds at the far end, while David took pictures of fishing boats. The wind had risen a little, blowing her hair about her face.

'I've got all I need now,' he said and came to her, offering his hand. 'Shall we find somewhere nice to have a sandwich and a drink?'

'Yes, please.' Her eyes were bright, her face a little pink from the wind and sun. 'It has been such a lovely day, David. I shall always remember this . . .'

'This is nice,' Jane said and snuggled up to David's warm body as they lay side by side in their bed that night. She sometimes worried that David could not make love to her in the way he would wish, but he was so tender and loving to her, bringing her to a climax as he kissed and caressed her body. 'Are you happy, David?'

He raised himself to gaze down at her face. 'Why do you ask?'

'Well . . . you make me happy but I feel that something must be missing for you because we can't . . .' She broke off and touched her lips to his. 'If I could I would make everything all right for you – you do know that I love you?'

'Jane . . .' David's arms went round her. He held her tight, his face pressed into her neck. 'I'm feeling so much better. I think soon perhaps . . .' He faltered and breathed deeply. 'I am a very lucky man. I thought I had lost you once and now you are here with me. What more could any man want?'

'Melia! I am so glad you are here.' Jane kissed her sister as they met at the railway station. David had picked up her sister's case and was carrying it to the car. 'Ned is at home with Nanny but he is excited about seeing you again.'

'I am so happy to be here,' Melia said and glanced at the baby in Jane's arms. 'Rosie is growing so fast and she looks wonderful – so do you. I don't think I've ever seen you look so well.'

'I've never been this happy before.' Jane laughed. 'I keep pinching myself to make certain it's real and I'm not dreaming.'

'Your arm must be black and blue.' Melia giggled. 'You don't know how good it is to get away. I had a couple of weeks looking after Aunt Alice before she finally decided to go into the nursing home to convalesce. She was really ill but she won't tell me what is wrong. I think I was impatient with her a couple of times, and she got upset and said she might have made a mistake and you were kinder than I am.' Melia arched her brows. 'I felt a bit mean, because I do have a long holiday from college, but I wanted to spend some of it with you.'

'She has never hinted at why she doesn't like me?'

'Well, yes, she sort of said that she fell out with father because you were on the way and she considered that he had let the family name down.'

'Surely it can't be just that?' Jane was shocked. 'I've been thinking all kinds of dire things, but if it was just that I was on the way before Pa married Ma . . .'

'Let's forget her shall we?' Melia followed her to the car. 'Your letters are so full of all the beautiful walks and the places you visit. I hope we can see some of them while I'm here?'

'David has put his work to one side for a few days. He is going to take us to Burnham Thorpe – that's where Nelson lived – and to Brancaster, Wells and we might get to Blakeney Marshes if we can manage it, though that is a longer trip. He also spoke about a trip on one of the fishing boats. We might visit the seals and have a whole day on the sea . . .' She smiled at Melia. 'But where we live is beautiful enough. We can take picnics on the beach and go for long walks together. We haven't had a proper chance to catch up for years. It is going to be wonderful, Melia!'

'Yes, it is, lovely.' Melia caught her excitement. 'Next term I start in a school in Hampstead as a pupil teacher. It means that I shall have a year of practical work before I take my exams – and I shall be near enough to look after Aunt Alice.'

'You don't have a romantic involvement?'

'No . . . I'm too young to get married yet. Teaching means too much to me to throw it away. I shan't make your mistake . . .' She clapped a hand to her mouth in horror. 'I didn't mean that, Jane. I am so sorry. I know you love . . .' She glanced at David and stopped.

'I'm not upset. I adore Rosie and I wouldn't change a thing.' Jane touched David's hand. 'I've been so lucky. So very, very lucky.'

'Ned, it's time we were leaving now . . .' Jane called him away from the rock pool where he was hunting for crabs and shrimps.

Ned turned and walked back to her, carrying the bucket in which he had collected various treasures. He picked a starfish out and showed it to Melia who looked at it with interest.

'You should draw this,' she told him. 'Make a project of your holiday experiences, Ned. You have a marvellous collection of shells and fossils.'

'Uncle David knows all the best places to go. I've done loads of drawings of seabirds and seals, Melia. I'll show them to you if you like.'

Jane followed behind them, carrying the picnic basket and the blanket. She marvelled at the way her sister got on so well with Ned.

Ned was growing up, becoming a charmer. As David had told her, he would be a perfect gentleman one day and with his looks he would break hearts.

As they entered the house Melia and Ned went straight upstairs, presumably to look at Ned's collection of drawings. Hearing voices coming from the back of the house, Jane dumped the picnic things in the hall and made her way to the conservatory. Surely that was David's voice?

As she got nearer it became clear that an argument was going on. Jane felt a cold shiver at her nape as she recognized the woman's voice, and then saw Maria Stratton. She was waving her arms about angrily and her voice was shrill.

'I won't have it, do you hear me, David? You may have chosen to marry that cheap slut but Ned is my son and I refuse to let him spend all his time with her.'

'You will take that back, Maria! My wife is not a slut and never has been.'

'All right, I shouldn't have said that – but remember what happened to her father. I don't see why I should allow my son to spend his holidays here.'

'Because I am one of his trustees. Stratton made me responsible for Ned's welfare in his will and I take my guardianship seriously.'

'I want him to come home with me today!'

'Be reasonable, Maria. Ned is happy here. He spent a few days with you but if he weren't here he would be at school or a friend's house. It took me a long time to persuade him to visit you even for a few days.'

'You have poisoned his mind against me – you and that bitch! You think I murdered my husband. I've known for years that you think I am a murderess.'

'Well, are you? No, don't tell me. I have no wish to know what you did.'

'He had pneumonia; you know he did!'

'If you say so . . .'

'Damn you!'

Jane felt as if her feet were glued to the ground as Maria screamed at him. She suddenly flew at him, her nails going for his face. David put up his hands to defend himself but she caught him a blow that made him stagger.

It was like watching something in slow motion. Jane screamed as David's knees seemed to give way and he fell, striking his head on the corner of the desk on the way down. She moved towards him but felt she was walking through treacle, unable to reach him in time to break his fall. Falling to her knees beside him, she looked down at his face. Blood was running from the corner of his mouth and his eyes were closed.

'David . . .' Jane cried. 'David, my darling . . . please don't be hurt . . . don't be dead . . .'

'He is all right . . .' Maria sounded scared. 'I didn't do anything.'

'You hit him.' Jane looked up at her as she bent over David feeling for a pulse. 'You knew how dangerous it could be if he struck his head . . . it could have moved the shrapnel . . . he could die . . .'

Maria gasped. 'No! I didn't want to hurt him . . .' she sobbed. 'I've always loved him . . . he was the only one who cared but . . .' She stopped, rage in her eyes. 'It is your fault. You took him away from me.'

'I have never once told David not to see you. If he stopped visiting you must have done something.'

She had found a pulse. David was still alive. His eyelids were fluttering. She felt tears wetting her cheeks as she bent to kiss him.

'David . . . it's all right my dearest . . .'

'He thinks I murdered my husband . . .' Maria said. 'Well, if I did give him something to make sure he never woke up, he deserved it – this is what he did to me . . .'

Maria ripped open the front of her silk blouse. She was wearing nothing beneath and Jane saw the jagged, disfiguring scars across both her breasts. It looked as if someone had attacked her with broken glass.

'Your husband did that? My God, that is disgusting! Why would anyone do such a thing?'

David was stirring, his eyes open. He smiled at Jane as she stroked his forehead, but seemed bewildered as if he weren't quite sure what was going on.

'He did it because he thought I was unfaithful to him and he wanted to make sure that no one would ever find me attractive again.' Maria glared at her, challenging her as she gathered her blouse together. 'Now you know my secret – so what are you going to do?'

Jane was helping David to sit up. He was obviously dazed and feeling unwell. She spoke to Maria without looking at her. 'I don't intend to do anything. It is your secret, your guilt – live with it or tell the police. Just leave us alone.'

'Damn you! You are so holy and self-righteous . . .' Maria was beside herself with fury. 'I wish we had never met you. David loved me until you came . . .' Her face was ugly with the force of her hatred. 'Damn you both to hell! I have nothing to live for . . .'

'Don't be stupid . . .' Jane said, but Maria had rushed from the room and David seemed to be coming to himself. She gave her attention to him. 'How do you feel? Does your head hurt? Maria pushed you. You banged your head on the edge of the desk.'

'I'm feeling a bit odd,' he said and suddenly wrenched to one side to vomit. His body jerked a few times and then he wiped his face with a handkerchief Jane offered. 'Sorry. I felt rough for a moment but I'm coming through it now. I am not sure I can stand up yet. My head is still swimming . . .'

'I'll get the doctor . . .' Jane tried to rise but David held her wrist, preventing her. 'Let me fetch him. You should see a doctor – you don't know what harm this may have done.'

'I shall visit the doctor at the hospital once Ned is back at school,' he promised. 'The dizziness is passing. Just stay with me for a moment . . .'

'She has gone, Jane . . .' they both looked to the door and saw Nanny standing there. 'I heard what she said to you . . . I always knew she killed my boy. He wouldn't do what she said. He had a bit of a temper . . . but he wouldn't do something like that . . .' Nanny looked distressed. 'She killed my boy. If he hurt her she deserved it.'

'Nanny . . .' Jane went to her, leading her to a cane chair. As Nanny sank down, she knelt beside her, holding her hand. 'Listen to me, please. Someone did something dreadful to Maria. She says it was her husband but none of us can know for sure. I know you heard what Maria said to me but you cannot tell anyone else.'

Nanny's expression was hard. 'She should be in prison for what she did. She murdered him . . .'

'Maria was talking wildly. She was upset. You can't say anything. Ned must never hear a word of this – do you understand me? The doctor didn't suspect anything at the time and it can never be proved. Please do not cause Ned more suffering. I am asking you this as a favour to me. If you care about Ned you won't say anything to anyone.'

Nanny met her eyes for a long moment and then nodded her head. 'If you say so. But she is a wicked woman.'

'Perhaps she was driven to what she did.' Jane gently pressed the old woman's hand. 'I know this hurts you. What she did to David hurts us – but for the sake of the family we have to forget what happened here.'

'You are a good woman.'

'Am I?' Jane shook her head. 'No, I don't think so. I am protecting what we have, Nanny. Holding on to it because I don't want to lose the special feeling we all have.'

'Have your own way. You've been good to me. I'll do what you say. I've known what she did for years and done nothing about it because I didn't want to leave the boy.'

'Maria's confession changes nothing. We can't bring him back, Nanny. We have to think of the living. If you told the police or Ned it would just make him unhappy – destroy us all.'

David had risen to his feet at last. 'I've suspected something for years and so has Ned, but it is best if we do nothing. Maria must bear her own guilt. I dare say that is punishment enough.'

Nanny stood up. 'Tears won't save anyone. She will burn in Hell and so she should.' She walked to the door, looked back reproachfully at Jane for a moment and then went out.

David sat down in one of the chairs. He looked white and shaken, his left hand trembling.

'Tell me exactly what she said to you, Jane.' His expression became grim as Jane repeated what had been said while he was unconscious. 'Stratton was madly jealous and a bully. If he did that to her he was asking for trouble. Maria is vindictive. You should watch your back, Jane. She hated you before and she will hate you more now.'

'I can understand her feelings, David. What happened to her was terrible.'

'She may have deserved it and she paid him back.' He closed his eyes for a moment. 'The fear that she might have killed him has played on my mind for years. It was the reason I got drunk that day . . . but not my excuse. There is no excuse for what I did to you . . .'

'I've told you to forget that, David. It is over. You have given me a wonderful life here.'

'We were an ill fated pair. Maria ruined her life when she married Stratton. I wasted years because of what I did to you.'

Jane sat beside him, leaned into his body to kiss him. 'I just want you to be well. Promise me you will go to the doctor – please?'

'It may not be good news.'

'I know.' Jane's hand trembled as she touched his cheek. 'I wish this hadn't happened. I wish you didn't have this shadow hanging over you – but if you have to face it then I shall too.'

'I've had headaches. I didn't want to tell you.'

'I know. I found an empty bottle of pills in the rubbish. I knew you were taking something for the pain.'

'Supposing they tell me I haven't long? Wouldn't you rather go on as we are?'

'Every day is precious to me, David. I've always known it could end suddenly . . .' She broke off as she heard voices. 'Melia and Ned are coming down now. I had better get tea ready. Sit here and rest – and promise me you will go to the doctor as soon as you can get an appointment.'

David pressed her hand. 'I promise. Do what you have to do. I'll wait until you call me.'

Jane leaned forward and touched her mouth to his lightly. 'I love you so much. You've given me more than I ever thought possible. Please forgive yourself, David. No more regrets ever.'

'No more regrets. You must promise too, Jane. Whatever happens to me. No regrets . . .'

'I promise.'

'One thing . . .' He held her hand in his, not looking at her. 'If the worst should happen, I want you to know that I've made you Ned's trustee in my place. His father wanted to protect him from Maria and I've done the same. Whatever she says to you, you will have to sign before his money can be touched – and you have a say in where he lives and what he does.'

'Nothing will happen.'

'Of course not, but I thought you should know just in case.'

'Go for a walk, Jane. I'll see the doctor alone – and then I'll come and tell you what he says.'

'You will tell me the truth? I want to share whatever the news is, David. Please don't lie to spare me.'

'I promise I will tell you exactly what he says. Go on now, have a walk. It's not a bad day, even if the wind is sharp.'

Jane kissed his cheek. He caught her, held her and kissed her on the lips, then stroked her cheek before giving her a little push.

'Come back in half an hour.'

Jane nodded. She left him and retraced her steps through the hospital corridor. The smell of carbolic and an underlying odour that she associated with chronic illness were familiar and haunting. For a moment she felt a surge of nostalgia for her nursing days but it faded as she remembered what had taken its place. She was so lucky! If only she could hold on to her luck for a little longer.

Outside in the hospital grounds there were signs that autumn had arrived. The leaves on the trees had started to change colour and the rose beds were beginning to look forlorn, their branches straggling and in need of pruning. A patch of dark red chrysanthemums brightened the otherwise empty borders, where a thrush was busy hunting for worms. She walked for a while, trying to enjoy the beauty that surrounded her, trying to forget that David was facing an ordeal she knew he dreaded.

Jane found a bench in a sheltered spot out of the wind and sat down. She glanced at her watch, counting the minutes. Suddenly, the tears welled up and spilled over. She covered her face with her hands, letting the grief pour out, her body shaken by deep hurtful sobs. If there was no hope for David she didn't think she could bear it. How could God be so cruel as to take everything away from her? Surely she had paid for her mistakes over and over again? David didn't deserve to die. It wasn't fair . . . it wasn't fair!

'I say . . . is something wrong . . . can I help, miss . . .'

Jane raised her head as the man's voice broke into her grief. Her eyes were misty with tears and she didn't recognize the soldier immediately, but he knew her.

'Miss Shaw . . . Jane . . .' Robert Hastings exclaimed. He sat down on the bench next to her, looking at her in concern. 'Sorry, Aggie told me you were married . . . is it Mrs Heron now?'

'Yes . . . Mr Hastings.' Jane fumbled for her handkerchief, wiped her cheeks and then blew her nose. She had remembered him now, though he looked very different in his uniform, older and more confident. 'Have you been seeing one of the doctors?'

'I was wounded in the final push last year but this was my last check up. I'm back to normal. Well, there's a slight limp but they tell me that may get better in time.' His brow creased. 'What are you doing here? Have you had bad news?'

'I'm waiting to hear. My husband is with the doctor now.' Jane lifted her head, forcing a smile. 'It was foolish of me to give way. Nothing is certain yet.'

'You are very worried about him. He was recently awarded the Victoria Cross for bravery. He saved the lives of about twenty men.'

'Was he? He didn't mention it.' Jane took her little silver powder compact out and used the puff to cover the redness on her nose and under her eyes. 'Of course he wouldn't think it was important. David prefers to forget the war.'

'I hope it won't be too many months before we can all forget.'

'It is over but for some people it will never end – the memories, their injuries . . .'

'We all carry the scars inside . . .' Robert looked at her uncertainly. He reached out and touched her hand. 'I've been told that I shall be given my final discharge soon. If you need help just let me know. Aggie will know where I am. She looked after my mother while I was away fighting.'

'Oh . . . that is kind of you to offer.' Jane glanced at her watch. She was less tense after her tears but her stomach was tying itself in knots. Another ten minutes to wait! 'How is your mother?'

'She died a few months ago. I was given compassionate leave and able to see her before the end.'

'I am so sorry. You must miss her?'

'Yes, of course.'

Jane stood up and he rose with her. 'I must be getting back. David must be almost ready by now.'

'You will be anxious to see him.' Robert offered his hand. Jane took it. He held it a moment longer than necessary. 'I do hope it is good news.'

'Thank you.'

Jane turned away and walked back to the hospital.

*   *   *

David was sitting in the waiting room, leaning back, his head against the wall, his eyes closed. Something about the way his body was slumped told Jane all she needed to know. Her heart caught and for a moment she swayed, feeling a wave of despair sweep over her. She was going to lose him. The ground seemed to shift beneath her feet and her head went spinning. Pausing, she took a deep breath and then went to meet him.

'David?' He looked up at her and she saw the fear and the grief in his eyes. Sitting down by his side, she took his hand and held it tightly. 'Tell me, my darling. Whatever it is we will face it together.'

'Jane, I am so sorry. I didn't want this to happen.' David's hand crushed hers. 'The shrapnel has moved. They want to operate. If I say no, it will be a matter of months, perhaps weeks. If I say yes and there is too much damage . . .'

Jane bent her head and kissed his hand, hiding the grief and despair she could not quite control, then she raised her head and looked at him. She would think of these things when she was alone. David needed her.

'What do you want to do?'

'I could have a few more months with you . . .' His eyes held hers, compelling and intense. 'I might die under the knife or go into a coma and never wake up again.'

'What chance have they given you?'

'About thirty to seventy against.'

'It has to be your decision, David. I shall be with you whatever you do.'

'I want to live, to be with you for as long as I can. It may mean some pain towards the end but . . .' He got to his feet, pulling her with him. 'Let's go home, Jane. I always knew it could happen. If we don't have much time we should make the most of what we have . . .'

Jane woke, turned and reached for David. The bed was cold and she knew he must have been too restless to sleep. It was often that way. He would be downstairs working on his articles or making himself a hot drink. She resisted the need to get up and go down to him. The worst thing she could do was to make too much fuss. David rejected sympathy but accepted love.

She had given him all she had to give as they lay together the previous night. Although David had never regained his full strength they had achieved a kind of loving soon after their marriage. David enjoyed touching her and kissing her, and she reciprocated. Since his visit to the hospital six weeks earlier they had been closer than ever. They had spent every minute of the day together, walking, talking, visiting the beautiful places that David knew so well.

Sometimes Rosie was with them, sometimes she stayed with Nanny; it didn't matter. They were a family, bound by the need to make the time stretch because every second was important.

These past weeks had been so very precious. She knew that David was taking a lot of pills, but he did his best to hide his pain from her and it made her heart ache because he was suffering.

Jane knew she could not sleep. She would go down and make a cup of tea. She would share it with David but she wouldn't make a fuss; she wouldn't ask if he had pain. Instead she would smile and talk about what she was going to do that day.

She could see the light was on in the kitchen. David must have wanted a drink but he had taken care not to disturb her. Opening the door she went in and then stopped, her heart catching. David was sitting in his favourite wing chair by the range, a glass of water and his pills on a wooden stool in front of him. His head was back against the chair and his eyes were closed. Jane felt a chill of fear as she moved towards him. She knelt down by his side, touching his hand. It was icy cold.

'David . . . Oh, David . . .' Looking up, she saw that his nose had bled on to his dressing gown. The blood had dried and looked almost black. He must have come down soon after she had fallen asleep. 'Why didn't you wake me?' Tears trickled down her cheeks. 'Why didn't you tell me you were in pain?'

She looked at the bottle of pills half expecting it to be empty but it was still almost full. David hadn't taken the easy way out; he had fought to the last because he wanted to live for her.

Jane bent over him, kissing his mouth. She stroked his face with her hands, the tears she had hidden from him falling like rain. It hurt so much to know that he had died here alone and in terrible pain. Yet David had known that at the end he would be alone; she couldn't go with him; she couldn't share the pain.

'I am so sorry, my love. So very sorry.'

Jane sat back on her heels looking at his face. She had fallen under his spell when they first met but then he'd ruined it all; they might have had years together. Even the love she had felt for Richard was overshadowed by the sweeping regret. Richard had loved her but she sensed that David had worshipped her, needed her in a way she had scarcely understood. She prayed that she had made him happy for a while.

'I loved you. I pray you knew that I loved you . . .'

Fifteen

'Jane, I am so sorry!' Melia ran to her and they embraced. 'I came as soon as I could. You said the funeral was tomorrow?'

'Yes. The doctor was satisfied with the hospital report so there is nothing to stop us going ahead. I've telephoned Ned's school and he should be here this afternoon. Mrs Hylton is coming this evening. She will stay for a few days. I sent David's sister a telegram but I don't know if she will come. I hope she doesn't but I had to tell her.'

'He didn't get on with her, did he?' Melia looked curious. 'Nanny said something when I was here but I wasn't sure what she meant.'

'Nanny doesn't like her. You shouldn't take any notice of anything she says about Maria Stratton.'

Melia nodded, an uncertain look in her eyes. 'Please don't be cross, Jane, but I told Aunt Alice.'

'I'm not cross but I doubt if she was interested.'

'I'm not sure. She sounded upset – concerned for you. I think she might come down.'

'Surely not? She has never bothered to write or send cards. Why would she come to the funeral of someone she has never met?'

'She has changed recently. I think she is really ill, Jane. She won't tell me what is wrong with her but I think it must be serious. Perhaps she wants to make her peace with you . . .' Melia twisted a strand of her long hair around her finger. 'You wouldn't quarrel with her if she came?'

'I never wanted to fall out with her. Providing she is civil I shall be civil to her.'

'I might have known you would say that.' Melia put an arm about her waist. 'I'm not surprised David loved you so much. I love you, Janey.'

'It is ages since you called me Janey.' She hugged her sister. 'Of course I know. I love you too.'

'It isn't fair . . .' Melia's eyes suddenly blazed with anger. 'Why does all the rotten stuff happen to you?'

'I've had my share of happiness.' Jane smiled. 'Don't pity me, Melia. I've loved and been loved; that is something not everyone is given. I wish David was still here with me, but he gave me so many memories. I shall survive. He wanted me to be safe here because he knew he couldn't live long.'

'I still think you've had a rotten deal. All that business with Ma and Pa — and Charlie, then Richard and . . .' She broke off as tears caught her throat. 'You deserve to be happy, Janey.'

'I am all right, Melia. I'm grieving but I know I have so much . . .'

'I thought we might go for a little walk?' Ned had been sitting with his drawing book on his knee for ages but making no attempt to use his pencil. 'I would like to talk to you. Put your coat on because the wind is cold.'

Ned got to his feet. He allowed her to help him on with his coat and wound a school scarf about his throat. He was clutching his drawing pad as they left the house and walked across the green that led to the top of the cliffs.

She gave him her hand as they carefully climbed down the steep incline to the beach below. Ned let go as soon as they reached the bottom. He stared at the sea but said nothing, his face tight with the emotion he was holding inside.

'I wanted to tell you,' Jane said. 'Your uncle has made me a trustee in his place . . .'

Ned stared at her, the tears very close. 'I don't know what you mean.'

'It means that I shall do the things David did for you — help look after your inheritance and what you do when you leave school . . .'

'What about coming here?' Ned's bottom lip trembled. 'Will you want me now he's . . .' the tears spilled over. 'Why did he have to die, Jane?'

'Oh, Ned darling.' Jane held out her arms to him. 'I love him too. I shan't stop loving him because he isn't with us any more. Nor will you. It hurts dreadfully now but one day you will remember all the good things you did together.'

Ned buried his face against her as he sobbed. She stroked his head. 'I want him to be here with us. Why can't he still be here?'

'I don't know.' Jane was crying now. 'I want him too, Ned. I miss him so much.'

Ned hesitated and then opened his drawing pad to show her a picture he had been working on of David.

Jane's heart caught with emotion as she saw David's face smiling at her. 'Ned, that is so beautiful. Better than any photograph. I don't have many of David; he was always taking them of me . . .'

'I was doing this for you for Christmas,' Ned said. 'I wanted to frame it for you as a surprise but you might as well have it now.'

'Oh, Ned, that is so wonderful. The best present I could ever have.'

Ned closed the book. 'Uncle David was going to get me a dog for Christmas. He said I could keep it here and take it for walks when I was home for holidays.'

'He told me.' Jane smiled. 'Why don't we go and buy one from the pet shop before you go back to school?'

She offered her hand and he took it as they began to walk along the beach together.

Jane was unable to sleep. She could only think about the next day and the funeral. Her dreams had been uneasy, causing her to wake suddenly. She still dreamed of the moment she saw her father's body hanging in his shed. There were so many other terrible memories; men with fatal injuries, her brother's tiny body . . . the day someone had told her Richard was dead, and now David dying alone because he didn't want to wake her.

Getting up, Jane went downstairs. She wandered into the conservatory, where David had spent so much time writing his articles. She sat at his desk and opened the folder in front of her. Instead of the article she had expected to see, she saw photographs of herself – shot after shot of her with her hair blowing in the wind, working in her garden, playing with Rosie. She hadn't even known that David had taken most of them.

Picking up a picture of her taken that day in Wells, she felt the tears trickle down her cheeks. It was a happy memory. David had given her so much to remember. She must remember the good things.

She dashed away the tears. She was dreading the funeral but somehow she would get through it.

Jane was hardly aware of the congregation as she followed David's coffin into the church. Ned was at her side. Dressed in his best suit he looked so grown up, his face pale but determined. He had begged to be allowed to accompany her and she couldn't refuse him.

Jane had been putting on a brave face for Ned's sake. Somehow she had shut out the reality until this moment, but as the final prayers were said and the Vicar led the way out to the graveyard reality hit her. David was dead. She would never see him again, never see the love in his eyes or feel the touch of his hand.

Tears trickled down her cheeks as she watched the coffin lowered into the ground. She listened to the last words of the Vicar's dedication and then moved forward to throw a handful of earth into the yawning opening. For a moment she swayed, almost wanting to be there, to join him. A hand at her arm steadied her. She threw a sprig of blossom from her garden on to the coffin and stepped back, still unaware of whose hand had held her.

People were coming to pay their last respects and to speak to her. She nodded and answered them somehow, feeling numb.

'Come away now, Jane.'

Jane focused on the person who had spoken. 'Aunt Alice . . . thank you for coming.'

'It is little enough.' Alice turned away.

'No, don't leave. Come back to the house,' Jane said. She became aware of the man at her side. 'Robert. It was good of you to be here. Will you come back for a cup of tea?'

'Yes. Thank you.'

Somehow Jane managed to leave the churchyard. She got into the waiting car. Melia was holding Ned's hand. He sat in the middle and took hers with his other hand, holding it tightly as they were driven home. She had been numbed throughout the service but now she was beginning to hurt. Her tears had been shed in private. She was pale and calm as she received her friends and a few neighbours who had attended the funeral.

A handful of David's army friends had turned up. They stayed for a glass of sherry, told her that David was a fine man and left. Jane realized that everyone had gone but her sister, Mrs Hylton and Aunt Alice. She began to clear the dishes and take them into the kitchen. Aunt Alice followed her.

'Let me do this for you, Jane.'

'I can manage. I would rather be busy. Besides, Melia tells me you are ill?'

'I have cancer in my breast. It has been there a while. They can't do anything more for me but I will thank you not to tell Melia. I don't want her giving up college to come home and look after me.'

'You can come here when you need to. We have plenty of room.'

Her aunt's face went white. For a moment she just stared at her, and then she gave a little sob and covered her face with her hand before looking at Jane once more.

'You offer me that – after the way I treated you?'

'I let you down. You wanted my help and I left you. You had a right to be angry.'

'I shouldn't have taken you for granted, Jane – but you know it wasn't just that, don't you?'

'My father married my mother because I was on the way. I suppose you resented that . . . thought she wasn't good enough for him.'

'She was a bad influence. He took money from the business so that he could marry her. It was true that it was owed him but he shouldn't have taken it without my father's permission. He took a gold bracelet and a brooch that had belonged to our mother too. I think it was the jewellery that made my father so angry.'

'Father shouldn't have taken them but he gave them to my mother. He loved her almost too much. It was the cause of their troubles. She didn't love him in the same way.'

'Helen made him miserable. He told me in his letter. He only wrote once even though I wrote to him all the time – but he sent photos of you and Melia sometimes.'

'I'm sorry. You must have been lonely after your father died.'

'I had my teashop. Father left everything to me. He made me promise not to give John a penny – but I would have if he'd asked me. He didn't.'

'He stole money from his employer. He should have come to you if he was desperate.'

'Yes.' Alice looked at her intently. 'Did you really mean it when you said I could come here at the end?'

'I never say what I don't mean . . .' Jane broke off as she heard Ned's voice raised in alarm. 'What . . .' The colour drained from her face as the door was thrown wide and Maria Stratton strode in.

'Having a cosy chat with your friends?' Her voice was bitter, angry. 'You didn't ask me to come back to the house but I came anyway. Damn you, Jane Shaw. I hate you. I wish it were you in that grave instead of David. He was mine. Do you hear me? He was always mine.'

Jane stared at her, shocked by the venom in her tone. Maria was beside herself with grief, desperate, her eyes wild.

'You loved him . . . more than you should, didn't you? It was David your husband was jealous of . . .' Jane saw the truth in her face. She should have seen it years ago, in the possessive manner Maria had shown when she took his arm that very first day. 'Did David know how you felt? Of course he did in the end . . . it shocked him, revolted him . . . it was the reason he stayed away from you . . .'

'Bitch! I'll kill you!' Maria picked up a carving knife from the kitchen table and lifted her arm. As she moved towards Jane someone caught her arm, twisting it so that the knife fell to the floor with a clatter. She screamed wildly, fighting and shouting until suddenly she was crying. 'Let me go. I hate her. She took David from me.'

'Let her go, Robert, please.' Jane had thought he had left earlier but he must still have been here, in the conservatory perhaps. 'Maria won't kill me.' She walked towards her, looking her in the eyes. 'David loved me, Maria. You were his sister. You could never have been more to him. He cared for you as his sister, nothing more.'

Maria was quieter now. She stared at Jane, her face twisted with hate. 'No, I shan't kill you. One murder was enough. I shall always hate you but I shan't come near you again. You won't have Ned. I am taking him with me.'

'You can't take Ned. He doesn't want to live with you.'

'You are no blood relation. I am his mother, I can do as I wish . . .'

'I am his trustee. David told me . . .'

'Damn you! I'll have it overturned. I'll blacken your name in the courts . . .'

'No, Madam, I don't think you can.' Nanny had come into the kitchen unnoticed. 'I know what you did that night. I know how you killed my boy and I've heard you confess. I've kept quiet for Ned's sake, but if you try to take him from us I shall go to the police and you'll hang for your wickedness.'

'Damn you! You evil old witch . . .' Maria hesitated, her eyes moving from Nanny to Jane, then she pushed past Nanny nearly knocking her down as she ran from the room.

'What an unpleasant woman,' Aunt Alice observed calmly. 'I don't know what she has done, but whatever it is I imagine that threat was enough to make her think twice in future. We all saw her attempt to kill you, Jane. You should go to the police.'

'She murdered her husband,' Nanny said, her mouth set hard. 'I know I gave you my word not to say anything, Jane – but if she tries to take Ned I'll go to the police.'

'She won't. I am sure this was all because she was feeling so desperately unhappy. She wanted David in a way that could never happen because they were brother and sister. When he realized it – understood just why she had killed her husband – it sickened him. He stayed away from her for years.'

'Well, she had better not come here again making trouble,' Aunt Alice said with a look of satisfaction. 'I'll have something to say to her if she does . . .'

'Are you all right?' Robert asked, looking at Jane. 'You're so pale. You've had a terrible shock.'

'She needs some brandy,' Alice said. 'Sit down, Jane. I'll bring you a glass.'

'Thank you but I think I need a little air . . . a walk . . .'

'May I come with you?' Robert inquired, and she nodded.

Taking her coat from a hook behind the kitchen door, she opened the door and went out.

'Do you want to walk on the beach?'

'Yes, please. Aunt Alice means well. Nanny was protecting me – but I can't take anymore for the moment. I just want to be quiet . . .'

'Would you rather I went?'

'No – but I can't talk for a while . . .'

Robert inclined his head. They turned towards a steep sloping path that led down to the beach. The wind was sharp and cold, stinging their faces. They walked on the stony sands in silence for a while until they reached the curving promontory. Jane stopped and looked at him.

'It is best not to go any further. The tide comes in quickly and the beach on the other side of the cliff is narrow.'

'We'll walk back then.' Robert looked at her face. 'Are you feeling better?'

'Yes, thank you. I wanted to scream earlier. I was so tense.'

'I could see that . . .' He smiled at her. 'It is amazing how calming a walk by the sea can be isn't it? I have always loved Norfolk – which is why I've taken a job down here now that I've been discharged. I am going to be a headmaster, Jane.'

'I am so pleased for you. It is what you've wanted, isn't it?'

'Yes. I always thought I should stay on at my old school forever, but the war changed things. I decided to make the break and I was lucky.'

'I am glad for you, Robert.'

'It isn't far from here, Jane. The preparatory school in Heacham . . .'

'We shall almost be neighbours.'

'Within cycling distance . . .' He paused, looking at her for a moment in silence. 'You know I am your friend, Jane. May I visit you sometimes?'

'I should like that. We have always been friends, Robert. Aunt Alice is terminally ill. She is going to move in with me so that Melia doesn't feel obliged to give up her studies and look after her.'

'You'll do that instead. It's what you always do, isn't it?'

'Perhaps – but it was my suggestion. I have trained as a nurse. It will be no hardship for me. I am afraid it means I may not always have time for friends – at least for a while.'

'We shall see each other sometimes.' He looked uncertain, almost bashful. 'I saw you were wearing my brooch today. I've always wondered if you received it.'

'My brooch . . .' Jane stared at him in surprise. 'My gold brooch

'. . . but it was sent to me when I was staying with Frances. There was no card . . . how did you know I was there?'

'I called at your aunt's house. Melia told me where you were staying. I came down on the train hoping to see you but then I lost my bottle. I just gave someone the parcel and left.'

'Oh, Robert. I wish I had known. I would have thanked you. It is a beautiful brooch.'

'I was going to ask you to marry me . . .' He looked self-conscious. 'Of course you would have said no . . .'

'At that time I wasn't thinking of marriage.' Her eyes were sad as she looked at his face. 'So much has happened to me since then. You know I like you but . . . David . . . Ned needs me . . .'

'I have plenty of time, Jane. The rest of my life.'

Jane saw the love in his eyes. He had always loved her, though he hadn't spoken when he'd had the chance. She didn't love him and she couldn't even think of him that way yet, but perhaps one day it might happen. 'Yes, I know,' she said. 'Thank you. I think we should go back to the others now, Robert.'

He offered his hand. She took it and they began to climb the steep path leading up to the top of the cliffs.